EACH MAN WAS A MENACE TO THE GIRL WHO TOOK THE NAME OF GEORGINA MOFFETT

Josiah Moffett—Could Georgina betray this old man who trusted her so much?

Wolfgang Quinn—Dare Georgina defy this foreign agent who made her what she was, and just as easily could destroy her?

Thomas Weston—Would Georgina give in to the words of love and honorable intentions of this far-too-inexperienced young man?

Viscount Autherly—What match was Georgina for the amorous wiles and sensual skills of this notorious rake?

Edward Peregrine—What chance did Georgina have to win the love of this breathlessly attractive man who could see behind her mask?

Gina Buxton was playing a desperate game as Georgina Moffett—with everything to lose . . . and just as much to gain. . . .

The Best in Fiction from SIGNET Books

The
Masked
Heiress

by
Vanessa Gray

A SIGNET BOOK

NEW AMERICAN LIBRARY

TIMES MIRROR

SIGNET TRADEMARK REG. U.S. PAT. OFF. AND FOREIGN COUNTRIES
REGISTERED TRADEMARK—MARCA REGISTRADA
HECHO EN CHICAGO, U.S.A.

SIGNET, SIGNET CLASSICS, MENTOR, PLUME AND MERIDIAN BOOKS
are published by The New American Library, Inc.,
1301 Avenue of the Americas, New York, New York 10019

FIRST SIGNET PRINTING, MARCH, 1977

3 4 5 6 7 8 9

PRINTED IN THE UNITED STATES OF AMERICA

I

Outside the great gray prison walls, the icy February rains drenched the city of London, swept in smoky silver curtains down the Thames, pounded the decks of ships of the line in drydock that were being hastily refitted to keep Napoleon from ruling His Britannic Majesty's Channel.

But inside Newgate Prison, court was in session, vainly trying to deal with the ever-growing mountain of small offenses occurring every day in the teeming city.

The prisoners' corridor outside the courtroom had been crowded with an odiferous press of accused women. The girl known as Gina Buxton stood wearily with the others, her mind so numbed by shock that she was hardly aware of her surroundings.

Throughout the long morning the number of prisoners had dwindled, until now barely a dozen were left awaiting trial.

"Trial!" sneered the woman next to Gina. "Might as well dump the lot of us now into Newgate and throw away the key."

The speaker shifted her gaunt weight from one hip to the other. Gina moistened her lips and spoke, for the first time that terrible day. "You don't think we'll get a fair trial?"

Her voice carried farther than she intended. Down the ragged row, prodded into line by rough guards, came a voice, gin-cracked and harsh. "Listen to the duchess! Fair trial! When did the likes of us get anything but a spit in the eye and a life sentence?"

"Life?" gasped Gina. "But I didn't do anything!"

"We're all innocent here," mocked the woman who spoke first. "Your first time, girlie? I remember mine. I wasn't as pretty as you, but I stood just as straight and proud. Thought I, I'll show the judge I'm not like the rest of them criminals."

"Ho, Fan!" jeered the cracked voice. "I suppose you got off? I *don't* think!"

"No, Sal, I was a great gaby. I never made that mistake again." Fan's wistful voice carried the unmistakable ring of truth. Gina's spirits, already sunken, dropped to a desperate new low. How had she arrived at this noisome place—how could she have been so innocent that she had not seen the trap, the deliberately set trap, in time?

There was no time for regrets, for going back over the sordid string of events that had led, inevitably, to this moment—that would come later. Just now the courtroom door opened and a file of half a dozen women prisoners emerged. The guards shoved them down the corridor toward the cells.

"See?" Fan breathed huskily, enveloping Gina in fumes of the gin that most of the women seemed to thrive on, smuggled by devious pathways into whatever jail they inhabited. Gina had been held only overnight in the women's cell, and already she scarcely remembered sunlight, freshly scented air, freedom to walk along the cobbled pavements. "See?" Fan repeated, jabbing Gina in the ribs. "Nobody gets off."

The owner of the familiar voice close to the door peered down the line, catching sight of Gina. "You're no better than the lot of us, Redhead, for all your fine airs!" Her jibe was taken up by the others until the corridor echoed with hoots and jeers, ending only when the courtroom door opened again and the guards thrust the women through.

Gina's eyes swam with stinging tears, brought on by the women's savage mockery, and she, the last one in line, stopped a moment to blink away the film so that she could see her next step.

She was unconscious of the picture she made against the background of the door. She was taller than average, with long bones that gave her elegance when she walked, a proud carriage that was unintentionally alluring. The fine bones of her face gave promise of an enduring beauty, but just now her cheek was smudged, her torn blouse gaped at the left shoulder, and her chestnut hair hung loosely around her shoulders, lusterless and uncombed.

It was the lack of even so small a comfort as water in the cell that she felt keenly just now, and she was shamed before the crowd of spectators in the courtroom. She longed to cry out—*Don't judge me by the way I look! If you saw me with my hair in order, my face washed, wearing my other dress, you would not believe me a thief, I promise you!*

The spectators were one vast blur before her teary eyes. She wondered whether Mrs. Potter, her employer (until yesterday, that is), would be there to accuse her. Or would young Mr. James Potter manfully take the blame for his role?

The other prisoners were dealt with swiftly. Gina was hardly aware of her surroundings. Fiercely she fought back the stinging tears, gathering her pride for her own trial. She was determined not to give the judge—or anybody—a hint of her deep pain.

Suddenly the judge was speaking to her.

"Your name?"

She faltered, uncertain, and the nearby guard jerked her arm savagely. She looked up at the judge, towering over her from the height of his bench, studying her with his cold light eyes as though she were an unexpected worm in a peach.

"Your name," snarled the guard.

"Gina."

"Gina what?" the magistrate prompted.

"I—I don't know," she lied, whispering so low that only the judge and the guard could hear.

"Gina," the judge repeated coldly, as though his worst fears had been realized. What was a girl doing without a name, anyway? The order of things was threatened, he seemed to think.

"The charge is stealing a valuable pin from your employer. How do you plead?"

Stealing that trumpery pin! It was, so Gina decided, and did not know how she knew, an ugly pin of brash bad taste. If she *had* taken it, she would never have worn such a thing, devoid of all beauty.

She mustered all her strength to say the truth. "I am innocent, my lord."

A slight stir sighed over the spectators, like a faint breeze lifting spring-green wheat. Was this going to be something new in the tired old court, something out of the ordinary? This, after all, was what some of them had come for.

And then her accuser stepped forward.

Mr. James, she breathed silently, *thank goodness you've come!*

Mr. James Potter, surprisingly, refused to meet her imploring eyes. Shared knowledge lay between them like a tangible bond, and she looked encouragement at him.

The words he spoke, in response to the magistrate's questioning, were an outrage. "After my mother had been so kind to her, taking her from the orphanage to train her as a maid-servant," James said without feeling, as though repeating a memorized speech, "the girl repaid her by stealing the pin. I don't know where she thought she could wear it, unless to impress some local fellow."

Tell him the truth, Gina implored silently. *Tell him how you pestered me, making my life a misery. Tell him about yesterday, when you followed me into the pantry and I couldn't fight you off! Tell the judge how your mother caught you kissing me, and blamed me—me!—for enticing you! Tell him, too, how it was, an hour later after I had cleaned her room, when the bailiff came to arrest me for stealing that pin—the same pin I knew was upstairs on her dressing table at that very minute.*

But of course James would not explain all that to the judge, no more than he would admit to tearing her blouse, the same ragged blouse she wore now.

His glance fell, almost by accident, on Gina, and she read in his eyes the end of her hopes. His eyes held more shame than he could live with, and she recognized his essential weakness for the first time. His mother would rule him, as would a wife later, and in that moment Gina forgave him. She had expected more than he had to give.

There was nothing to be gained by telling her side of the story.

She hardly heard the judge's sentence. She knew only that there was no way out of the courtroom, except for the door by which she had entered, the door that would lead back to that abominable cell.

The other women prisoners started out that door. She was again at the end of the line. Dully, she looked around the courtroom, in an obscure wish to take a last look at the freedom that was no longer hers.

Her eye fell upon women from London's upper world, dressed in the height of fashion, with little beribboned and fetching hats, feather-trimmed cloaks, and beside them, hand-some men oozing prosperity, even luxury. *Come to look at us like animals in a menagerie? Like the lions in the Tower?* Gina thought with a sudden hardening of her senses.

She straightened her shoulders unconsciously and looked at them all, giving back stare for haughty stare, and swept with all the pride of her lithe, young body through the door.

Outside in the gloomy hall, she followed the rest of the prisoners back the way they had come that morning, across the gray courtyard under heavy skies, into the inner prison. The iron gates clanged shut behind her, and the resounding echoes pounded in her ears.

The first night, she could not sleep. She huddled in a corner of the cell that she shared with half a dozen other women and stared ahead of her, unseeing. Her inner self retreated, refusing to accept this monstrous fate, but the facts would not go away.

Mrs. Potter, a greengrocer's daughter whose husband had somehow amassed a small fortune, had ambitions for her eldest son. Marriage was to be the lever to pry her way into a social world she could, by her own birth, only dream of. But money could open doors for her son, and she disposed ruthlessly of any obstacle in her way.

Gina ruefully thought, *Just my luck that I was in her way. If Mr. James had had any sense of honor, even rudimentary decency—*

But of course he hadn't.

She looked around her at the other inmates, the grimy gray walls, the tiny window far above her head. The grilled door that opened only to admit what was intended as food. A merciful numbness crept over her and slowed the frenetic racing of her thoughts.

Fan tried to coax her to eat, but her stomach churned and she turned away from the ill-smelling dish.

It was the third day. *I'll die in this place*, she thought, and knew it was the simple truth. Even the orphanage, the only home she had known since she was three, had not been this miserable.

The cell door opened.

"It's not mealtime!" cried one of the women. The others, avid for a break in their deadened days, joined in.

"Come to take us for a walk in 'yde Park?"

"The Prince invited us to a fancy ball?"

The guard in the doorway grinned. "More likely a trot up the gallows steps!"

"I mind when there was the long trip to the gallows on Tyburn Hill, in my granny's time," Fan reminisced. "Got your last breath of fresh air on the way up Holborn Road. And the crowds that came to see the hangings! Better than a month of Sundays, Granny said. Not the same anymore."

"Enough of this!" the guard cut her off sharply. He was middle-aged, judging from his grizzled hair and the deeply

9

cut seams bracketing his thick lips, reflecting years of indulgence. His mean eyes searched the cell. "Where is she? The redhead?"

Not until Gina found herself following the guard down the long corridor and out into the courtyard did she believe that he had really come to liberate her. But why? Her sentence was for years, and she could not imagine why she had been removed from her cell.

Unless—the thought struck her—Mr. James had recanted his testimony. Could that be true? She remembered that abject look on his face in the courtroom, when he had tacitly begged her forgiveness, and knew it was contrary to nature to expect him to act honorably. The impulsive youth who had pursued a lowly servant girl into the pantry was not likely to confess that he had lied under oath.

She was given no time to reflect further on whatever lay in wait for her. It was enough, for the moment, to gaze at the milky sky of early February, to breathe the cold air with acute gratitude, even for these few moments.

Then they were inside the square building just within the outer gates, and climbing worn stone steps to an upper room. The guard rapped on the door, and in response to a word from inside, opened the door and thrust her inside.

The room held little furniture. It was possible that convicts were interviewed here, and the warden granted a minimum of possible weapons—two chairs, a small wooden table for writing, an odd cabinet or two.

The only occupant of the room was silhouetted against the sole window. Her first impression of him was of a squarish man, broad of shoulder, without, apparently, any neck at all. Upon the sound of her footsteps, he turned around. Slowly he took in her draggled dark skirt, her once-white blouse (Mrs. Potter had claimed that Gina had no clothing of her own, and would give her none), and finally reached her face.

Her knees, weak from days of fasting, trembled dangerously. She prayed she would not faint, and held herself stiffly against—well, against whatever was to come. She was totally mystified. Searching his foxlike features for a clue, she saw him staring with disbelief at her.

"I wouldn't have credited it!" he said softly, more to himself than to her. "Exactly so!"

"Sir?" Gina said.

"I am Mr. Quinn," the man said, with sudden briskness. "Let us get down to business. I am satisfied that you are the person we want."

"I don't understand," she protested warily.

"Of course you don't. I am not recruiting for a house of ill repute, so don't stand in the doorway, ready to fly away." Mr. Quinn nearly approached kindness then. "Here, sit down in this chair. We have much to talk about."

Obediently she sat where he indicated. More than ever, she was conscious of her dirtiness, her hair—the guard had called her a redhead but her hair was only deep auburn—untouched, and her gown in a state unfit even for scrubbing rags. Mr. Quinn, after that first long examination, paid her appearance no heed.

"First, let me ask you, Gina—your name is Gina?"

"Yes, sir."

"What else? You have a second name?"

"They gave me one at the orphanage," she acknowledged, "but I won't use it."

"Why not?" he asked, leaning forward as if a great deal depended on her answer.

"Matron named me after a street near the orphanage," Gina told him. "Buxton, she said. But it wasn't my own name, so I don't like to use it."

"And what is your own name?"

"I don't remember it."

"You were only three, after all," Mr. Quinn said with a sigh. "Oh, yes, I've looked into your past. But I can give you a new name. If you accept it—"

He stopped and looked at her with a curious, squirrel-like gleam in his eyes. "What would you give me to put the prison behind you?"

She could only stare at him. "Give you? Nothing! I mean—what *can* I give you? I have nothing in the world except these"—she spread her hands to indicate her rags—"except what I am wearing."

Suddenly the ludicrousness of the situation overrode all her misgivings, her woes, her gnawing hunger that had suddenly become clamorous. How ridiculous it was for her in her stale-smelling clothes, her tousled unbrushed hair, her work-reddened hands, to consider seriously what she could give the sleekly shaved, obviously prosperous Mr. Quinn.

She laughed, a little shakily. After all, she had not laughed for some days, and the habit was almost broken. "What would you do with my rags, Mr. Quinn?" she said, almost saucily. She lifted her chin to look at him squarely. She didn't expect to see approval, but it was there.

"You'll do very nicely," he said. "But you didn't answer

11

me. What would you do—let me put it this way, what would you be *willing* to do, to be free of the prison? Forever."

She considered him. Obviously he had escaped from Bedlam, somehow eluded capture in Lambeth, and made his lunatic way across the river.

"Come, come," he said testily. "Answer me."

Better to humor him, she thought, and said, "Almost anything."

"Almost?"

A picture of the crowded, filthy, stench-ridden cell she had just left, and the women who had come from the gutters of the London slums who shared the small space with her, swam before her eyes.

She answered with all the sincerity she was capable of.

"Anything, Mr. Quinn. I'll do *anything.*"

II

Mr. Quinn nodded in satisfaction, and rubbed his hands briskly together.

"Just so," he said brightly. "I thought as much."

She half rose from her chair, but on a gesture from him she sank back. "Now then, the first thing is to get you out of here," he told her. "Wait a moment, and I will take care of a few details." He went out, leaving her alone in the room.

Alone! She ran to the door and peeped through it. The corridor was empty, and she opened the door a little wider. She could escape! No one was on guard. Mr. Quinn, of the bewildering speech, was not in sight.

She edged through the door, when a sobering thought struck her. Where would she go? She had no friends, no place to hide, no one to shelter her.

Looking down at her pitiful clothing, she turned to go back into the room, to wait for the man who might be her benefactor.

If indeed he were not an escaped lunatic!

Even later, in the carriage rattling over the uneven cobblestones, wet with the unspeakable refuse tossed as a matter of course from tenement windows hemming the narrow lanes, Gina could not believe.

Had she just drifted off into a dream? Would she wake inevitably to the ghostly gray walls and the rough shapes of her cellmates?

She peered from the grimy windows of the hired conveyance, greedily soaking in the sights and sounds, the vibrant hurly-burly of London street life. Even the cold wind, whistling across chimney pots and moaning down dilapidated stairways, could not keep Londoners inside.

13

"Don't show your face," commanded Mr. Quinn.

Puzzled, she turned to look inquiringly at him. The tone of voice was sharp, suggesting that a blow might follow, but he sat unmoving in his corner of the seat. He looked at her with his little blue eyes, under bushy, sandy eyebrows, steadily, and she realized that she was being tested. Biddable in small things, she thought, blindly obedient in great.

With a secret smile she sank back against the straw-filled padding, feeling it luxurious after the cold cement of her recent days, and gave herself over to unbridled speculation.

None of the reasons she could think of for her unexpected jail delivery made any sense to her. Nor, in fact, did the idea that Mr. Quinn was a fugitive from Bedlam across the river, and would soon be taken up by the authorities and returned to St. George's Fields.

The cab turned one way and then another. They had reached a more prosperous neighborhood. The houses sat a few feet back from the street, with little iron fences in front and area steps leading downward to lower floors. Trees, too, lifted their rounded, bare tops against the sky, and the air, away from the river, seemed clearer.

She stole a nervous glance at her companion, but he apparently had forgotten her presence. At any rate, he rested his chin in his hand against the window, screening his face from outside view.

At length, after so many changes of direction she lost track of them, the sound of the wheels changed, and she realized they were moving more slowly, into a bricked courtyard.

The sun was overhead. Only the middle of the day, she realized with wonder, as Mr. Quinn helped her down from the carriage. It had taken only an hour for the transformation— from her prison cell to this walled space, wherever it was. She was not allowed time to look about her. Someone came running from the building, which formed one wall of the courtyard, to deal with the driver. Mr. Quinn ignored him, taking her by the arm and hurrying her into the house.

The sudden darkness made her stumble on the steps, but his arm held her from falling. Without knowing quite how it happened, she was in a warm kitchen. Tantalizing odors came from the depths of the great iron range. She was left alone with a stout black-haired woman called Molly, apparently the cook. Molly possessed the unmistakable blue eyes of Ireland, apple-red cheeks, and an alarming efficiency.

No matter how it turned out, Gina thought shortly, no matter whether she were hustled back to Newgate before

14

nightfall, she would be grateful for that next hour. A copper tub, set up before the blazing kitchen hearth. Abundance of hot water poured into the slipper bath, and clouds of soap-scented steam enclosing her in near-privacy. A comb and brush.

And when she emerged, and put on a new russet skirt and white blouse, similar to those she had been wearing but fresh and clean-smelling, she felt that the old, jailed Gina had been discarded, as worthless as the rags that Molly, with an exclamation of disgust, thrust into the range.

Live this moment, her cautious self reminded her, *that's all you've got—the next moment may bring disaster!*

That philosophy had become hers by experience, almost from the first days at the orphanage. Those days were almost the first she could remember. Before that—

She was seated at the deal table, savoring a bowl of stew, when Mr. Quinn reappeared. She looked at him through a euphoric haze. He stared at her, first in obvious amazement, and then in dawning approval. Surprised into speech, he said softly, "Remarkable! He was right!"

Gina almost asked, "Who was right?" but wisely judged that his exclamation was not directed at her. She concentrated on spooning the last of the stew, and eating it. Who knew when she might eat again?

He pulled out a chair opposite her, and sat down, elbows on the table. Now in the kinder light of the fire, he did not look quite so much like a fox. His nose and chin lost their inquisitive sharpness, and his little eyes looked out at her from their bushy overhang with approval.

Gina was no longer afraid. The bowl of soup, the freshness of clean skin and clothing, had worked their miracle. Now she was exceedingly curious. If he had spoken honestly, that he was not running a resort of ill repute, as he had called it, then his purpose was beyond the limits of her imagination.

He settled down to business. "Still of the same mind?" he queried. "Still willing to do what we—that is, what *I* ask?"

It took her only a moment to look squarely at her choice. On the one hand, if she refused, she must return to the squalor of Newgate. On the other hand—

"Yes."

"Good girl. Now your name is Georgina Moffett."

"It is?"

"From this moment on. Remember it well. I am going to take you shortly to a house near Berkeley Square, to restore you to your great-uncle."

She stared at him in wonder. For the first time since she had left the orphanage, the familiar fierce need to know swept over her. "How could you find out, when even the orphanage didn't know who I was? Who were my parents? Why did they abandon me? *Who am I?*"

"Who you really are doesn't interest me," Mr. Quinn told her, coolly. "The identity you assume today is the important thing. Now listen to me."

Gina listened. Georgina Moffett, the real Georgina—Mr. Quinn told her—was the daughter of Sarah Moffett and her husband John, nephew of old Josiah Moffett, a man of considerable wealth with estates along the Kentish coast southwest of Dover.

John and his wife and the baby Georgina had been traveling for some months through the Continent, and by an ill chance had reached Paris in June of 1789. They had been fascinated by the rising of the populace, seeing the birth, so they thought, of a new democracy in troubled France.

"At least, so they wrote home," Mr. Quinn said dryly.

"But France is an empire now, isn't it?"

He shot a quick glance at her. "You're interested in politics? That is unusual—"

"For someone as lowly as a kitchenmaid?" she finished for him. "I waited at table sometimes. I listened to the talk."

He waited for her to continue, but when she said no more, he commented cryptically, "That will make things easier." He went on with his story. . . .

The Moffetts, beguiled by their enthusiasm for what they believed to be a genuine, well-intentioned, and bloodless revolution, such as the English had accomplished almost exactly a century before, had lingered too long. As onlookers, they were swept up with the mob on the Fourteenth of July, and those who found their trampled bodies believed they were dead even before the gates of the Bastille swung open.

Their three-year-old daughter, left for the day with a *concierge*, vanished without a trace.

"Old Josiah Moffett had a search made for the child. Exhaustive though it was, the state of Paris in those days and for a long time afterward was such that a small child was as easy to find as a particular drop of water in the Thames."

"She's been found," Gina said suddenly.

Mr. Quinn nodded enthusiastically. "You've got it in one! Georgina Moffett is alive. *You!*"

"Me?"

Astounded, she stared at him across the table. He might as

16

well have told her to walk to Dover and swim the Channel. At this moment, even that impossibility seemed more reasonable than his suggestion.

"You want me to pretend I'm—that child?" Her voice was scraped raw by disappointment. Whatever she had expected, it wasn't this. "I can't!"

He eyed her calmly. She jumped to her feet and started to pace back and forth, her shoes slapping smartly on the brick floor.

"You're asking me to take the place of a *lady*. Me, Gina the kitchenmaid! He'll see through me in a minute." She whirled to face Mr. Quinn, her dark skirt fanning out behind her, her long legs outlined by the thin fabric. "Then it's back to prison with me—forever, this time!"

His smug smile goaded her past discretion. "I'm not going to ask you why you want me to do this—this *impossible* thing—"

"That's wise of you," he interjected. "In due time, you'll know."

She ignored his remark. "But I can't do it! I won't. I can't even give you back these clothes. She burned the ones I was wearing when I came here. But I'll say thank you for the bath and the soup. And now, if you please, you can take me back to my cell!"

Her voice broke on the last words. For a delirious hour she had believed she might be free. Even a moment ago, she could believe in the story of Georgina Moffett, could even fancy that story could have been her own, for all she knew. But the dream was only a poor thing, a child's toy, broken in an hour.

Through brimming tears, she caught sight of the astonishing Mr. Quinn. He was leaning back in his straight wooden chair, his face alight with enthusiasm.

"Bravo!" he cried, applauding lustily. "Don't worry, he will not expect you to be other than you are. Remember, Georgina would have been reared in an orphanage, the same as you. But the orphanage taught you how to speak, how to walk. That can't be counterfeited."

"What?"

"You'll do magnificently, my dear," he told her. "There's something in the way you hold your head, some of your mannerisms—oh, yes, *Miss Moffett*, you'll do."

She summed him up in one word—*Bedlamite*! But she did not say it aloud.

When they were once again seated in a closed carriage,

17

evening had begun to fall. The haze of twilight was an incredible blue, and the flickering lights of other vehicles approaching them blurred in the fog rising from the river. Molly had thrown a woolen shawl over Gina's shoulders, dismissing Gina's stammered thanks with a shrug, and now Gina pulled the wrap closer and clutched it tightly.

Even so, the February cold penetrated, damply searching out even her bones, so it seemed, and she shivered. Mr. Quinn looked disapprovingly at her. "Don't take a chill," he warned her. "You don't want to give the old man any trouble." Suddenly he chuckled at some private joke. "At least in the beginning!" he added.

After a moment, she ventured, "Who is this man? If he lives in Kent, why is he in London?"

Carelessly, Mr. Quinn replied, "Something to do with the government, I think. Anyway, it makes no difference, does it?" He eyed her keenly.

"I suppose not."

After a moment, he added quietly, "He's not 'this man' to you. He is your uncle Josiah, and you are not to call him anything else. Not even to *think* anything else."

She murmured, "Unless I fail."

He twisted on the seat to peer at her in the darkness. Perhaps it was only a trick of the lights of a passing vehicle, but in the obscurity of the cab's interior, she thought there was an unpleasant gleam in his eyes. She was suddenly reminded of a stray, starving cat she had seen once, while she emptied kitchen refuse into the pit at the back of the Potters' yard. She had interrupted the beast at his feeding, and he had snarled with genuine menace at her. For a moment she had been terrified of him.

Now, she was held in the grip of unpleasant memory for an instant. Mr Quinn held her gaze steadily locked with his, and gritted, "You will not fail. Don't forget that. It's up to you, and I strongly advise you—don't fail."

Suddenly she was afraid. What was ahead of her? An impossible impersonation, one at which she could not succeed and dared not fail. Strangely, her fear was not of Mr. Moffett—the unknown Uncle Josiah—but of the bulky man next to her, who had generously delivered her from prison and fed and clothed her.

The cab rumbled over rough stones and smoother roadways, changing direction now and then, on a journey that stretched, so it began to seem, into infinity. At last, the rapid pace of the vehicle moderated, the clip-clop of the horse's

18

shoes on the cobbles slowed. Apparently they were nearing their destination.

Curious, Gina looked from her window. They were traveling around a minuscule park, surrounded by imposing, well-lighted houses, and then at a tangent down a small street that led away from the square. Mr. Quinn spoke to the driver, and they stopped.

Now that the moment of trial was at hand, she found that she was even more frightened than when she stood next to Fan in the prisoners' line outside the courtroom. That, she realized with a start, had been only four days ago. Another day, in another world. Another Gina.

They stood on the pavement before a house not quite so grand as the ones behind them in Berkeley Square. This one was imposing enough, she decided swiftly. The windows were lighted rectangles against the dark facade of the house. A fanlight over the door shed a luminescent glow on the doorstep.

By its light she could see iron railings along the street, small carved iron gateposts marking the walk. She was suddenly petrified. Her feet refused to carry her forward. Her tongue was dry and withered in her mouth and her heart pounded in her ears.

"Don't panic!" Mr. Quinn said fiercely, seizing her arm in a grip that went through to the bone. "Come on!"

Forced by his grasp to move with him, she stumbled up the broad steps. Vaguely, above the beat of her blood in her ears, she heard the knocker rap sharply.

The door opened. Broadly, across the step, spread the generous yellow light of many candles, and a butler stood on the threshold.

"We wish to see Mr. Moffett," Mr. Quinn said sturdily. "I have brought his great-niece back to him."

The door began to close quickly, and then, hesitating, stopped before it shut completely. The butler peered at them nearsightedly throught the crack.

"Miss Moffett?" The man spoke in a shocked whisper, and then lost his imperial aplomb completely.

"Best you come in," he said, and opened the door widely for Gina to enter.

III

Gina stepped across the threshold and halted, momentarily blinded by the blazing light after the soft turquoise twilight. As her eyes grew accustomed to the brilliance, she looked around her. Behind her, Mr. Quinn was telling plausible lies to the old servant, and a part of her consciousness heeded them. But for the rest, she was stunned by an excess of heat, light, and the clean smell of a well-scrubbed tile floor.

She knew that this entry hall pleased her, but she did not know why. She had never heard of harmonious proportions, of the elegance of restraint. She thought perhaps its charm lay in the spaciousness of the broad oaken stairway on the left, climbing straight to a balustraded landing. Perhaps it was the slender-legged table along the right-hand wall, flanked by two graceful, gilt-touched chairs.

But most likely, she decided, it was the lavishness of light— real wax candles in wall sconces, in the chandelier overhead, reflected twofold in the gold-framed mirror over the little table. The flickering candles gave an impression of hospitality, generosity, kindliness, and she responded, expanding almost tangibly in the welcoming warmth.

The contrast between her recent surroundings and this house, like midnight and high noon, warned her to be wary. This would be something to remember, all right, when she was sent in disgrace back to prison. For, of course, the whole scheme was the lunatic product of a deranged mind—Mr. Quinn's secretive and quite mad mind.

Only one phrase remained in her memory of all that Mr. Quinn had urged fiercely on her, gimlet eyes boring into hers—*you must not fail.*

On her part, she agreed entirely. She *could* not fail. No

fate could be so unfeeling as to show her this, this *heaven*, and then snatch it away.

Mr. Quinn loosened his hold on her elbow, but it was only a token. He still held her in thrall, even though the bonds were invisible. She was, at this moment, neither orphan Gina Buxton, nor the new girl, Georgina Moffett. She was merely the creature of Mr. Quinn—her own identity lost, her new character still shapeless. She had never had much identity, only a fierce, almost animal, instinct to survive.

And survival meant, although she had not analyzed it so, a saving oblivion of all that had happened to her before she arrived at the orphanage. A child of three could be expected to remember, for example, how she had arrived at the orphanage—by boat, by carriage—but she did not.

Could she even remember the kind of home she had lived in for those uncertain years—the question had not bothered her for a long time, but Mr. Quinn had brought the aching wonder back to her. Mr. Quinn, and the subtle effulgence of this small room.

Who was she? Did she remember—for instance—a room like this one? A nurse to take care of her? Did she have servants to bring meals, fresh dresses? Someone to tuck her into a warm safe bed at night?

Or were her first three years simply an extension, backward, of the hard drudgery she knew in the orphanage? Had her mother had such work-reddened hands as these she thrust now into the folds of her skirt to hide them?

Possibly the one, and possibly the other. Gina did not know, because long ago she had *chosen* not to know.

Mr. Quinn brought her back to the present with a start. He touched her elbow. "Now, my dear," he confided with a chuckle hidden in his voice, "we must wait. I wager it will not be long."

They were alone. She had not noticed the butler leave. She moistened dry lips. "What happens next?"

"Hard to say. But I will gamble that the old gentleman cannot resist the bait."

"Bait," she repeated, the word sour on her tongue. She knew that what he was asking of her was—unusual, at the least. She refused to take it out and look at it, to weigh the question in the balance of her uncomplicated scales of right and wrong. After all—she had earlier this day decided—what could they do to her but put her back into prison? And that was only if she were found out.

Whereas, if she turned back now, before the game was

21

played out, prison was an infallible certainty. A dreadful, gray, unavoidable result. She knew she would do anything to keep from going back to the stinking cell she had left—only a lifetime ago—that morning. Besides, she would never know, if she gave up now, whether she could in fact carry off the impersonation itself!

Mr. Quinn glared at her with a mixture of anxiety and menace. The anxiety, she knew, was bent toward the remote possibility of a lurking scruple or two on the part of a convicted thief, and the menace gave her fair warning that she must go on with the deception.

For the first time, it occurred to her that the result of failure might not be prison. Might, in fact, be something quite vague in her mind, but exceedingly unpleasant, even disastrous. She swallowed hard, but the lump that had risen in her throat refused to go away.

"I—I can't!" she whispered desperately. "I can't pretend to be something I'm not!"

He gripped her arm above the elbow and she felt the pain coursing down her arm, numbing her fingers. His sharp little eyes, half buried in unhealthy rolls of flesh, pierced the shield of bravado she had hastily flung between them. "You what? Don't you forget, girl, everything you are wearing is mine. And, if you so much as quiver, I'll take it back. Right here."

"You wouldn't!"

But she suspected he would, and enjoy the process as well. He read submission in her eyes, and his cruel fingers eased on her flesh. "After all," he said with a cajoling geniality she was learning to know as false, "you're not pretending to be somebody else. You really don't know who you are, do you?"

It was the simple truth. She was surely not Gina Buxton, but she was nobody else, either!

The alternatives were clear. Do as she was bidden, or lie forgotten in the putrid straw of an airless cell, and die.

Unconsciously she squared her shoulders and lifted her head. It was a proud gesture, the more impressive because she did not know she was doing it. She was tall, nearly as tall as Mr. Quinn, and she looked into his eyes almost on a level.

"Don't worry, Mr. Quinn. I'll do the best I can."

After a moment his face relaxed into a smile, but she could detect no amusement in it. They settled down to wait.

It seemed to her that they waited a long time. She recalled hearing, at some time, a door closing in some remote area of the house. Hesitantly, she mentioned it at last to her companion.

A worried frown appeared between his eyes. "Where was it? Did you hear anything else?"

"No, nothing else. Probably a servant," she guessed.

"I don't like it," he said, half to himself. He began to pace back and forth in the narrow hall. "Sending for the watch? No, I don't think so. His curiosity has to be pricked. His great-niece, found at last. He could not be sure whether it was true or not. And he'd have to be sure. No, he wouldn't hand me over, not without seeing you first."

His own arguments convinced him, she judged, by the way his face brightened. The restiveness that pervaded the entry hall, growing as the delay prolonged itself, was partly banished by Mr. Quinn's sudden confidence. Partly—but not entirely.

Her nerves were screwed tight enough to hum. What kind of man was this Josiah Moffett? Kind? Possibly. Shrewd? Probably. And gullible? Dryly, she doubted it. She was dimly aware of an expanding ambition, dilating from the tiniest pinpoint of a seed until it threatened to fill the horizon. There was more in the world than a life of servitude. Whatever happened here tonight, she would not be the same person tomorrow. There were houses of luxury, such as this. Coaches, fine clothes, even jewels—and none of them like that brooch of Mrs. Potter's!

The visions in her mind were vague of outline, but the essence was unmistakable. Gina's determination spun round and round. The panoramic view of countless rewards set her dizzy. She sank involuntarily down on the second step of the oaken stairway, and leaned her throbbing head against the banister.

Could she reach up from the lowest step on the social stairway, where fate had thrust her, and gain—she was not quite sure what she wanted, but the conviction came to her that she could, she *could*. If not here with the mysterious Josiah Moffett, then by some other pathway. Mr. Quinn was sure to send her back to prison. Her logic was infallible. She must think of a way to avoid—

At that moment the old butler returned. If possible, she thought, he was shakier than before. His ashen face was long, and the long creases that ran down his cheeks made it appear even longer. His eyes protruded in a look of permanent astonishment, his thin old eyebrows making tents of inquiry above.

Whimsically she thought that nothing in his long life could

23

have astonished him so much as her own appearance in his master's foyer.

"Mr. Moffett—" He swallowed, and began again. "Mr. Moffett will see you, sir." He cast a look at Gina. "And the young lady, too."

Inwardly, Gina exulted. She had passed the first test—the butler acknowledged her quality. She had been in service long enough to pick up certain nuances used by servants, whose keen eyes were often sharper than their masters. Gina had been quick to learn, greedy to know all the things of the world that the orphanage had omitted in her education—which was a great deal.

The butler had called her a "lady." She stepped ahead of Mr. Quinn, avoiding his brutal grip on her arm, and went through the opened door. She was hardly aware that Mr. Quinn hesitated fractionally before following her, a considering frown creasing his forehead, as though assailed by sudden doubt. When she did glance his way, his expression was once more bland, even affable.

The room into which they entered was cavelike, almost gloomy after the brilliantly lighted hall. In a few moments, she could see sufficiently to take stock of her surroundings. The furniture was heavy, dark, masculine. The color of the carpet, thick beneath her feet, was lost in shadows cast by the massive desk. At one side of the room was a fireplace, and a little fire burned neatly on the hearth. A sole candle on the desk brought pale glimmers of light to a burnished standish and two ornate boxes of brass, which were the only objects on the broad polished surface of the desk.

She thought at first they were alone in the room, but a thin voice spoke from the obscurity beyond the desk.

"Come, let me look at you, child."

Startled, she sought the source of the voice. In the shadows, almost as though he reveled in secrecy, sat a man dressed in dark clothing. One hand shaded his face from the faint light, or, possibly, supported a weary head. He must be ill, she thought, and his voice reinforced her guess.

"Mr. Moffett," interposed Mr. Quinn, his voice unnecessarily loud in the quiet, "I am Wolfgang Quinn, at your service. I have, at great trouble and expense to myself, located—"

"I was addressing the young lady," said Mr. Moffett, in the same thready voice that, even as insubstantial as a reed blowing in a forest, carried sufficient authority to stop her mentor in mid-breath. "Come here."

Obediently, she moved forward. She still could not see the

man well, and she wondered what he expected to see in her, with her back to the firelight, and only one candle illuminating an oblique angle of her face. But she was drawn nearer almost as a magnet draws iron. He was her future, and on what happened in the next few minutes, her fate would rest. It was good he did not ask her a question, she thought wildly, because her dry mouth could not have shaped a single word.

The butler, whose name she learned was Hastings, was quickly remedying the lack of light. He brought a branched candlestick, setting it on the desk near Mr. Moffett, and lit the candles. He watched her surreptitiously, as he lit one candle after another, and the swelling light fell upon her. Had he too known the real Georgina? she wondered. Considering his age, she thought it was eminently likely that he had been in Mr. Moffett's service far longer than her own life span. Probably in her father's time—.

Stilled by surprise, she caught her breath. *Her father's time!* She hadn't even noticed the moment when she made the transformation, moved from Orphan Gina to Imposter Georgina, whose life could open up into a beguiling, fantastic vista.

Mr. Quinn had been right—she must not even think that this man was any other than *Uncle Josiah.* And suddenly she knew it would be easy.

Without even stumbling, without more than a fumbling hesitation, she accepted, with silent gratitude to the vicar's version of Providence, this magnificent gift that had been presented to her. Summoning all her considerable intelligence, she bent her attention to the wisp of a man in the chair before her. She must learn how to please him. . . .

"And you say you found her in an orphanage," Josiah was murmuring when Gina attended him again. "And how did you know to look for her there?"

"I am sorry, sir," purred Mr. Quinn. "I see I did not explain myself fully. I found your niece in Newgate Prison. Then I searched out her origins, and found that she had come from the orphanage. She knew little or nothing of her background. But I knew—from certain indications that I am not at liberty to discuss just now—" His voice trailed away effectively. He allowed just the faintest hint of confusion to appear in his manner, and then went on. "Even her name, though, fits. Gina. Georgina."

Mr. Moffett seized on the crucial point. "Why were you in prison, my child?"

Mr. Quinn again seemed about to speak, but a wave of

Josiah Moffett's slender hand stopped him. She wondered just how this imposture would profit Mr. Quinn. She was certain that success here meant a great deal to him. Well, not as much as it now did to her!

She wished she knew how Mr. Quinn wished her to answer the question, and yet, weighed in the level gray eyes of the man in the chair, she was compelled to tell the truth. Later, she realized, she could have done nothing more advantageous to her.

"For theft, sir."

"Of what, my dear? A loaf of bread? A shawl against the cold?"

"No, sir," she answered steadily. "I was accused of stealing a worthless piece of jewelry."

"Accused, you say," Mr. Moffett pounced. "But you did not steal it?"

Her gesture spoke volumes of contempt for the trumpery pin. Even now she could not think of it as valuable. It was so garish in its design, so—the word vulgar came from somewhere in her mind.

"Then why—" Mr. Moffett's voice lapsed into silence. He seemed lost in thought, while his eyes studied her.

"A young man—" Mr. Quinn began, but Mr. Moffett glanced austerely in his direction, and he lapsed into frustrated silence.

Mr. Quinn teetered on the brink of mixed emotions. On the one hand, he had a healthy respect for the acumen of the man before him. Josiah Moffett had a formidable, if not wide, reputation for brilliant shrewdness, and Mr. Quinn might find it very uncomfortable, he believed rightly, if he were detected in this illicit scheme.

And yet, uncomfortable was not the word for his situation if he failed, even though through no fault of his own. He was the one who had discovered the girl, having been told what to look for. He was therefore responsible for her success. He did not care to think of the consequences to his own person if his superiors deemed him incompetent. He barely refrained from shuddering. Fortunately, Mr. Moffett seemed fairly hooked. Yet there was still suspicion in the old man's face.

"Hastings, bring the light closer," Mr. Moffett said suddenly.

The candelabrum, held with old palsied hands, shook its shimmering light in flickers over her face. Obedient to a slight gesture from Mr. Moffett, Gina moved her head so that the revealing light fell full upon her face. This was the test, she knew, aware that he was searching her features for something—an accident of bone structure, a quirk of eyebrow perhaps—that he alone knew.

Her blood pounded like a drum in her ears, and she wished she had eaten either more soup, or less.

She stood so, interminably, looking steadily into vacancy. A sharp cry roused her, and she turned with a whirl of her long skirt.

Mr. Moffett had fallen sideways in his chair. His face took on, as she watched, an unearthly pallor, and if he still breathed, she could not detect it.

"His heart," Hastings explained, almost sobbing.

Mr. Quinn's reaction was equally indicative of shock, but of a different order. In an undertone that only Gina could hear, he muttered, "If the old crock fades on us now, we're as good as dead ourselves!"

IV

Josiah Moffett was not dead.

Gina moved the candleholder, rescued from Hastings's heedless hands, so that the light fell full on the invalid's face. The butler fumbled in his pocket for a small vial. He moved it back and forth under his master's nose. Soon he was rewarded by a long, shuddering groan.

Mr. Quinn, fidgeting behind her, sighed gustily. Her own anxiety faded in inverse proportion to the returning color in the old man's cheeks.

Mr. Moffett fluttered his eyelids, and took a deep breath. "I am subject to these—occasions," he said by way of apology, and letting his hand hover for a second on his servant's sleeve in thanks. "Now then, my child, I want to hear your—experiences; but not tonight. I find that I am a little tired."

So. It is not over yet. This intolerable strain will go on and on, and on, she thought, *and I cannot bear much more of it.*

It was the measure of Mr. Quinn's vast relief that he made his first mistake. The old man in the chair seemed, to Wolfgang Quinn, to be, of a certainty, fair hooked on the cunningly contrived bait. They were right, Mr. Quinn exulted silently—those who had told him the girl would do. And how clever to find her in prison—she would not be overly burdened with scruples.

"Mr. Moffett," he began officiously, "I'll bring the girl back tomorrow—"

The old man in the chair roused, the candlelight showing anger, feeble but unmistakable, in his eyes. "*Girl?*" he said, in silken reproof. "My great-niece?"

Mr. Quinn was fairly caught. If Gina were the person he

28

claimed she was, then he should never have used a word usually applied to a servant. And if she were not Georgina Moffett—he might as well confess the plot at once and have done with it. Hè had succeeded with the impersonation better than he had hoped. He must take extreme care not to be brought down to disaster, not now when they were so close.

"I—I only meant—"

But Mr. Moffett was no longer listening. "Hastings, send Mrs. Beddoes upstairs with the young lady." Was there a faint stress on the last word?

"Very good." Hastings bowed. "In—in which room, sir?"

His master had closed his eyes. He was dreadfully fatigued, Gina thought, or else really quite ill. And if he were too ill to take her in—

But he aroused enough to open his eyes. "In the Wedgwood Room, of course," he said with a touch of petulance. Then he closed his eyes again. The interview was quite definitely concluded, and Mr. Quinn's error, so he thought with rising cheerfulness, was forgotten.

Hastings bade them wait in the foyer. He disappeared behind the baize door at the back of the hall, beneath the oaken stairs. As soon as they were alone, Mr. Quinn allowed his jubilation to appear. He all but whirled her around the hall, she thought, and even standing still, his spirit danced visibly within him.

"We've made it!" His words were ecstatic, even though he retained sufficient caution to whisper. "Now then, Gina—"

With a wicked twist she had not known she possessed, she said, "Please, sir, remember I am *Miss Moffett*," and was gratified to see a grudging admiration in the glance he shot at her. With a return to her ordinary manner, she added, "What happens now?"

"You stay here, of course," he said, surprised. "I'll be back bright and early to see what's going on."

She was suddenly afraid of losing the sole anchor she had to reality, fouled though it was. This man had befriended her, no matter why, and he had miraculously delivered her from prison. As to Mr. Moffett, she realized she had no idea of what went on in his mind. Did he believe her? And even if he did, who was he? What manner of man was she entrusting herself to?

She could be packed off to Bedlam this night, or back to Newgate, and no one would know what had become of her.

Darkling rumors, once heard and all but forgotten, ran through her thoughts.

Luxurious though her future might be in this house, on the other hand her fate, already reversed once today, could as unpredictably, as unreasonably, take off on some new, unsuspected tangent. The price, she thought fearfully, might be more than she could afford to pay.

Clinging to the known, she faltered in contemplating the unknown. "Can't I go back with you?" she asked suddenly.

Mr. Quinn's approval turned into frost. "What are you thinking about, girl?"

With the deliberate derogatory word, she was dumped back into the cell, in her mind, into the fetid straw.

She could have cried with hurt, like a bewildered puppy dropped from a carriage and left behind. But pride came surging to her rescue, and she said, "I'm all right, Mr. Quinn. I'll look forward to tomorrow." Gratifyingly, her voice did not shake.

Mr. Quinn appraised her with a long look. So much depended on this woman, and he knew so little about her. Would she break under pressure? Would she, if the old man pretended to be kind, betray everything in a gush of gratitude? Genuine kindness was not a part of Mr. Quinn's daily experience, but now and then it had crossed his path, always to his detriment. He hoped that in this house, with so much at stake, he would not be so unlucky.

Best make sure of her. "You play your cards right, and you won't be sorry. I'll see to that. You understand me? Don't play me false—"

Footsteps sounded behind them, and Hastings returned, in his wake a plump motherly woman, substantially more respectable than Molly of Mr. Quinn's kitchen.

The housekeeper dropped a curtsy to Gina, sent the departing Mr. Quinn a level, assessing look, and with quick competence shepherded Gina upstairs.

"To the Wedgwood Room, he says," panted Mrs. Beddoes on the last flight of steps, "and I sent Agnes up to light the fire, but they'll yet be a chill."

Wise in the ways of the back stairs, Gina wondered, *The fire already laid? A well-run household.*

The housekeeper held the door to the pale green Wedgwood Room for her. A young girl, obviously Agnes, was on her knees before the hearth, coaxing a tiny flicker into a blaze. The room still held the bleakness of a February night, but the coverlet was turned back and Gina suspected that a warming pan was already taking the chill off the bed. The room was clean and orderly, and in fact had an air of being in constant use.

"You're surprised, miss," said Mrs. Beddoes, "and I don't wonder at it. But Mr. Moffett's instructions are to keep the room in readiness for Mr. John and Miss Sarah, if they ever come back from France."

Shocked, Gina exclaimed, "But that's been so long!"

"Aye, but he thought there was a chance that they might have escaped, in all the trouble. Poor man, I think he's given up by now, but he puts off having the dust sheets put on. And a good thing, too, for I don't know where we'd put you, else."

The woman's artless explanation dismayed Gina. A room kept for—she calculated quickly—sixteen years, in readiness for a beloved family who would never return. Surely old Josiah Moffett's faith must have wavered over the years, waned until there was only an unreasoning hope left.

Suddenly, she felt cold, on the bitter outside of life, like a homeless urchin pressing her nose against a steamy bakery window. There was ineffable bliss, she believed, just beyond the limit of her clouded vision, a happiness she had not known could exist. She did not understand its shape or texture—she only knew it was there, and if she were strong enough, bold enough, she might reach far enough to touch it.

What if Josiah Moffett believed she was in truth his great-niece? The only relative he had left, somehow salvaged from the tragedy he refused to face? He would love her, not for herself, but certainly for the person he believed she was—and then, suppose he found out she was someone else?

Heartbreak.

With a flash of insight, she knew that whatever happened here in this house, it would mean heartbreak. For Josiah, if he found out she had deceived him. For herself, if she had to leave, unwanted. Uncherished—and that was the key word, the *open sesame* to all she craved in the world. It was not the soft comforts, the warm fires, the fine clothes, silky against her skin. It was the *cherishing* that her innermost self cried out for, with the aching of a lost child, crying in the cold outside a lighted window.

The fulfillment of her craving was almost within her grasp. Something deeper than thought fastened on to the hope of being truly loved, and would not let it go.

She was mildly surprised to come back to the present, and

find that only instants had passed, though she had traveled so far.

Doggedly, Mrs. Beddoes was still following her own avenue of logic. "His nephew John," she said. "From the way Hastings put it—and a rare shock it was, too, I don't mind saying—that would be your father, miss?"

Brightly she waited for an answer. Gina, torn between her need to survive, and the dread of bringing disappointment, even grief, to the old man, found the scales weighing heavily on one side. Perhaps she could truly take the place with him of the toddler lost in Paris, or in London, or in any of the myriad, possibly fatal, stopping-places in between.

"Yes," Gina said steadily, decisively, in her mind irrevocably, "my father."

After Mrs. Beddoes had exhausted all the excuses for lingering that she could devise, she left, dragging an equally reluctant Agnes with her.

Gina curled up in a chair drawn near the hearth, and sat for a long time, chin in work-reddened hand, letting the leaping flames warm her body and make pictures for her imagination.

The pendulum was swinging back, carrying Gina from tiptoe assurance to uneasy distrust. She feared to move, lest her reverie of bliss be broken into shards. For it was a phantasm—it had to be. By no stretch of the odds of probability could she have waked up shivering this morning in matted, seamy straw, in torn tunic and skirt, with three cellmates greedy for her share of an odious, greasy breakfast, and come to sleep that same night in a room of surpassing comfort.

A soft green room, yet riotous with color. Tones of gold glowed at the windows and on the chairs, echoed in the multicolored floral colors of a huge needlework rug; embroidered Jacobean flowers climbed up the bed curtains.

She hung on to her fantasy, born, she suspected darkly, of Newgate fever, not moving until the fire died down and the room turned cold. Then, regretfully, she stirred.

But even after she rose from the deep-cushioned chair, the sense of unreality stayed with her. Marveling, she moved around the room, touching—to make sure of their tangible texture—the curtains at the windows. Feeling the soft silky wool of the rug beneath her bare feet. And when she reached the bed, she found that Agnes had laid out a nightgown for her—made of soft white flannel, with cunning lace ruffles around the neck and at the wrists of the long sleeves.

She must not wake up, she thought, and deliberately tossed aside all her doubts—at least for now. In some fashion she must have strayed into lunacy—perhaps joining Mr. Quinn's aberration, or perhaps, and even worse, finding a sort of madness that was peculiarly her own.

At any rate, her situation, real or not, was incomparably satisfying to the senses, and there was nothing to be done but to enjoy it. Whether it endured until the morning, or whether she had in truth slipped into derangement that would last the rest of her short life, she could not determine. Tomorrow would tell, she decided, climbing into bed and feeling the welcome softness of the long flannel gown folding about her feet, next to the heavenly warming pan. . . .

She dreamed that night, the dream that she had forgotten. Long ago, so long ago that she could not tell when, she had dreamed the same dream night after night, and always the dream had ended in sobbing hysterics.

It began gently enough. There was music in it, a woman's pure voice softly singing. *"Mon amie Jeannetot"* were nearly all the words she could remember. The music held a sweet rocking rhythm, like a cradle, and as the dream went on, she knew she was being held by the singer, closely and dearly, and then the dream vanished, fading away unaccountably, and leaving her bereft.

Matron would come then, summoned by one of the older orphans, and hold her until, exhausted, she would fall asleep again.

So it was now, the old dream bringing her nothing new, except for the shiny white animal with four bright hooves. But the same sense of desolation was there, pervasive and insistent, and she woke with wet cheeks.

The wisps of the dream lingered like an old perfume, until, at last, she slept again.

When she awakened again, the maid Agnes was making up the fire. A tray holding a pale green Wedgwood chocolate pot, and cup and saucer to match, stood on a nearby table. Gina realized suddenly that she had eaten nothing for days except for the bowl of soup at Mr. Quinn's, yesterday.

"Ah, you're awake, miss," said Agnes, roused from her task by Gina's sharp exclamation. "Now I'm glad to see that. You were sleeping sound as a baby when I came in before."

She brought a fluffy, feather-trimmed bed jacket from a drawer, and helped Gina into it, plumping up the pillows behind her with more energy than skill. Then she brought the tray and set it across Gina's lap.

"Just chocolate?" Gina said, sounding disappointed in spite of herself. She was so hungry that she did not think she could get out of bed without being strengthened by at least a roast chicken, and perhaps fortified by a few side dishes.

"I'll bring your breakfast straight," Agnes promised.

Gina had a prudent second thought. "Will Mr.—my uncle expect me at breakfast?"

"No, Miss Moffett," Agnes assured her. "He always breakfasts in his room. He is not well, most days. But then I expect you know that."

Agnes vanished. Gina leaned back, savoring every sip of the hot drink. *I could get accustomed to this,* she thought.

How many times had she done just the same chores that Agnes was now doing for her? Make up the new fire, light it so that the mistress would be warmed while she dressed. Lay out the best silver and the Staffordshire china on a worked linen napkin, and struggle upstairs to Mistress Potter under the staggering weight of the mammoth tray. No simple, ascetic hot chocolate for her! No indeed—it was eggs, and kidneys, and mountains of toasted bread, and three kinds of preserves, gooseberry, Damson plum, and a sweet orange marmalade brought down from Dundee.

Thus she had done every morning of the four months she had worked for Mrs. Potter. Now it was incredible that she herself could be waited upon in the same fashion.

She lifted her work-roughened hand and looked at it. Tentatively, she placed it on the soft sheet and smoothed the small wrinkles out of the fine linen, feeling the unaccustomed silkiness against the roughness of her skin.

The day stretched ahead of her. Josiah Moffett would doubtless send for her soon, to resume the interview terminated last night with his collapse. And he would decide for himself the truth of her statements.

Mr. Quinn's words came back to her. "You don't know who you really are," he had taunted her. "So you might as well be this one as that one, hey?" His shiny little eyes were vivid in her recollection, and his pudgy fingers clamped on her arm. She decided she didn't like Mr. Quinn very well.

I'm not a gullible goose, she told herself. Somehow, in some way, Mr. Quinn would have to be paid. He was not a man who gave anything away—even a bowl of soup—for charity, she was sure.

But, with any luck at all, she thought with entirely unjustified optimism, perhaps he won't present his bill, at least for a while!

34

V

She looked down at the gown Agnes had dropped over her head, smoothed over her slim hips.

Her mother's gown, so Mrs. Beddoes told her.

This white muslin fabric, these slippers, had been chosen by a woman she could not have known, yet whose life—and tragic death—had come, in the intricate maneuverings of fate, to entwine with Gina's. It was an odd kinship—not of blood, Gina reminded herself austerely. Let there be no question of longing for that. And yet, she stood here in Sarah Moffett's room, dressed in Sarah Moffett's clothing. And slept last night in that woman's bed, wrapped in a cheerfully warm gown, smelling strongly of the lavender in which it had been laid away.

Mr. Quinn might well prove to be an ugly ally, but she, quite simply, could not summon sufficient self-denial to leave this house. Where would she go? What could she do? A housemaid without a reference would inevitably find employment, such as it was, on the streets. Besides, even though she could not prove she was the missing niece, neither could she prove she was in fact someone else.

She entertained a grudging respect for her rescuer. He had been careful to tell her nothing that she could use against him, even supposing what he considered her orphan-bred scruples unaccountably rose against him.

Rapidly she reviewed their brief conversations. The story of the child Georgina. His discovery of Gina Buxton herself in Newgate. The resemblance—in his eyes—to Sarah. Nothing that anyone might take exception to. Only the lurking undertone in his voice, the veiled ominous note in his words.

You must not fail! he had said. And something in the way he said it gave her pause to think.

She did not intend to fail. Perhaps her success might not lie in the precise form envisioned by Mr. Quinn—but everyone had different dreams, and Gina's had traveled far afield from their previous directions during the last twenty-four hours.

She could tell the truth, she determined—the truth that she knew. And if the old gentleman downstairs chose to accept her, it would not be her fault, would it? Her conscience would be clear, and Mr. Quinn's could safely be left for his own accounting.

But don't count too much on being accepted, an inner voice warned. *The event sounds too good to be true—or even honest. Somewhere a pitfall has been dug for you, most likely.* She resolved to walk warily.

Now her uncle was asking for her, she was told, and, encouraged by the fact that at least the servants accepted her assumed identity, she descended the stairs to the lower hall, where old Hastings waited to guide her.

She found Josiah Moffett in the same room where he had interviewed her the night before. But today, the heavy maroon draperies were pulled back from the window, and watery February sunlight flooded the room.

The man himself appeared also to have opened up a window in himself to the daylight. The seeming invalid of the night before was transformed into a vigorous man of, if not middle age, at least only preliminary senescence.

Josiah Moffett was taller than she thought. His face was long and bony, his arresting eyes under near-transparent lids flashed blue, and he was thin as a heron. An air of unquestioned authority sat upon him, and she thought the set of his prominent jaw indicated a stability to rely on.

"You slept well?"

"Yes, sir. Thank you."

"Please sit down. Over here, next to me. I think you'll find this chair to your liking."

He spoke with polished civility, but she noticed that her chair was so placed that her face was in full light, and his own, once he had seated himself, was in demi-shadow.

Now, she thought, *Mr. Quinn can't help me anymore.*

The questioning began, kindly enough. "Tell me, my child, what you remember first. Your very earliest recollection. And then we will see—"

She spoke slowly at first. She did not tell him about her

36

dream of the night before. It was too precious to her, the only security she remembered. Even wispy as it was now, vanishing in the light, she clung to it as to a loved toy relic.

"The orphanage, of course," she said. "And Matron—she was really very kind, as much as she could be with so many children to care for. But—"

Gina told him as briefly as she could about her life at St. Clothilde's Home for Indigent Children. He did not interrupt her, and at one time she thought he had fallen asleep.

She hadn't realized how little there was to tell. She had lived nineteen years, all but the first three in the orphanage just off Buxton Street. They had slept on little pallets on the floor—all the girls together in one big unheated room, the boys in another. They had eaten at long wooden tables from wooden bowls. There were lessons three days a week, and when they were not at lessons they were learning useful chores—so Matron had classified them—scrubbing floors, cleaning windows.

On Sundays they had gone to the nearby church, two by two, down the street, to be herded into the last three pews of St. Margaret's, unheated in winter, stifling in August.

"Everyone pitied us," she remembered suddenly, "but they kept their children away from us. As though we had loathsome diseases." Her eyes flashed as she spoke in recollection. With a sudden, rueful laugh, she said, "I'm sorry. I thought I had long ago buried my resentment."

Mr. Moffett stirred. She could not read his thoughts, could not tell whether he believed anything she said, whether he even cared, whether he would call for the constable to take her back to prison.

"And now tell me why you stole the brooch."

It was over. Her tiny little interval, one night, of being cherished—that was it, she realized with dawning recognition—like a loved niece was gone. Not the soft bed, not the fire nor the generous breakfast tray. It was not these she would miss most, but the cherishing they reflected.

Having known it, fleetingly, she would know the measure of what life could be and was not. And in Newgate Prison, if she were taken back, she would die of that knowledge. It was as simple as taking a plant from a sunny window to the coal cellar.

She raised her head to look squarely at him. She wished she could see his face more clearly. Somehow she had to convince this man that she had not lied. Surprisingly, his goodwill was more important to her than all the rest.

37

"I did not steal it," she said earnestly. "It was worth very little. I am positive that even as the watch took me away, the brooch was still on the woman's dressing table."

"Then why?"

"Because she wanted to marry her son to some distant connection of a knight." The contempt in her voice edged her words like a saber.

An odd sound came from the shadows, and she realized with some astonishment that Josiah Moffett was laughing. This was the final blow. She had been picked up and handed around like a small item of no great value, and now—he found her *amusing.*

Something was happening to Gina, she thought with alarm, and she grasped with both hands at her considerable self-control, dinned into her every day at St. Clothilde's. But some emotion long forgotten and buried stirred within her.

"I am glad I have served to divert you," she said with immense and very angry dignity. "No doubt Mr. James Potter shared your amusement as he testified—no, *lied*—about me in that courtroom. But to me it was something more than a torn blouse, an ugly episode in a pantry. It was my reputation, my chance for a respectable position, and, actually, my liberty that furnished his entertainment."

She stood up, ignoring Josiah's imperious gesture. "I will relieve you, sir, of my care, as soon as I have found my own clothes again."

Tears stung the back of her eyes, and she dreaded the imminent possibility of breaking into tears before this formidable man. Somehow, he seemed even more daunting than the bewigged judge at Newgate Prison. But she resolved she would not let Josiah frighten her, either.

She walked away with that peculiar elegance she did not know she had, a matter of long, cleverly articulated bones. When she reached the door she paused, fumbling with the catch.

The man behind her spoke. "Georgina."

My name is Gina! she would have cried out, childishly, but she could not make a sound. She could only stand at the door, not turning, rigid in pride.

"Where did you learn how to speak, Georgina?"

Over her shoulder she flung at him, "The vicar at St. Margaret's. The orphanage thought we had souls to save, if nothing else, and the vicar—"

She finally worked the catch and swept through the door. She started blindly for the stairway. One thing at a time, she thought. First, she would go upstairs as she had told Mr. Moffett, find her shirt and the dark skirt, the stiffly clean woolen shawl of Mr. Quinn's providing, and leave the house. She would not even look around her, upstairs, at the room she had slept in, had dared to dream could be hers.

She had tricked herself again. Aching for someone of her own, someone to belong to, she had agreed too easily to Mr. Quinn's scheme. Well, it hadn't worked, as her inner doubts had told her all the time.

She would be gone before Mr. Quinn returned. Suddenly that was important. She did not know where she would go. But she was positive that she was not going to be taken back to Newgate. It was imperative to be gone from this house before Mr. Quinn returned.

Careful even in her blindness to close the door behind her, she did not even see the two men in the hall. She had swept to the first step in the grand staircase when she heard a word that stopped her short.

"Formidable!"

The word was pronounced in French, and startled as though someone had struck a familiar note on a harpstring, she turned.

One of the two men in the hall was Hastings, and she passed over him quickly. The other man aroused her immediate interest. He was like no one who had ever visited at Mrs. Potter's, and she examined him intently.

Of medium height, he was of slight build. A well-cut coat covered what she shrewdly suspected, from the way he carried himself, to be incipient, bulging evidence of good living. His tailoring was impeccably English, but his moustache was not, nor was the spirited and frankly admiring gaze he favored her with.

"Is this the young lady?" he said to Hastings, and not waiting for an answer, he stepped to the staircase. Hastings followed him, not quiet knowing how to deal with the vagaries of foreigners, but permitting approval to appear briefly but clearly on his old face.

When the stranger came close, she saw telltale signs that he was older than she had at first thought. Bright, probably amusing, she guessed, but for just a moment she glimpsed a queer, sad, searching look in his lively eyes.

"Mademoiselle," he said, giving an impression of gallantly sweeping a plumed hat from his head in her honor, even though he stood perfectly still, "permit me. I am René Valois, *à votre service."*

A voice spoke from the doorway of the rooms she had just left. "I should have known," said Mr. Moffett, dryly, "that you could not approach the question without prejudice."

"*Mon cher*," responded the stranger quickly, "a pretty girl is reason enough to send a man's wits wandering. But I see something is amiss here. Do not tell me, Josiah, my old friend, that you have somehow offended the young lady?"

The delicate, humorous innuendo in his voice left no doubt as to the offense he meant, and suddenly Gina felt herself blushing to the roots of her hair. However, in spite of her embarrassment, she was charmed.

She reached her hand out to the stranger, and smiled at him. His pebble-brown eyes darkened in a peculiar fashion, and she thought for a moment that he caught his breath in surprise. But when she looked her question at him, his face was bland, telling her nothing.

"Nothing is amiss," she told him in her pleasant, throaty voice. "My—Mr. Moffett has a penetrating sense of humor, that is all."

"Ah?" The Frenchman looked from one to the other.

"Well, René?" challenged Josiah Moffett. "Is this the child?"

Suddenly she realized that René Valois was not a chance visitor. He had been invited for a specific reason, and she could guess what that purpose, humiliating indeed, was. He knew something about the real Georgina Moffett. And he was about to tell Georgina's uncle that this girl was an imposter.

Why hadn't Mr. Quinn thought ahead? Why didn't he know about this Frenchman, a man who knew something about the lost child—perhaps had even known John and Sarah Moffett in Paris?

Seething inside with resentment at Mr. Quinn, she kept her face as impassive as she could, while the two men, with Hastings hovering impotently in the background, dueled strangely over her.

She believed that on Valois's next words rested Josiah's belief in her. If Valois were to say "Yes, this is Georgina"—on what evidence she could not fathom—then Josiah would greet her, and cherish her, as his long-lost niece.

She willed the Frenchman to lie—and yet she knew that if he did, she would never be secure in this house. Never would she know who she really was, or who the sweet-singing woman was who held her so tenderly.

"I cannot tell, Josiah. You must remember that I saw the girl when she was much younger, a mere *enfante* of three years. That is all. And—the years are tricky. No, Josiah, I cannot tell you as a certain thing. This *demoiselle* could be your niece, and then again, I am not sure. *C'est possible.* That is all."

Back in the study, seated between the two men, her mood was different from before. This time she had grown defiant. And this time, too, she had a foreboding sense of Mr. Quinn's imminent arrival. By that time she must be gone. Without trace.

Josiah Moffett might not believe her. That was his privilege. But he was not going to put her into Mr. Quinn's ungentle hands!

She faced the men with outward composure. Inwardly, she had at last laid hold of the germ of a plan, and while she smiled at Josiah Moffett, and glanced sidelong at René Valois—a glance she did not know was flirtatious—she allowed the mainstream of her mind to flow along channels to be used, if necessary, to accomplish her escape from this house before Mr. Quinn's arrival.

"Now, René," said Mr. Moffett, "you do not think this lovely young lady is John's daughter?"

"N-no," said the French visitor. "I say only that she does not look as that one did at the age of three."

"Three?" He had captured Gina'a attention, and she cried out, "You knew me when I was—before I was placed in the orphanage?"

"That is the question before us, is it not?" Valois spoke impartially. He was truly an attractive man, she recognized, with an air of grace even in the way he moved his eloquent hands. Had her past been linked with his?

She could barely breathe, impatient for what would come next.

"Perhaps I should explain," Mr. Moffett interposed. "My nephew John and his wife Sarah, and their child, were in Paris when the Revolution began. The Bastille fell that July day, and, by all accounts that reached me, they were killed. But their daughter Georgina was smuggled out of Paris by Monsieur Valois here, and taken as far as Brussels. Then—he lost the little girl."

She had fixed her eyes on the speaker. He wore an appearance of aloofness, as though all this had happened to some people he had never known, but Gina thought, acutely, a live emotion still throbbed beneath the surface. A man who kept a bedroom in constant readiness for the return of the lost for sixteen years was not a man of steel.

41

"Through no fault of mine, Josiah," Valois thrust quickly. "I had the utmost faith in—those to whom I confided the child."

"I never said otherwise," Mr. Moffett said mildly. "But the fact is that no one knows what happened to the baby. She disappeared from friends in Brussels, when René here had to return to Paris."

"By command of His Majesty," René interposed.

"Of course. I hired persons to trace my niece, and one found evidence that she had been brought to England, by people who did not know who she was, and—"

Had this long story been hers? Had she been that baby, three years old, too young to know her name perfectly, abandoned on the doorstep of the orphanage where hands—if not overly kind, at least not cruel—had drawn her in and fed her, sheltered her, and given her what they had to give?

She came back to the present with a jolt, to find both men looking inquiringly at her. She roused as though from a dream, and flushed. "I'm sorry. It's such a sad little story, isn't it?"

"And not yours," Valois said sharply. "Is that right?"

Nothing but the truth would serve. "I don't know. Truly I do not remember any time before I was in the orphanage." *Except the singing,* she thought, *and the sweet rocking.*

Surprisingly, after a moment, Mr. Moffett said briefly, "I believe you. I have known occasions when the mind remembers only what is best to remember, and forgets things too cruel to dwell upon. I shall not trouble you about the past, at least the long-ago past, again. But now"—his voice suddenly tightened, hard enough to probe unpleasantly—"what of this Mr. Quinn?"

"What can I say, sir? I know nothing of him. I never saw him before yesterday."

"Vraiment?"

"Vraiment," she echoed René unconsciously. "I was taken out of my—my cell, and into a room somewhere in the prison. I don't know where it was, except that we crossed a courtyard, and up a stairway inside a tower, and there he was. When he told me"—she had to go very carefully here, because she had the frightening feeling that she was walking on a narrow causeway, with dark waters on either side—"that he thought he could see that my sentence was—set aside, I think were his words—I listened. I knew I was innocent of the crime they accused me of, and I thought that perhaps the family was working secretly to get me off."

42

"Did you think that was likely?" said Josiah Moffett. He adopted a more kindly attitude, for reasons he did not share with his companions. Her lapse into French had been—*interesting*. Either she was an unconscious mimic, or—something else that he would not look at now. But he found her resemblance to his nephew's wife not so sharp as it had seemed at first. This girl had her own ways, charming ways, and he had taken a liking to her for herself. His house, elegant in style and comfortable in service, suddenly seemed barren to him, and the years ahead—how many or how few only his ragged and worn heart could decide—loomed as a wasteland. Until now.

Her reply was candor itself. "No. I did not think that the Potters would stir themselves for me. Mr. Potter might have, but I'm sure his wife would have prevented it. But truly, Mr. Quinn did not say they did."

"And you agreed to go along."

"At first I did not know there was anything to go along with, Mr. Moffett. He told me nothing, not until he had taken me to his house—I suppose it was his house—and I had a chance to clean up, and he gave me clothes to wear."

"That ugly outfit you wore last night?" queried Mr. Moffett with distaste.

"At least it was not torn," she answered simply.

Different pictures rose in the minds of the two men, set into motion by her words. Mr. Moffett's picture was of a neglected and abandoned waif, no matter whether three years old or nineteen. He glanced at René's rapt expression, and guessed that the French royalist's mental imaginings might be better left unsaid.

So many questions Gina longed to ask! What was the little Georgina like? What of her mother, her father? What did they think? Did they laugh much? She dared not ask. The men seemed to have forgotten her.

After a long moment, Mr. Moffett cleared his throat. "I am rather out of touch, Valois. Is there a lady who could do the job?"

Puzzled, Gina looked from one to the other. What job? she wondered frantically. Was it to do with her? *What job?*

René Valois understood the cryptic question. "The countess," he said.

"It must not take long. I will not want to give up my niece for more than a month. See to it, will you, Valois?"

Without a word to her, Mr. Moffett and René Valois rose with one accord and strolled together toward the door of

43

the library. Gina thought she must have heard wrongly. There was no fanfare of trumpets, no sense of portentous announcements—nothing. Nothing but the words she could not believe, had he really said "my niece"?

And what of the man who had brought her here? What was Quinn after, and how would she pay him? She thought again of the jolly fat man, the essence of good humor, until one saw the cold malice in his eyes.

She thought—but there was nothing to think. She could only sit in that library, the wintry February sunlight on her face, the tickling smell of wood smoke and old leather in her nostrils—how wonderful after the gray walls of Newgate, or even the tiny attic window of her unheated room at the Potters'—and let odd words, pictures, fragments of thought, swoop through her mind like so many birds. . . .

Mr. Quinn . . . that poor little Georgina packed from Paris to Brussels to oblivion . . . the kind blue eyes of Mr. Moffett—she already respected him enormously, but now she began to feel the burgeoning of affection for the first man she had known who was really kind. If she had indeed heard rightly, and if in truth Mr. Moffett was going to let her stay, she would make it up to him. No true niece could be more affectionate than she would be. She could never be grateful enough.

Yet—he had not said precisely she was to stay. Burned too many times by her cheerful optimism, she forced herself to hold down the sudden, strange bubbling of happiness that started somewhere near the pit of her stomach. But the strong exertion caused her hands to shake on the arms of her chair, and her breath catch so that she thought her ribs must crack with the effort to breathe.

Mr. Moffett returned to the library, alone. "One thing, Georgina," he said, crossing the room to stand before her. "You will not need to worry about Mr. Quinn."

She rose shakily. Things were happening too fast around her. She needed time to sort out all the pressing things bombarding her with urgency. She needed to *know* who she was. Or who Mr. Moffett thought she was—genuine or imposter.

"He is coming—"

"He has come," Josiah Moffett said with a reassuring smile. "And he has gone away again. Early this morning. I will see that he is recompensed for his expenses and his trouble in bringing you to me. In bringing my own niece back to my house where you belong."

It took a moment. Blood thrummed in her temples, her

tongue turned dry, her knees shook. The long silence lay between them, unsettling, looming large.

The old man shattered the heaviness. "Welcome back, Georgina!" he said, and held his arms wide.

She was dreaming again. It could be nothing else. But while she could, she would enjoy it.

With a glad cry, she flew into the arms that held her tightly.

VI

"It's the most romantic story I ever heard!" exclaimed Miss Singer, around a mouthful of pins. "To think of it! All those years not knowing who you were, and then to be found—"

Miss Singer only just refrained from adding, "in jail, of all places." She had heard the entire story, including some embellishments that would have surprised Gina herself, before she was brought upstairs two weeks ago to the sewing room, in the house belonging to the Countess of Strathford. But somehow, although in the ordinary way very little stirred the seamstress, the outfitting of the beautiful and mysterious Miss Moffett, under the direction of the formidable countess, was not only a windfall of prosperity but touched a sentimental chord Miss Singer rarely felt.

Lamely, she finished, "And to find out who you are."

The plain young woman sitting in the windowseat spoke acidly. "Who she *says* she is, Singer."

"Now, Lady Hester." The reproof came from old Parsons, personal maid to the countess since her marriage, some thirty years before, and at this moment serving as her mistress's deputy in the delicate matter of providing a new wardrobe, at Josiah Moffett's expense, for Georgina Moffett.

Gina stood in uncomplaining silence. What was there to say? Hester, the countess's daughter, was a mature twenty-two, with an undistinguished face and an air of self-importance. She spoke only the truth just now, and even Gina, possessed of a growing dislike for Hester, could not fault her for that.

Almost a month had passed since Gina had stood before the judge in Newgate courtroom, and marched out a convicted felon, head high, her long strides taking her majestically out of the room.

The countess had said, the first day they met, "One thing I don't need to teach you is how to walk. Just remember, Georgina, your clothes, your elegance, if you attain such perfection, will depend on the way you carry yourself."

Gina thought with suppressed amusement, *I've been walking for a long time without someone to tell me how.* But nearly everything else she had learned, she found now she must unlearn and be instructed anew.

She was awkward in the extreme at first, so she thought. There was so much to learn. How to dress for every occasion—from receiving one's friends in one's morning room, but not before eleven o'clock, to a ride in an open carriage to an *al fresco* at Richmond on the River. The degrees of formal address. The newest ways of dressing one's hair—Gina was pleased to note one particular fashion that covered the noticeable three-cornered scar at the top of her left ear. The niceties of curtsying. The practices that must be avoided at all peril—"not quite the thing"—walking alone on the streets, for instance.

The countess was as difficult to please as ever Matron had been. The countess, unlike Matron, did not beat her, but her disapproval was meted out by a rapier-sharp tongue that spared nothing. A look into the future showed Gina the kind of person Hester would surely be. Already they were much alike, but perhaps Lady Hester had a stronger will.

Uncle Josiah had given the countess a month to instruct Georgina in the ways of society. For that month the countess insisted that Gina live with her in the great house on Belgrave Square. It was proving to be a miserable month, and Gina was counting the days now, almost the hours, until she would be back in her room at Uncle Josiah's, for good—possibly.

How far she had come in confidence she did not realize, not until this day, when she stood in the midst of folds of primrose silk, Miss Singer on her knees before her, and Parsons watching from the basket chair in the sewing room.

Tossed over a clothes horse along the wall out of the way were other gowns that Miss Singer had already tried on her client, and found wanting. The fabrics made a kaleidoscope of color—gold. The most delicate pink with ruching in a deeper shade of the same color. Gloves and little hat to match. A bottle-green dress with folds of cloth cunningly caught up and draped about the hips. A half dozen round gowns, the fabric fulled comfortably at the back, to wear at home—the colors light and young.

The white shapeless blouse and the dark plain skirt had disappeared long ago into the rubbish bin, and the slippers Mr. Quinn had provided her were tucked away in the bottom drawer of the highboy. She could not throw them away, not for any sentimental value they might have, but simply because to dispose of them thusly would be wasteful.

Her new slippers fitted so well they were a joy to put on. Some of soft Moroccan leather, others of satin, embroidered to match her new gowns. Little soft boots to wear in the winter snows, with white fur bordering the tops, and soft warm linings.

She felt guilty about the expense her uncle was put to. But he bent a serious eye on her and told her, "I've had no one to spend my money on for such a long time, my dear. Don't keep me from enjoying it now."

She had dropped a kiss on his cheek for thanks, and to cover her guilty flush. How fortunate the real Georgina would have been!

She had struggled often with her conscience in this past month, but since her conscience was an untried thing, her behavior having been motivated by Matron rather than by what the vicar called an inner light, the battle was unequal. Perhaps someday she would know what was right. Just now, she decided, it was not right for her to be in prison for a crime she had not committed; so which of the two wrongs was the lesser?

It took only a slight exercise of intelligence to decide that it was only common sense to choose the wrong that was most comfortable.

But still, she was not entirely happy. And when the Lady Hester, a disagreeable girl, so far forgot Christian charity as to jibe at Gina, her wounding words struck deeper than she could have hoped.

And on this morning, with only three days left in this oppressive household, Gina stirred, feeling the wounds throbbing, and spoke with a silky sweetness that she did not feel. "If my uncle Josiah is satisfied that I am in truth his niece, then that is sufficient for me. And I am at a loss to understand your interest, Lady Hester."

Surprised as though a chair had suddenly developed talons, Hester stirred in her perch on the windowseat. "Ah, but is he satisfied?" she prodded. "How could he be sure about a jailbird? Everyone knows they lie."

48

Gina allowed amusement to show. "You are well instructed, I see, on the subject of jailbirds." She pulled sharply away from Miss Singer's pin-filled hands. She knew she ought to overlook Hester's constant carping, but her temper had for too long been reined tightly. Now she crossed the room to look down at her tormentor.

"But you see, Lady Hester," Gina said with deadly gentleness, "I cannot lie, because I don't know the truth. And I never said I did."

Lady Hester's sharp eyes were pinpoints of light, flashing for a moment. A retort trembled on her thin lips but the words remained unsaid. The countess spoke from the door.

"Hester, I am ashamed of you. All I have ever taught you seems to have been of no use. Already you have suffered from your sharp tongue, and one might hope you would learn from that. Now mind what I say, if you can."

"Yes, Mama," Hester said, plainly unrepentant.

And the matter was closed to all appearances.

The ugly little incident soon faded from Gina's mind, even though it did not from the Countess's. She had told no one—including her husband, who kept his residence on the family estates in the north of England, indulgently allowing his countess to spend the season in London, and quite possibly enjoying himself fully while she was gone—that Josiah Moffett had offered her a staggering sum to give his niece the polish that she would have had, had not an adverse fate torn her from her family in her formative years. The sum was sufficient to pay a few of the countess's pressing creditors, and while she would have died, quite literally, before she would have confessed to it, she regarded Josiah as an instrument of a kindly Providence.

The countess knew little about Josiah Moffett and his vocation, but she paid attention to the good supply of rumors, and concluded that he was not one with whom it was safe to trifle. If she did well with the girl, who knew what other small tasks might fall to her lot?

And, completely honest with herself, she knew that Gina was the kind of girl she would want as her own daughter, if she had had a choice in the matter, but instead—through an undeserved blow of fate—she had Hester.

And Hester was not going to spoil things by antagonizing the object of Josiah's charity. The countess was determined upon that. The best thing was to get Hester married off. Let a husband school her. Already Hester had driven away three prospects, who never came up to the mark.

But Peregrine! The countess could hardly believe such a prize dangled within Hester's reach. If they did make a match, thought the countess with nonmaternal malice, Hester would not rule the roost!

That afternoon, Gina made her first appearance at the countess's weekly reception. On Thursdays certain of the encapsulated little world of London society repaired to the drawing rooms of the Countess of Strathford. The food was good, and the gossip was better. But in considering this ultimate test of the countess's accomplishment, Gina's nervousness held her in a grip that turned her blood to ice and clamped her mind as though in a vise.

She remembered, later, her first sight of Thomas Weston, though. How could she forget? In the midst of her acute social discomfort, he was frank and open-faced, an eagerness to embrace the world glowing in his eyes, and a naïve belief in that world's benevolence.

Tom, in his turn, saw the girl that all London was talking about, and found her even lovelier than rumor shouted.

He had finally drawn Gina to the window looking out upon Belgrave Square. The window was draped in pale green, tied back with gold cord, and the background suited Gina's auburn hair. He told her so.

"Then, Mr. Weston, you have brought me here on purpose?" she teased, her eyes bright. This was the first person in the room who made her feel comfortable. She could not have told why, but he was in such contrast to the last young man she had encountered, to her own disaster, that she felt warm toward Tom.

He was not an accomplished flirt. He blushed and stammered, "Oh, n-no, of course not. But you are s-so lovely, any background would suit."

"Not just any background," she objected, remembering the age-blackened walls of Newgate Prison. Involuntarily she sighed. Tom was so young, so—so unworldly. She felt ages older.

She coaxed him to talk. She had learned an attitude of total absorption in her companion that drew him out more than any adroit questioning might do. Without saying more than a word now and then, she learned that Tom was possessed of a small amount of wealth, but it was still under the control of his uncle. This was Tom's first year in London, and he was finding it difficult.

"My uncle Ned is fine," Tom asserted stoutly, "but—he doesn't approve of anything I do."

"How gothic!" she exclaimed. "Does he lock your doors at night, letting hounds loose in the halls?"

"You've been reading novels," Tom reproved her with gravity.

"Don't blame the countess. I read no novels these days. But Mrs. Pot—a woman I knew," she amended hastily, "devoured them all. They're such fun!" Then, seeing her companion unamused, she turned, with an inward sigh, to the subject that seemed to engross him.

"You'll soon be of age, I shouldn't wonder. And then your fustian uncle will retire from the scene."

"Soon? Two years yet! My father thought twenty-five was the earliest age I could be trusted."

Twenty-three? He acted five years younger than that. But the approving warmth in his blue eyes made up for his lack of polish. Feeling the countess's appraising glance on her, she stirred herself to display the results of the countess's teaching. Saying casually, "I should like to meet your uncle one day," she steered Tom away from the window and toward a group consisting of, she noticed too late, Lady Hester, and a girl Gina had just met, Adelaide Gough—pleasant, blond, with a look in her eyes as though she contemplated some inner scene of more interest than her surroundings—and a man of medium height, stocky build, and bored eyes.

"The Viscount Autherly," Lady Hester introduced Gina. "He lives, when he is in the country, on the estates bordering our own, and I have known him all my life."

"A very short time, after all," said the viscount gallantly. "And you are the famous Miss Moffett. My pleasure, ma'am."

The viscount's words were all that was proper, but Gina did not quite like the expression in his light brown eyes. She told herself she was too sensitive. Autherly was Hester's old friend, and that must be voucher enough.

Gina acknowledged the introduction civilly, but Lady Hester paid no heed. Instead, she was rallying Tom. "Your uncle has not come today. Is he in town?"

"As far as I know," said Tom. "I have not seen him since yesterday."

"In the same house?" Adelaide protested.

"Edward's business," interposed Hester, "keeps him overly occupied. I have often told him so."

Autherly flashed a speculative look at Hester, but she ignored him. Turning to Gina, she explained, "Miss Moffett, Tom's uncle is Edward Peregrine." She waited expectantly.

Gina thought rapidly. *Peregrine*——had she heard that name somewhere recently? Was it a name she should remember *if* she were Georgina Moffett? She could not hesitate too long, she knew, and fell back on the truth. "Peregrine?" she asked blandly. "Did I meet him here today? I confess I do not remember the name."

Hester's light blue eyes narrowed, and she said slowly, "The Peregrine estates lie next to Josiah Moffett's, on the Kentish coast. And you don't remember?"

The implication was almost tangible. Gina stepped warily around the pitfall dug by Hester. "I'm sorry. I should be surprised if anyone remembers names and places too well if they had not thought of them since the age of three."

Gina wanted to add, *And what do you remember of the days of your infancy?* But of course she could not. The manners that the countess was teaching her marched with her own innate sense of dignity and consideration. Gina thanked Matron, not for the first time, that she did not have to overcome the handicap of gutter manners. The nuances of her new state were difficult to master, at best.

"Then Mr. Peregrine was not here today?" Gina asked innocently.

"No," Hester said curtly, her face flushing momentarily. Then she turned again to Tom. "Be sure to tell your uncle that I missed him, and hope he will come to see me soon."

Gina raised a mental eyebrow at Lady Hester's familiar tone. Her curiosity was aroused. Edward Peregrine——a source of exasperation to his nephew. A great friend of Hester Reading. And, stealing a glance at Autherly, she thought she detected a strong dislike on his part for the absent Peregrine. Jealous of Hester? Gina did not think so.

But no matter what anyone else thought of the man, she herself recognized him for a potential danger. This Edward Peregrine lived, when he was home in Kent, next to Josiah Moffett.

Not Josiah Moffett——*Uncle Josiah*! She must remember to call him that, even in her thoughts.

And quite possibly Edward Peregrine might remember her mother and father, and——heaven forbid!——even Georgina. She

52

must take great care, she decided, never to meet this Edward Peregrine.

The countess signaled to her then, and she crossed the room to be introduced to some new arrivals—an older woman with two attractive daughters in tow whose names she did not catch. She was caught up then in another round of gossip that, fortunately, she was not expected to understand. She thought wryly that Mrs. Potter would have given her teeth to stand where her despised maid stood this moment, listening to tales about names and titles that were so far only hearsay to Gina—the Marquis of Chirk, Lord Barham of the Admiralty, Colonel Somebody, even the ranking royalist refugee from France, the Duc de Chaillou.

René Valois, she noted, was not here, although Chaillou mentioned his name—"Good thing Valois doesn't take advantage of the amnesty for us refugees. He'd *kill* Bonaparte!"

Gina listened politely, her thoughts elsewhere. She began to feel unreal. The room was stifling, and the faces began to pass before her eyes as they might in some phantasmagoria, and she had a feeling of falling, falling through space, knowing inevitably she would land on wet, matted straw on the floor of a narrow, overcrowded cell.

Murmuring an excuse to ears that did not hear her, she moved away. She felt she was tottering, that any moment she would slip through the insubstantial floor. She must get to a window, to some cool air.

After a century she reached the door into the hall. Parsons was on duty at the door, the butler having business elsewhere for the moment. She took one look at Gina, and a muffled explosive sound escaped her.

"I told them—" she muttered. Gina found herself on the satin settee in the small reception room off the hall with a vial of strong-scented salts pungently under her nose. She had no recollection of how she came there.

At length the mists cleared, and she could smile at Parsons's long worried face peering intently at her.

"Best go upstairs to bed," said Parsons. "I'll call Sally."

Gina shook her head. "I can't do that, Parsons," she demurred, adding with a touch of dry humor, "It's not the *thing*." Parsons snorted, but Gina caught an answering glint in her eyes, and at once felt not so lonely. *At home with maids*, she thought with amusement, *and not with viscounts. That should tell me something.*

Parsons was summoned away then, and Gina sat where she

was, prolonging the quiet, postponing the required return to the drawing room.

Somewhere a door opened and a gust of cold air swirled through the room. She did not open her eyes. It was far away, and she didn't care.

Sound of footsteps, and cold air as though clinging to someone just arrived from the March winds.

Her eyes flew open, and she saw with dismay that a stranger was standing before her. She noted fawn small-clothes, brocade vest worked in an abstract design of gold threads, pale blue surcoat. She finally worked her way up to his face. It was an interesting face, one part of her thought, a sensitive mouth, an overlong but very straight nose. Heavy straight eyebrows, over eyes so dark blue as to be nearly black.

And just now those disturbing eyes held an expression she could only have described as reflecting some great inner upheaval. A fancy, she decided, gone in a moment.

She hoped her own countenance did not mirror her own immediate dislike, flaring up unaccountably under his fierce regard.

But when he spoke, in a pleasant voice, his words were ordinary in the extreme.

"You are ill?" he inquired. "May I call someone for you?"

"No, sir," she said, rising to her feet. He was immediately the most disturbing man she had ever met, and she did not know why. "It was only the stifling heat in the drawing room. I felt faint for a moment."

"You are restored now, I trust. But it seems that I have not seen you before, have I?"

"I am Georgina Moffett," she said, with a touch of defiance.

Something flickered in the back of his deep-set eyes. She thought, *Already my name is as famous as the regent's. Already the London world buzzes about the great impersonation—maliciously opting for the negative side of the situation.* She guessed that she could count on the fingers of one hand those who rejoiced with Josiah that the lost had been found. *Well, if Uncle Josiah were satisfied—*

"I have heard that his great-niece had been found," the stranger said stiffly. "We must all be most happy about that—if it is true."

"If!" she gasped angrily. "You have no right to say that. If my uncle is happy, it does not concern you!"

"Doesn't it? You must have a peculiar code of ethics,

54

indeed. I collect that you consider perpetrating a hoax on a sick old man as altogether admirable?"

His savage words touched the doubts she had stifled, and woke them. Who was this man, that he could so talk to her? Whoever he was, his suspicions were live and flourishing. And she could not combat them alone. She longed to fly—upstairs, into the drawing room, home to Uncle Josiah. But she could only stand as though rooted, and glare at him.

"Who are you?" she demanded.

The answer came from an unexpected quarter. Lady Hester stood in the doorway. Her glance as it fell on the two, clearly engaged in no ordinary conversation, was murderous. But her voice dripped honey as she advanced.

"Edward Peregrine, at last! I had quite given you up!"

The dangerous stranger—stranger no more—greeted Hester with relief. As though he had stepped into deep water and didn't know how to reach shore.

Foolish thought! He had no qualms. In fact, he was completely odious. She longed to tell him so, but the opportunity was lost. The barest of introductions by Hester—Edward Peregrine, Uncle Josiah's near neighbor, a man who could, possibly, unmask her. And yet, his danger to her identity was almost forgotten.

Gina watched him offer his arm to Lady Hester, and without a backward glance the two disappeared through the door into the drawing room.

She acts betrothed to him, Gina thought fiercely, *and all I can say is those two deserve each other.*

If there had been a vase near at hand, she would have smashed it against the wall.

VII

The parlor of the Moffett house on Kennett Square was ablaze with light. Always generous with wax candles, at least for the front of the house, Mrs. Beddoes had outdone herself at last.

"After all," she had told Sir Charles Derwent, Josiah Moffett's assistant, "we've got sixteen years' worth of wax that was never used, you might say, and if we go on a bit over now, it's no more than we would have spent over the years anyway." She finished with a defiant sniff, "I'm sure Miss Georgina's worth every single one of them!" She turned to flee to the kitchen before her happy tears overflowed.

Her attitude toward the refurbishing of the house, under Josiah's meekly spoken but iron-willed direction, was of a piece with the prodigality of the wax tapers. "Even Scripture tells us so," she kindly advised Agnes, struggling up the back stairs with a copper boiler of hot water. "Just be glad that it's not your lot to butcher the calf."

To do her justice, Agnes was far from resenting the work to be done to make the house on Kennett Square fit for the entertaining that Josiah was sure to want. "Makes a nice change to have a lovely young miss in the house," Agnes confided to Meg, the newly hired kitchen maid. "Before she came back, the master never smiled from one end of the day to the other. Work as you would, he never noticed. Seemed like he grieved in his heart, and never let it show. Like it was broke, you might say. And that astonished he was when Mr. Hastings opened the door and there stood Miss Georgina!"

Agnes allowed a tear to escape and run down her cheek in tribute to the overpowering effect of the sudden appearance of the new mistress. Meg was of a less romantic turn of mind. "And you say she's just a housemaid? Like me?"

Agnes regarded her with disfavor. "Not like you, I'm sure. You could tell the minute she walked into the house she was *quality*."

Meg objected. "I thought you weren't there when she came in."

"I meant in a manner of speaking, as you'd know if you weren't addled in the head," Agnes told her. "Best do that copper kettle over again. Mrs. Beddoes won't like that job above half."

Meg, left alone, looked about her to find a confidante worthy of her skeptical thoughts, and found only the cat, an ugly, antique, three-colored animal who had seen many of the back alleys of London. "Between you and me," Meg said wisely, "it's more than enough to think I'd believe such good luck to happen to anybody." But before the cat's disinterested eyes, the new maid began to pirouette in the flagstone-floored hall, vigorously agitating one hand as though it contained a fan, until the sound of footsteps in the nearby kitchen brought an end to her pleasant dreams.

In the front of the house, Gina's thoughts were far from reflecting upon her good fortune. Instead, the evidence of lavish preparations for her homecoming, and the clear expectation of visitors to come, burdened her with an unaccountable depression. She had returned from her month in residence at the countess's home only yesterday afternoon. A magnificently far cry from her earlier arrival in Mr. Quinn's carriage, this time Uncle Josiah had sent his own carriage after her. It was a splendid equipage, requiring four horses to draw it, and unwieldy in the narrow streets of the city. But it was well-sprung and vastly roomy, and even the ancient style of the body, and the worn velvet on the seat corners, could not detract from its great elegance.

The door of the house had been thrown open before she set foot on the bottom step, and her uncle greeted her as warmly as though she were indeed his long-lost great-niece.

And this recollection brought her by an inevitable progress to consideration of Mr. Quinn. She had not heard from him since the night he had brought her here. He had returned early that next morning, and Josiah had sent him away.

She thought she had seen him later across the street, but Hastings had told her she wasn't to worry about "that man that escorted you here, Miss Georgina. The master has taken care of him."

She dared not ask just how the master had accomplished that—paid him off, or given him in charge. Uncle Josiah could have done either with justice.

If Mr. Quinn expected payment from her, he had not come again to collect it. Or, if he had, he had been sent away. She considered what manner of payment he could have expected, and finally come to the conclusion that if it were money he wanted, Uncle Josiah had taken care of it.

Her thoughts running along this fashion, she decided she must simply forget Mr. Quinn. Her head had been stuffed in the past four weeks with so much else that indeed she found it hard to envision the man's foxy features, but only the recollection of a formidable, and quite ugly, strength behind his fat, genial eyes.

But he had got her out of Newgate, and deposited her here in this delightful fairyland, and she would be grateful forever for that.

"Brooding?" A voice spoke behind her. "I'm surprised. But of course this establishment is less lively than Strathford House."

Sir Charles Derwent stood in the doorway. She smiled at him dutifully, remembering his great worth to her uncle. She had learned much in the last weeks. She could now discern that he was far from a fashionable figure—no diamond pin in his cravat, no rings on his fingers. Merely a dark, serviceable coat, padded at the shoulders, and dark breeches. A purely businesslike apparel.

"Liveliness can encroach too much, Sir Charles," Gina said. "I must confess I am happy to return to my uncle's house. Pray tell me, this reception tonight of Uncle Josiah's. Will there be many visitors?"

He smiled. "Your uncle has invited only his near acquaintances to meet you. But of course your family is so well-connected, and he is so well-liked, that there may well be the crush of the year on his doorstep."

"Oh, I do hope not!" she cried, distressed. "What will I ever do?"

"Be your own charming self," advised Sir Charles. She glanced up quickly, thinking she detected a wry note in his voice, but there was no sign of disapproval in his countenance. She must have imagined it.

Quickly, she turned the subject. "I am told you assist my uncle in many ways, Sir Charles. With his country estates?"

"No, Calder—down at Seahaven—deals with that end of your uncle's affairs. Myself, I abominate the country."

She smiled quickly. "I do not know yet whether I agree with you or not, Sir Charles. At the orphanage there were no excursions into the countryside." *Nor anywhere else*, she added silently. But perhaps she remembered something deep inside her, for she had a real need for blue sky and the tracery of trees against it. Perhaps some memory from those locked-away days? She did not know.

There was no opportunity to go further into Sir Charles's duties, for Josiah Moffett himself joined them. He entered the room with a step that was not quite sprightly, but hinted at a jauntiness left behind in his youth. Now she saw clearly those wrinkles that had been kindly hidden by the subdued candlelight of last evening. The pallor of his complexion told her that the weakness that had overcome him that first night of their acquaintance had not been vanquished, but only lurked in readiness to pounce upon him again.

She felt such a strong rush of affection for him that she could not speak. She turned away to hide the tears that welled to her eyes, and began to fiddle with the ball fringe along the edge of the heavy damask drapery.

"Come now, Georgina," rallied Mr. Moffett gently, "did the countess perform her duties so poorly that you have no self-assurance, even with me?"

"Oh, no, sir," Gina exclaimed. "It was just that—well, sir, I am so excessively grateful—"

"Now, my child," said Josiah with great kindness, "you have already brought such pleasure to me that I am amply repaid. Now that we have settled that between us, tell me what you think of the way the carpets have been cleaned. I am sure I know nothing of such matters, but it seems to me they have turned out quite handsome."

Speaking gently, and of small things, by degrees he brought her to a condition of composure, where she could smile back at him, her eyes crinkling slightly at the corners, and her spirits soaring again.

"Well, my child, I see that all is well again. Now as the evening goes along, I may find the affair too much for me. If I retire from time to time, promise me you will not allow my absence to worry you."

Gina impulsively touched Josiah's sleeve. "Uncle Josiah, are you sure this party isn't too much for you? I am convinced you ought not to overdo."

"Don't fret, child," he said warmly, covering her hand with his own and giving it a reassuring pressure. "I know the countess wanted to show you off in her own home, but that's not the thing, my dear. An afternoon reception of an informal nature does not signify, since it was part of her training. You belong here, and so the world will know, after today."

"You think anyone will come?" she said, frowning doubtfully. "Nobody knows me, and I am persuaded they have little desire to make my acquaintance. Why should they?"

Her thoughts turned upon the orphanage, where she was merely another bantling, as like the others as one pea to another.

"Precisely because they do not know you," said Josiah with lurking amusement in his eyes. "They will fall over themselves to see the long-lost orphan."

Thoughtfully, she wondered, "But many will doubt me. Even Monsieur Valois could not be sure."

"I am satisfied," Josiah said simply. "That will be sufficient for most, I'm sure. And Valois will be convinced when he sees you."

"Tonight, sir?"

"No. He is out of London. Not, this time, on my business."

"What does that mean, sir?" she asked, after a pause. "I fear I do not know precisely your interests. Something to do with the government, I surmise."

"And that is enough for you to bother your head about now," he told her swiftly. "Later, perhaps, but just now you are to enjoy yourself. I should like to see that Newgate shadow leave your eyes, Georgina."

He touched her cheek with one long, finely kept finger, and smiled encouragingly. "Now smile, my child, for if I am not mistaken, I hear the first of our guests arriving."

Someday, she vowed, she would be able to express her gratitude to him. Just now, it was sufficient to know that she would gladly die for him. In the meantime, hearing the Countess of Strathford's shrill voice in the foyer, she unconsciously squared her elegant shoulders, lifted her head, and prepared to meet her uncle's guests. Close enough to dying for him, she thought wryly.

But conscious of the fact that her new gown, cunningly, and very expensively, contrived in sea-green with a gauzy scarf delicate as the spray of surf around her shoulders, was vastly becoming, she managed to sustain the first shock of the early arrivals. Then, finding her tongue, and remembering the myriad admonitions of the countess's tutelage, she began to enjoy herself.

60

The rooms began to fill. The drawing room contained so many people that Dabney, under Hastings's eye, must inch through the press with his tray. Names and faces whirled in Gina's mind. So many new people—how would she ever be able to remember them all? Eventually, there came a lull in the procession of guests. Gina ventured to the door to peep out.

Carriages, having discharged their cargo, were lined up around Kennett Square, waiting for the shouted summons that would bring them back to stand before the front entrance again. Soft carriage lights traced the outlines of the square in the darkness. The cool March air touched her fevered cheek like a balm, and for the moment she was transported beyond herself.

What a strange intricate weaving of fate had brought her to stand, tiptoe with happiness, in this doorway! But even as she thought blissfully that she would never ask for anything more, not after tonight, a chill breeze gusted around the corner of the house, and she shivered. Across the street one figure turned his back to the wind and sought the shelter of a waiting carriage. A lone coachman, tired of the company of his fellows, probably.

The cold wind blowing could be an omen. After the comfort and the warmth of this home she had found, would she be dragged away and thrust into the outer darkness of gutter, of jail?

Hastily she stepped back into the hall. Fortunately no one had noticed her absence. Josiah stood at the door of the drawing room, from whence came a high-pitched hum of voices.

At Josiah's side in the doorway, his back to her, stood the man whom at all costs she did not want to see again. The set of the shoulders in the maroon velvet coat, the dark hair curling in studied carelessness at the nape of the neck—it must be Edward Peregrine! She had not seen him come in.

Josiah spoke with an impatient gesture to his companion, apparently giving a sharp order. Gina was surprised—Edward Peregrine, to bow in that subservient manner?

Then the man in the maroon coat turned into the hall— and she could see how mistaken she was. For the man was not Edward Peregrine, at all—but Sir Charles Derwent! She was so relieved that she scarcely noticed Sir Charles's face darkening with suppressed anger as he hurried past her.

The third wave—or was it the fourth?—of arrivals poured

through the front door then. Lady Hester Reading, Gina saw with a swift glance through the drawing-room door, was talking vivaciously wth Thomas Weston. Gina felt a pang. *Of course*, she thought, *all these people have known each other for simply years, and I'll always be an outsider, on the fringe, never really accepted.*

And then Hastings announced, with strong approval ringing in his cracked voice, "Mr. Edward Peregrine!"

Her first thought was panic. She did not know quite what she expected from him, perhaps another set-down as he had given her before. Well, tonight she was in her own home—at least he must recognize that—and she hoped she would know how to deal with such an odious, self-important man as the tall, lean-faced gentleman bowing this moment over her hand.

"Good evening, sir," she said, her voice dismayingly unsteady, but then she gathered strength, knowing that her uncle was nearby, and added, "It was good of you to come this evening."

Amusement flickered once in his eyes, and then vanished, to be replaced by something she interpreted as contempt, veiled in deference to her uncle, and she was conscious of a strong wish to give him the set-down he had clearly avoided for far too long. The opportunity would come, she thought, and giving him her most brilliant smile, she retrieved her hand from his, and turned to where her uncle had been standing, only moments before.

"I perceive that Mr. Moffett has deserted you," said Mr. Peregrine. "I trust his health has not deserted him, as well?"

He glanced at her for an answer, but the note in his voice told her that he very likely held her responsible for any adverse influence on Josiah Moffett's physical state, and she resented his inquiry instantly.

"I am sure the excitement has been beneficial," she said, her eyes dancing with indignation, "for he has enjoyed so much planning for this evening's entertainment."

He bowed in acknowledgment and turned away. Then the thought struck him forcefully. "But I must not leave you here alone!"

"Be sure that it is not your duty, Mr. Peregrine," she said tartly, "to look after me."

Affronted, he said with sudden savagery, "Believe me, I rejoice in the thought." His eyes glittered, and she was relieved when an interruption kept him from saying whatever was in his mind.

"There you are, Edward," said Lady Hester gaily from the door to the drawing room.

Gina would have sworn that Peregrine was unpleasantly jolted by Hester's voice, but her impression lasted only a moment. When he turned to Hester, his expression was amiable and his manner civil.

"I've been watching for you," she cried archly. "I thought you would find it easier to come in the carriage with us, but then—your affairs are more important, I am sure!"

By the time Hester had drawn Edward into the crowd, Josiah returned to her side, and Sir Charles began to circulate in the drawing room. The party wore on to its inevitable conclusion, and only after all the carriages had driven away, leaving the square once again lit only by the soft moonlight through the rising mist from the river, did her thoughts return to Edward Peregrine.

She had been able to exchange only a few words with him later, over supper. He looked smiling down at her—the smile that might have lit up his face, except that it never reached his eyes.

"I must admit," he said stiffly, "that Josiah seems happy tonight."

"You have known him a long time?"

"All my life," said Edward Peregrine. "My family's lands run beside his, in Kent. As I am sure you remember."

"Then you must have a great affection for him," she said impulsively. She glanced up to find Lady Hester's eyes on her, glittering in angry speculation. For that reason, Gina favored Edward with a fetching smile. Lady Hester was too far away to hear the words that accompanied her smile, as she added to Edward, "And I wonder that you grudge him his happiness."

"In finding you?" Edward gritted in an undertone, inaudible to those around. "Believe me, if he had truly found his niece, all who know him would rejoice. But you see—" He set down his cup hard enough that the saucer clinked a protest. "You see, my dear Miss-Whoever-You-Are, I knew the real Georgina! And I have an excellent memory."

He bowed over her hand after supper, and made his way swiftly from the house. And now, with the carriages departed, Gina had time to remember his parting words. To remember, and let worry come to fret at the edges of her mind.

For Edward Peregrine must have proof that she was not

who she said she was. He knew the real Georgina; that meant he, and probably he alone, could prove she was an imposter!

Without lifting a finger, she had made, she was positive, an exceedingly powerful enemy.

VIII

Gina took one last look at her reflection in the pier glass before leaving her room. The April sunshine fell full across the floor, touching into cheerful morning light the green rug on the floor, the gilt edge of the mirror. She could not help but admire the figure she saw in the glass.

Her luxuriant auburn hair was dressed almost in the latest fashion. She had no recollection of the injury that had resulted in the white triangular scar that disfigured the top of her left ear. Now she pulled the wings of her hair down over her ears, hiding the scar. She topped the arrangement with an elegant little green bonnet, tied with satin ribbons.

For the rest, she wore a close-fitting dress of French silk, made with a full skirt, and a short tailored jacket to match, all in a shade of medium green a little darker than her eyes.

She thought she would never be happier in her entire life than now, and she sketched a wave at the smiling reflection in the glass.

As she reached the ground floor, she hesitated. All was settled in its accustomed place—young Dabney, the footman, in his place near the front door, nodding as he slumped sleeping in his chair. The sound of carriage wheels and the clip-clop of smartly trotting horses filtered into the hall from the square. The impulse struck her to exhibit her new outfit to her generous uncle.

Tapping lightly on the door of his study—the room that had so frightened her that first night—she heard his voice bid her enter.

"Uncle!" she cried as she entered. "I came to display to you your own generosity. See?"

She pirouetted before him, and when she turned back she

saw open pleasure in his eyes. "I thought you might like to see what a fine figure your protégée will cut in the park today."

"Not my protégée, my child," he said softly. "My dear *niece*."

She lifted his hand impulsively to her lips. "I can't thank you enough for your kindness—" she began, but the peremptory wave of his other hand stopped her.

"There must be no talk of gratitude between us," he said gravely. "Love, yes. But for every instance of what you call kindness on my part, I am repaid tenfold by your affection and your high spirits." He smiled upon her, and she felt tears start to her eyes. He was the architect of everything she had ever dreamed of, and much she had never even known, and her answering emotion seemed more than her body could contain.

The moment was fragile, and Josiah closed it up and tucked it away for the present. "Where are you bound?" he asked. "To the park, you said?"

"Yes, sir. Lady Hester has invited me to go in her carriage—no, I think is her aunt's carriage—for the morning promenade. Is it the thing to do?"

Indulgently, Josiah smiled. "I think in such company— Lady Hester Reading and Lady Granville—you will come to no harm. Be off with you, and—Georgina, enjoy yourself. You have much unhappiness to make up for."

She stooped swiftly and kissed his cheek. "I'll leave you to your dusty old government papers," she said with a twinkle, indicating a stack of official-looking documents on his desk. "I am sure the fate of England must rest in them."

A voice spoke behind her. "Rather say, the fate of the world, *mademoiselle*." René Valois drew off fawn washleather gloves and handed them to Hastings, already holding a beaver hat of an exaggerated height and a marvelously curly brim.

She regarded the Frenchman uncertainly, never sure whether he was jesting or not.

"Now," he added ruefully, "I have distressed the *petite* Georgina. Forgive me?"

He lifted her hand to his lips. In a burst of frankness, she said, "How could I not?"

"I noticed a very grand carriage pulling up to the door as I came in," Valois told her. "Fit for a princess!"

She laughed. "Hardly that," she said, "but I must not keep

66

Lady Granville waiting." With a cheerful wave at Uncle Josiah, she was gone, leaving the two men to their business.

She went down the steps to Lady Granville's equipage. Lady Hester was already seated beside her aunt, and the footman helped Gina up into the back-facing seat of the barouche. The head over the back seat was folded down, an arrangement allowed by Lady Granville only on the finest days.

Gina hid her thoughts behind a bland expression, but she noticed there was sufficient room on the forward-facing seat for three to ride comfortably. Uncle Josiah was no doubt right—no harm would come to her in the presence of such overwhelming respectability as Lady Granville radiated, but probably not much enjoyment either.

Lady Granville was a billowy woman, who took to herself such elements of fashion as accentuated the prodigality of her figure. Thus her poke bonnet was possessed of a wider brim than most, and her dress seemed to be made up of scarves upon scarves, all of which were in constant need of adjustment. Gina revised her opinion. It would be most uncomfortable to sit in proximity to such undisciplined garments.

But Lady Granville was kind, and Gina smiled at her and settled back against the dark but very comfortable squabs, and prepared to enjoy her outing.

"A fine day," said Lady Granville to Gina, as they approached the gate into the park. "Jones, let us take the right turn today. It may be that we can see the regent—I heard he had returned to London from his sojourn in Bath. I do hope that doesn't mean that the invasion has begun."

Hester cried, "Oh no, Aunt, I am sure we would have heard. After all, what can Bonaparte do? Lord Nelson's fleet—"

Her aunt paid her no heed. "Look, Hester. There is Landon. I wonder at seeing him alone. Do you think that Miss Wright has cried off? Surely she could not care about his liaison with that Brent woman, do you think? A good marriage must overlook any disadvantage, and all men are alike. Even your Peregrine, Hester. I heard that he has suddenly found a new interest!"

"Mr. Peregrine is all that is noble," said Lady Hester, severely pursing her thin lips. "I am sure this gossip must be unfounded. Have you heard—who has taken his interest?"

"No," said Lady Granville, too quickly. She glanced secretively at Gina, believing herself unnoticed.

But Lady Hester had seen the glance, and interpreted it

much as Gina herself had done. So gossip was now linking her name with Edward's! How startled the *ton* would be if they knew that Edward's sole interest in her was to prove her false!

"Nor have I heard," Lady Granville continued with devastating frankness, "that he has developed a *tendre* for you."

Hester flushed unbecomingly. She changed the subject, speaking of parties she had attended, and of many people that Gina did not know. Gina had a strange feeling that she had evaporated, leaving only her ears and eyes behind. Hester was deliberately excluding her from the conversation, and Lady Granville was engrossed in watching for the prince regent, the very sight of whom seemed to assure virtue to the beholder.

This was Gina's first view of the park. To her city-bred eyes, the broad expanse of drives and the great grassy stretches beyond, dotted with clumps of trees, were breathtaking. She had not believed that such stretches of open country existed, at least in London, and she suddenly missed the close-built houses she was accustomed to. Here she felt exposed, like a gull on a rock along the river, and she moved uncomfortably in her seat.

She glanced at her companions. They paid no attention to her. It was a very belittling feeling.

The barouche moved smartly along the drive. Nearly everyone was going in the same direction, and looking backward Gina could see a procession forming behind them. It was a daily occurrence, she had learned, where all the *ton* met their friends.

"Looking for Edward Peregrine?" said Lady Granville presently. "He rarely comes out to the park, you know."

Hester was profoundly irritated with her aunt. "I know that. But I think he will be here today."

"Oh? Then you are on better terms with him than I supposed."

Gina sank back in her seat. How desperately she wished that Edward Peregrine kept to his custom, as reported by Lady Granville—avoiding the usual drive in the park. She could not bear to think of him, not after that encounter at her own party. She had not seen him for the three intervening days.

What would he say to her? And worse, suppose he just looked at her with those cold blue eyes and said nothing, as though she were beneath his notice?

He knew the real Georgina, he had said. And sooner or

later, she must suppose he would reveal her imposture. Would it be some place in public, such as in this barouche with the arrogant Lady Hester as complacent witness? Today?

Gina began to think energetically of ways to evade the man. A headache? No. Nothing that she thought of would do. And at times Gina thought it might as well all come out into the open at once. She cringed at the thought that somewhere in London existed a man who could—at his own pleasure—unmask her and snatch her from this very comfortable life she had. And she knew that what she dreaded most was not the loss of her luxury, but the hurt that must come to Josiah Moffett, who had shown her the only affection she had known since—well, since she had come to the orphanage, from whatever shadowed place she knew before that.

Gina became aware that those who had arrived on the promenade first had turned and were now coming back, so that the Granville carriage began to meet other carriages and riders that they knew.

"Look at that!" cried Hester. "What a beautiful sight! The driver is certainly a nonpareil!"

Gina craned her neck to look at the sight—and sight it was! A phaeton, very light in its build, with enormous wheels, drawn by a pair of identical gray horses. They stepped out smartly, heads high, in rhythm, and the driver was in perfect control. He drew his pair over as he approached Lady Granville's equipage, and doffed his high hat.

"How well you handle your pair!" cried Hester. "I do envy anyone who can control such prodigious animals! My cousin won't even let me try with his blacks, and I must say it is too bad of him."

"Don't think you can cajole me into teaching you to drive!" retorted Autherly. "I know your heavy hand on the ribbons of old! Now perhaps I might teach Miss Moffett. A pleasure indeed!"

Languidly, Lady Granville said, "Don't tease, Autherly. Besides, I'm dying to know, have you seen the prince regent?"

"Prinny? No," said Autherly, amused. "But I must tell you about the sight I did see. A shopkeeper on a high-perch phaeton. I vow the perch was all of five feet above the axle."

"Not really!"

"Very young, and overly ambitious, I should say. He is sure to find himself in trouble before long," said the viscount,

69

and added with malice, "No more than he deserves. These Cits that try to ape their betters should receive a good set-down. I should like to administer such a rebuff myself. But the occasion will in all likelihood never arise."

The viscount was speaking to Lady Hester, but his penetrating glance swept Gina far too often for her comfort. She moved restlessly, and met his eyes by accident. There was a quality of interest in them that took her breath away.

She welcomed the interruption provided by the arrival of Tom Weston. He was riding alone, and he approached the barouche on the side opposite to where the viscount was holding his fretful grays.

"I must say thanks for your entertainment the other evening." The gallantry that Tom affected turned stiff because he could not refrain from sending darkling glances toward the viscount. Since the viscount had not been invited to Josiah's party for his niece, Tom's remark was hardly tactful.

"I understand that Mr. Moffett's rout was quite the thing," said Autherly to Gina. "His guest list, I imagine, must have been taken out of his hands."

Gina, not knowing that Autherly's name had deliberately been omitted, was bewildered. She knew antagonism when she saw it, however, and the signs between Autherly and Tom were clear and sharp.

"It was a fine occasion," she said sweetly. "I have never seen such a fine expanse of park as this. The air is so fresh and—everything is so beautiful!"

Her enthusiasm illuminated her face and her green eyes, and Tom warmed under their influence like a flower expanding in the sun.

Autherly and Hester seemed to have much to talk about, of people Gina did not know. She concentrated on Tom, holding a tight rein as he was on his bay horse and on his tongue. Swept by a fellow feeling of irritation at the others, she bestowed a dazzling smile upon Tom, and said, "What a beautiful horse!"

Tom expanded visibly. "He is, isn't he! I must say, he's far more manageable than I expected."

His hand moved caressingly over the shoulder of the animal, and Gina could see his pride fairly bursting through his skin. How boyish—

She thought briefly of the boys at St. Clothilde's. At twelve, they were beginning their apprenticeships, and by Tom's age they were halfway to being old men. Unconsciously a shadow passed fleetingly over her face.

"Do you ride, Miss Moffett?" Tom essayed.

She nodded. "I have had a few lessons. But truly I don't ride well. I must have the most docile beast, and even then—" She laughed ruefully. How lacking she was in ways that most of those around her had known from their cradles! Would she ever catch up? And the sobering thought came to her—would she be given time enough to try?

She returned to her surroundings to find that Autherly had engaged Tom in brittle conversation. "That hack?" said Autherly with the faint suggestion of a sneer. "I see old Wisham saw you coming, and trotted out his prize!"

Tom's face grew alarmingly red, and he said stiffly, "My uncle selected this horse."

"And paid for it, too? I confess I had not thought your uncle so generous. But perhaps," Autherly said, affecting pained surprise, "with your funds, he may be open-handed. Although it appears to me he is overly anxious to conserve your income." He eyed Tom's mount with contempt that he was at pains not to conceal.

Since Hester surprisingly was enjoying Autherly's malice, and Lady Granville seemed not quite to understand the subtleties of the exchange, out of kindness Gina plunged into the conversation with the feeling of holding off two unequally matched swordsmen. "I should be frightened to death of your horse, Tom," she said.

The viscount's drawling voice rose. "Frightened of such a poor beast? Miss Moffett, you surprise me. I shouldn't think you would be frightened of anything."

Whether there was an underlying barb in the words, she did not know. Tom, nettled, pulled at the reins. "I told her she needn't be alarmed."

Perversely, Gina cried, "I shouldn't be frightened—I think. But I see I must prove myself." She reached to open the door, and before the scandalized footman could divine her intent, she stood on the ground, looking up at Tom's horse only a yard away.

"Miss Moffett, pray be careful! It's far too daring—take care! Look at those enormous ugly teeth!" Lady Granville nearly groaned, and Gina, looking obediently at the enormous yellow teeth, so close to her·bonnet, involuntarily took a step backward, and devoutly wished she had been less headstrong. But she saw no way to retreat, except to climb ignominiously back into the carriage.

She stood her ground with dignity, hoping her trembling knees would not betray her altogether. Tom quickly slid to

71

the ground to stand beside her, and thoughtfully maneuvered the horse backward away from her. She was able to breathe normally again. But Tom suddenly appeared crestfallen.

She looked to see what had overset him. Small wonder, she thought, catching sight of Edward Peregrine on a magnificent black horse, just ahead of the Granville barouche.

It was strange, she thought, how one man could so immediately become the focus of all attention. Hester, dropping Autherly, now displayed an excessive air of delight at seeing the man she prized above all else. Gina hardly noticed that Edward's delight, if it existed, was admirably concealed. Lady Granville leaned back against the squabs with an air of turning the whole situation, which hovered on the edge of unpleasantness, over to Edward Peregrine, and promptly assumed the air of one who contemplates a far horizon.

Autherly and Peregrine exchanged curt nods. Tom's cheeks flamed red. Gina's indignation stirred anew. How dared that odious man embarrass Tom to such a degree? Even though he was Tom's uncle, that surely didn't give him the right to reduce Tom to the condition of an awkward schoolboy.

She put out her hand toward Tom, to encourage him, but found Edward's stare had now shifted to her. As he looked at her, his eyebrows slightly lifting, she became conscious of her awkward situation, standing on the ground between the carriage and the stomping horse, in a situation that, to say the least, lacked grace.

There was nothing else to do. Gina summoned all the teaching of the Countess of Strathford, and lifted her chin with inborn resolution. Returning Edward Peregrine's stare with all the hauteur she could command, she did not respond to his greeting. Instead, she turned to Tom and smiled her most winningly at him.

She was conscious of Edward's stare burning somewhere near her left ear, and of Autherly moving away, saying words of farewell. Hester was talking over Gina's head to Edward, and Gina had to admit that—no matter how arrogant Hester's fiancé might be—his arrival had put an end to what might have become a nasty encounter between Tom and Autherly.

She had the utmost sympathy for Tom, but was also a little irritated. Tom presumably had had every advantage of tutoring, of being brought up well—and yet he was such a gapeseed as to allow Viscount Autherly's needling remarks to unhinge his decorum, and precipitate what was at the least an embarrassing situation. She sighed.

Cutting sharply across her reflections came Autherly's amused drawl, carrying for the moment an undercurrent of excitement. "Here he comes! I beg of you, see what a ridiculous figure the idiot cuts! I wish he would not offend my eyes again."

All eyes were upon the approaching driver indicated by the viscount. "The fool in the phaeton," Autherly had described him, and Gina could agree.

The low carriage was rapidly approaching them from the depths of the park. Drawn by two matched chestnut horses, straining into their harness, there was at first an air of dashing triumph to be seen in the driver, sitting on the absurdly high perch where he could handle the ribbons more easily. Or so the designer must have assumed.

From where Gina stood on the ground, her view of the equipage was unimpeded. Tom was slightly behind her, and Edward had moved away, probably, she thought, to avoid speaking at any length to Autherly.

"He's pelting too fast!" cried Tom impulsively. "He's lost them—he'll never pull them in!"

It all happened in an instant. The oncoming horses took fright and the near horse reared back, his terrible hooves cleaving the air before him for an endless second before touching the ground again. And as the near horse straightened, he swerved in her direction.

The chestnuts were swallowing up the yards between them and Gina. She could not avoid being trampled. She was too paralyzed with fear to move. She opened her mouth to scream, but no sound broke the drumming of hooves upon the ground.

All she could see was the rolling eyes of the horses, the enormous size of the wheels—

A high-pitched scream rent the air, but it was not hers. Gina's thoughts dwelt on Uncle Josiah's coming grief, and she took a deep breath.

And it was all over. Something dark moved across between her and the runaway horses, something knocked her out of the way against the great carriage wheel. And the phaeton hurtled harmlessly by.

She sprawled on the ground, feeling the stinging in her palms, and the blood thrumming in her ears. She lay prone for a long time, while she waited for pain to start somewhere. But it didn't.

When she was helped to her feet, the terrible scene of carnage that she expected did not appear. But—if not a scene of broken chariots in the Coliseum—it was bad enough. Lady Granville was providing a diversion of great interest by having whooping hysterics in her carriage. Hester was totally intent upon soothing her aunt, an endeavor that could easily take some time.

The footman had grasped the reins at the head of Lady Granville's horses, those staid old animals looking mildly at the havoc wrought by the obstreperous youngsters.

The driver of the high-perch phaeton had turned his subdued team over to some bystander, and himself ran over to the scene. All apologies, he began to offer disclaimers before he arrived.

"My horses ran away. I—lost control of them. The dealer assured me they were proper steppers. What's the damage?"

Edward was on the ground, his face white and drawn with pain. Aghast, Gina dropped to her knees beside him. "My dear sir, what happened?"

"That idiot of a driver," explained Tom. "The wheel came within an inch of grazing Uncle Ned's leg, and the surprise—" He broke off sharply. "See to him, will you, Miss Moffett, and I'll get some help."

Gina decided that this was not the time for the thanks that trembled on her lips. She had seen enough to know that Edward had put his horse across as a barrier to divert the runaways, but the phaeton was too near. "What is it?" she said, in place of her thanks. "Where are you hurt?"

She sent a swift glance over him, a glance that had assessed damaged small boys quickly, in her days at St. Clothilde's, and with deft hands she located the injury. "Shoulder," she said briefly. "I wish it may not be broken. There, sir, can you move your fingers?"

Reluctantly, he opened and closed his fist at her instruction, and she said in an encouraging manner, "I collect that your nephew will see that you get home. He is seeing now about a carriage." She bit her lower lip in relief. "You did save my life, you know," she said softly.

Tautly, Edward said, "It was really not such a dangerous incident, after all. Are you hurt, yourself?"

"No. Tom pushed me away." She surveyed her torn gown, and the inground dirt on her palms. She could not help but observe, "I had no idea that life in exalted social circles was so hazardous!"

Peregrine, astonishingly, chuckled, and then, pain surging over him, closed his eyes. Tom took charge then, and helped Gina to rise.

74

"Here comes Goodwin with the carriage. Over here," he said, raising his voice. "Did you bring Fortnim?"

She turned away, as Edward was helped into the carriage. She surmised that he would not wish his agony to be seen, and Fortnim, Edward's groom, and Tom were well able to manage.

Lady Granville was somewhat subdued, but clearly, seeing her eyes roll, Gina judged it was only a matter of time before her unstable control was shattered.

Hester said impatiently, "Get in the carriage, Georgina. I've got to get my aunt home. No time for your mooning around here."

For the first time, Gina, seated in the barouche, saw the face of the guilty driver, the Cit trying to rise above his station. He was staring at her in astonishment, his eyebrows threatening to rise entirely into his dark hair.

And all the way home, she thought, *He recognized me, and I recognized that crafty look in his eyes.*

The same look she had seen when his mother had burst into the pantry where he was forcing his awkward kiss on Gina.

What more could James Potter do to her now?

IX

Lady Granville's coachman exhibited no signs of panic as he carefully maneuvered the open vehicle through the crowded streets. If he moved more slowly, it was not, Gina surmised, because he wished to spare his mistress the ordeal of jolting over the cobbles, but solely because he was concerned about his elderly horses.

Hester was proving competent, if a trifle cold. In a bracing tone of voice, she said to her aunt, "I do think it's too bad, now that the season is coming into full swing. I must commiserate with you that such an accident should befall you, particularly today of all days. I don't know—" She let her voice trail reluctantly away, biting her lower lip in obvious indecision. "I'll send word to the duchess that you're ailing. The news of the accident will certainly reach her before evening, and I am sure the duchess will understand."

Lady Granville stopped in mid-whoop, and eyed her niece narrowly. "You will do nothing of the kind. I should hope that my spirits are not so poor they cannot overcome such a small shock as this. A mere trifle, after all. It was poor Mr. Peregrine who was injured, and not I," she cried. In a heartening manner she added, "I'm sure I hope your fiancé will not be crippled for life, Hester. But then, you are not formally engaged, so that's all right."

Lady Granville leaned back upon the soft cushions, and closed her eyes. Thus she did not see a speculative look creep into Hester's tight face.

At Granville House, Gina perforce must follow the others inside, feeling much like a forgotten parcel left on a shelf. Hester and Lady Granville's maid, hastily summoned from the kitchen and still wiping biscuit crumbs from her lips, were totally engaged in the difficult task of propelling Lady Granville's ample form up the broad staircase.

The butler held open the door to a small drawing room, and Gina passed through. "I do not wish to trespass longer than necessary," she informed him. "We had the most frightful experience. I'm sure the coachman will want to see to his horses. If you could send word to Mr. Moffett in Kennett Square that I am here, and request him to send someone for me, I will not bother you longer."

The butler, whose name was Peel, bowed and left the room. She was not quite sure how far Kennett Square was, nor exactly how to get there. She did know that she must not set out alone on foot through the streets. She settled herself to wait.

One thing she was abundantly grateful for, she reflected, was that she was not required to minister to Lady Granville. That lady reminded her forcefully of Mrs. Potter on the occasion of a rare visit to the kitchen area, having heard that the Marquise of Ravenall made regular tours of inspection throughout her household. The Potters' kitchen cat marked the event by dropping an object, unidentifiable but very dead, at her feet. The resulting screams were, in fact, heard in the street. How much the same—the baron's lady and the greengrocer's spouse! She speculated pleasantly upon the reaction were she to point out to Lady Granville the resemblance. A small chuckle escaped Gina.

"How delightful to perceive that you, at least, have suffered no ill effects," said Viscount Autherly from the doorway. "I trust I am correct?"

Gina whirled, embarrassed at being overheard, but Autherly was bland and smiled at her with such friendliness that she was immediately mollified. "I—I really was not hurt. It seems a miracle, but poor Mr. Peregrine, I fear, is seriously injured. Have you news of him?"

She looked anxiously at Autherly. She could not know how appealing she appeared, her large green eyes full of concern. If Autherly at that moment came to a fateful decision, no one was to know. Certainly Gina, so slightly acquainted with him, read nothing but consideration on his face.

He was not handsome, but somehow he emanated a magnetic current that many women, of all classes, found irresistible. Lines of indulgence were making inroads around his discontented mouth, and suddenly she thought he looked vulpine, like Alderman Moyes every time he watched her serving dinner at the Potters. But surely Viscount Autherly was not of the same stamp.

"Only a dislocated shoulder, I believe," Autherly informed her.

"*Only!*" she exclaimed. "How painful it must be! And I have only these small cuts to concern me." She looked down at the palms of her hands, crisscrossed with tiny scratches where she had fallen, hands outstretched, to the ground.

Now that she turned her mind to her own injuries, she found they stung unpleasantly. A trifle, compared to what might have happened—or even what had happened to Peregrine.

"Let me see." Autherly took her hands in his and turned them palms upward. "You must have these seen to. How shocking that they have been neglected."

"A mere nothing, sir," she interrupted, frowning, and withdrew her hands from his grasp. She moved away, vaguely uncomfortable. Automatically she rubbed her smarting palms together, and wished she hadn't.

Feeling the silence lengthen between them, she forced herself into speech. "I think that Lady Hester will be down shortly," she offered. "Her aunt was much recovered even before we arrived," she added, not feeling the necessity of explaining the reasons for that lady's quick recovery. "But of course Lady Granville will want to rest."

"Truly, Miss Moffett," Autherly said, "I was not much concerned about Lady Granville. You must remember that I have known her for a long time, and her moods are well known to me. My purpose was to see that you had suffered no harm."

"Me?" Gina stared at him. To think that a viscount, especially of such polish and experience, had spared even a thought for her! Seeing James Potter again had set her mind running along old paths. This would not do, she thought. She must remember that she was Miss Moffett!

"It was apparent that Lady Granville, under whose protection you were this morning, had quite forgotten you," said Autherly, warming to his theme, "and that boy Weston was too occupied to see to your welfare."

"His uncle could have been seriously injured," protested Gina. "He saved my life."

"You think so?"

Autherly let the skeptical note hang in the air while he moved to the window, peered into the street, and returned to stand near the fireplace, leaning indolently against the mantel.

"I am distressing you," said Autherly at last. "Pray forgive me. My intention was to allay your very natural distress over someone you feel an obligation to, however unjustified. But it occurred to me that perhaps I could escort you to your home. I am persuaded that Lady Granville has not so much as thought of how you were to go on."

Gina had collected her spirits. Viscount Autherly was merely being civil, she persuaded herself; his unnecessary lingering over her hand meant nothing. And she was not to be drawn into a discussion of Edward Peregrine's movements in that split-second of imminent disaster. She had in truth been in too much of a fright herself to see clearly, but she was still fairly calm, a surprising fact. Perhaps she would indulge later in hysterics, as Lady Granville had done. They had appeared to afford that lady much relief.

"You are kind, sir," said Gina, "but I have sent word to my uncle, and I must wait for his instructions."

"Then I am too late, and my disappointment must be my punishment," said the viscount smoothly, bowing. Just then from outside came the near sound of carriage wheels. With a quick word of farewell, Autherly left her.

Josiah had sent his trusted aide Sir Charles Derwent to bring his niece home, Gina found as she hurried down the steps of Granville House. Derwent helped her into the carriage and sat beside her.

"Thank you," Gina said. "I was becoming excessively uneasy at overstaying my welcome." Autherly had not overstepped the bounds of propriety, but nonetheless, he had made her uncomfortable.

"What is all this?" inquired Derwent. "Are you hurt? Your uncle most particularly charged me to find out the extent of your injuries, and to summon a doctor to meet us in Kennett Square."

"Oh, there is no need for that," Gina disclaimed hastily. "Only shaken up a bit, that is all. A few scratches, but I am sure Mrs. Beddoes has a healing salve that will fix them up at once."

He surveyed her, eyes narrowed, for a bit, and then, apparently reassured by her steady gaze, relaxed and leaned back on the cushions. "The footman who brought your message said there had been a terrible accident," Derwent said after a moment. "Was anyone killed?"

Gina gave a quick exclamation of irritation. "I told him nothing of the sort. I simply said that I was at Lady Granville's and asked for someone to come. How foolish—" She

79

turned in quick alarm. "My uncle, Sir Charles, how is he? Was he distressed?"

"Not when I left," said Derwent. "I told him you were quite clearly all right, or you would not have been able to send a message. But he is of course alarmed. Tell me what happened, and perhaps we can see whether some details of the incident should be withheld from him."

Gina accepted his logic. Besides, the incident had been exciting, and she was pleased to be able to tell it, now that her fright was past, and no one had been injured. Except Mr. Peregrine. Gina noted fleetingly that the word "odious"—almost a part of his name in her thoughts before this—did not spring unbidden to her tongue this time.

"It was of all things the most unexpected," she began, and finished the tale just as the Moffett coach began the turn into Kennett Square. "And Lady Granville was too ill to think of how I was to get home."

"Too selfish, you mean. Is that all?"

"All I can remember."

She had omitted nothing—nothing of importance, she amended. Only the identity of the culpable driver. She might tell Uncle Josiah, even though she considered it only a disagreeable coincidence. Nor did she see any purpose to be served by detailing her tumultuous feelings as she saw Edward Peregrine lying on the grass, his face frighteningly white, his piercing blue eyes hidden behind closed eyelids, and looking surprisingly vulnerable.

An exclamation from her present companion drew her back to her surroundings. They had arrived in Kennett Square, but a carriage blocked their way, and she saw that it was standing before their own door.

"The doctor!" she cried, alarmed, but Sir Charles demurred.

"Not likely," he said. "That is Lord Barham's coach."

Aware of an unusual quality in his voice, she glanced at him. He appeared worried, perhaps even vexed. He made as though to get out of the carriage, but she touched his sleeve.

"What does this mean? Something, I feel sure," she whispered urgently. "What is amiss?"

"I don't know," answered Sir Charles abstractedly. "Perhaps the French have landed."

"And Lord Barham—whoever he is—comes at once to inform Uncle Josiah?" Her tone was skeptical.

"Something like that," said Derwent. "I fear we cannot ask Barham's coachman to move away for us."

"Of course not. Who is he?"

"First Lord of the Admiralty."

"He runs the Navy? But what does my uncle have to do with the Navy?" she wondered. "Surely they do not expect him to take command of a ship!"

She was impatient with what she considered her companion's unreasonable impulse to secrecy. "What worries you, Sir Charles?"

"I'm not worried," he answered, too quickly. He paused, debating some question in his mind. Finally, he turned to her and with a frank air said, "You may as well know, I suppose. It's not something that is much talked about but—" He shrugged his shoulders, as though to say that it was out of his hands now, and added, "Your uncle is the head of all intelligence operations."

The look of bewilderment on her face spurred him to add, "You know, military intelligence. Army and Navy, both. All reports come to him, and he keeps all the threads in his own hands."

Without being aware of it, a note of bitterness crept into his voice, but she scarcely noticed it then.

She had not known exactly what she expected, but this was beside the mark. Intelligence? What exactly did that mean? Spying?

She did not know she had spoken aloud until Sir Charles responded pettishly. "Spying? No, no! A matter of national security, of the highest priority in time of war. As we are now."

"But—I don't understand!"

Looking at her with ill-concealed irritation, he nonetheless said with forced patience, "The Navy and the Army need to know certain things—such as, where is the French fleet? Off Boulogne? Coming up the Channel? Can Nelson overtake it, or can he take the time to protect the Sugar Islands? How well founded is the enemy? Have they put to sea with provisions for a week, a month? Or is their maneuver merely a training exercise? Things like that."

Gina revolved his words in her mind. Yes, she could see the need for knowing those things. But how was the information procured?

"Do you really need to know that?" asked Sir Charles dryly. "Just this moment?"

"No," she said slowly. "I don't think I even want to know that at any time. But"—as a new thought struck her—"is my uncle's employment common knowledge?"

"No. And I need hardly add that I would be much obliged to you if you did not let it be known that I had so informed you."

She nodded agreement. "So Uncle Josiah's affairs are secret. But then—why is Lord Barham's visit so unexpected?"

"A man of the first consequence," said Sir Charles succinctly, "whose own convenience is paramount in his eyes. It is rare for him to leave his comfortable office."

"Then something is gravely amiss with my uncle!" she cried, and threw open the coach door. Not waiting for the coachman to drive closer, she was hurrying down the sidewalk and up the steps before Sir Charles could stop her. With a grimace, he too alighted and followed her.

Inside the house, Gina's worst fears were realized. The household was in a state. Hastings was nowhere in sight. Fingle scurried through the hall as she entered, not noticing her.

A man of portly figure, dressed in dark and very expensive broadcloth, stood in the hall. He bent a penetrating gaze on her. At any other time she might have been intimidated by his severity, but she scarcely knew what she was saying. "Is my uncle ill?" she cried.

Harshly, he answered. "What do you expect when he believes you have been killed? And here you are, to all appearances unhurt."

"Killed?" She was astounded. "That cannot be. No one was killed. The message I sent—" Suddenly she became aware that she was wasting time. "I should like to see my uncle," she said with dignity. "Pray excuse me."

She was prevented from passing by Lord Barham. "The doctor is with him," he informed her. More kindly than before, he said, "Best wait until the doctor has restored him somewhat before you see him. Your appearance might alarm him even more."

She looked down at her torn gown, and suddenly felt the blood rush to her cheeks. "I am sorry, my lord," she faltered. "I had no idea how dreadfully mussed I am. Believe me, I had not noticed until now." She glanced into the gilt-framed mirror, and noted the smudges on her cheek.

"Perhaps the doctor should see to you," Lord Barham suggested.

"Oh, no, sir. I am truly unhurt."

"What really did happen?" he persisted.

"There was an accident," she began. "In the park. I was with Lady Granville and Lady Hester Reading, and we had stopped. To visit with acquaintances. A driver coming toward us lost control of his horses, and they bolted toward us."

She had succeeded in capturing Lord Barham's entire attention. When she had explained how she had happened to be standing on the ground when the horses bolted, driving directly toward her, he was visibly moved.

"And Mr. Peregrine suddenly was between the horses and us—"

"Was *he* hurt?" Lord Barham demanded.

She nodded, biting her lip. "I do not know how severely, sir," she said. "But Viscount Autherly seemed to think it was not serious."

"Autherly? How came he into this business?"

"He was standing at the other side of the carriage, talking to Lady Granville," she recalled. "But you see, my lord, Lady Granville was distraught, and I could not intrude my affairs on her. So I sent—"

The doctor emerged from the study. He was a stranger to Gina, but apparently not to the First Lord. Barham said swiftly, "Mr. Sayers was away from home, so I sent for Fellowes here. . . . Miss Moffett," he added, addressing the young and very serious doctor, "your patient's niece."

Mr. Fellowes eyed her curiously. In response to her agitated question, he said, "He'll be all right. He'll sleep the night away, and I'll be back in the morning."

Hastings interrupted. "Miss Moffett," he said, "your uncle is calling for you."

With scant ceremony she left the two men, and hurried to her uncle's side. He seemed very ill—she saw with a pang the pallor of his thin face, and the tightness in his lips holding back the pain.

Wordlessly, she sank to her knees beside him as he lay on the couch. He took her hand in feeble fingers, and the smile on his face as he realized she was safe stirred her to her depths. In such a short time had she become important to him, she knew, but in that same short span he had come to be the foundation of her life.

He closed his eyes, and was instantly asleep. She brushed her lips against his forehead, and tiptoed out, leaving Fingle sitting nearby in case her uncle should waken.

When she emerged, the doctor was gone, and Lord Barham was taking his leave of Sir Charles. Both men turned to her as she said, "He's asleep now."

"Tomorrow," Lord Barham said. "My news will wait until tomorrow."

Sir Charles interposed, "But in time of war, my lord, perhaps every delay is vital. At any rate, I could go along with you to the Admiralty, and perhaps stand in Moffett's place?"

He made as though to reach for his hat, but Lord Barham said shortly, "No need for that, Derwent. I'll come again tomorrow." With that he was quickly gone, leaving Sir Charles staring after him with an odd expression, before he too departed.

She paused at the foot of the handsome staircase and looked down the corridor to where Uncle Josiah was sleeping. Hastings emerged then from the back of the hall and said softly, "May I say we are all happy that you escaped injury?"

Suddenly she leaned forward and whispered urgently, "What brought on this attack, Hastings?"

"I really could not say, miss," said Hastings. "The messenger came, and Sir Charles answered the door. Which is not the usual thing in this house, as you know."

"I know," she said automatically. "And he told my uncle I was injured, or worse? How utterly foolish of him! Almost as though he wanted—"

She did not finish. The thought was too fantastic. Hastings stood with eyes averted, and said only, "I could not say, Miss Georgina."

She had begun to feel very odd, her shaking knees giving clear evidence that the morning's toll was about to be collected. She reached her room before the delayed shock overwhelmed her.

She began to shake, and could not stop. She was cold, her room shady after the early morning sunshine. She found she could not stand, and dropped into the green velvet chair, one of a pair that flanked the fireplace. The fire was newly laid but she did not trust herself to light it. She did not know how long she sat there, but it could not have been very long before Agnes, breathing heavily from her exertion, rushed into the room.

"Hastings said—" she began, and then peered closely at her mistress. "Land sakes, child—I mean, Miss Moffett—what's amiss here?"

She stepped to the bellpull and rang it vigorously twice.

"Let's get that torn dress—what a pity, and it's probably ruined—and what about you, miss? A pity you poor child had to undergo it all—"

84

There was more, all of it merely soothing syllables to Gina's numbed mind. Suddenly Mrs. Beddoes was there. The two of them got Gina undressed, and wrapped in a flannel robe, and, at Mrs. Beddoes's injunction, the fire lit in the grate.

"Nothing like heat to do a person good no matter what ails them," said Mrs. Beddoes wisely. "Now, miss, I'll have Agnes turn down the bed—"

Gina came to life. "No!" Then more kindly, she repeated, "No, thank you. I couldn't rest in bed in the middle of the day. Thank you both. I'll be warm in just a bit."

They settled her, still protesting, on the new yellow chaise that was Josiah's most recent gift to her. Wrapped in a lamb's-wool coverlet, and propped up by a multitude of pillows, Gina began to feel more herself. Meg appeared with a luncheon tray, setting it across her lap.

Gina toyed with chicken, sipped tea, ate a crumbly biscuit with damson plum jam. And thought.

Mr. Peregrine had certainly acted with dispatch and nobility in sustaining the brunt of the maddened horses. And it was surprising that his injury was not of more magnitude than it seemed to be. Perhaps she had overrated the danger, and yet she knew that in the second of decision, Edward had acted without, apparently, taking heed of the possible cost.

Odious he might be, arrogant he certainly was, but also fearless and decisive. And, so far at least, he had not seen fit to unmask her identity, by whatever memory he had summoned up as infallible proof. And, after today, she could be sure that he would not hesitate to act when he saw fit. His throat had been a sword hanging over her since the night of Josiah's party. Now, she had seen the sharp edges of his weapon.

And James Potter? What kind of fate pursued her that she should see again the unwitting architect of her disgrace? And under such strange circumstances? Pure chance that he should be driving in the park the same day—and yet, when she thought about it, it was not so strange after all. For Mrs. Potter possessed an overweening ambition, and Gina could see that woman's fine guiding hand behind young James and his purchase of a high-perch phaeton and the team to draw it. But Mrs. Potter could not instill in her son the ability to handle the high-spirited horses, nor the strength of character to refuse what he must know made him appear ridiculous.

She was uneasily disturbed about the odd look on his face as he took in the circumstances of Gina's new life. It was

85

clearly a shock to him to see there in fashionable Hyde Park the girl he had last seen in the dock. Now she was surrounded by members of the *ton*, prosperous and happy.

What would James do? What *could* he do? Her answer, based more upon wish than on fact, came promptly. Nothing!

Of the viscount Autherly, she thought not at all. And that was a mistake.

When Agnes came for the luncheon tray, she found her mistress sound asleep.

X

Gina was learning the ways of the fashionable world of London. For someone of her quick intelligence, the many intricacies of manners—for example, the half dozen degrees of curtsies, the correct way to address a mere baronet, or a royal duke—were easily mastered. Gina had a hunger to know everything that could be useful in this new world into which she had been catapulted unceremoniously. The four rigorous weeks she had spent with the Countess of Strathford had been ample tutelage.

In response to the customs she had recently learned, she set out the next day to pay a courtesy call on Lady Granville. She chose a gown of pale green, of a deceptive plainness, since the material itself was shockingly expensive and the making of it had been in the hands of an unexcelled dressmaker. Over it she wore a short jacket of a darker green.

She stopped at the door of the downstairs rooms of her uncle, and tapped. Hastings brightened at the sight of her.

"He's been asking about you, miss," he said, nodding toward the room behind him. "First thing this morning."

"Agnes told me he was still sleeping. You should have sent for me."

"He had his breakfast to eat," said the butler simply.

She nodded in perfect understanding. "Is he better?"

For answer, he held the door wide so she could enter. Josiah was propped up in a vast chair near the window, the remains of an invalid's austere breakfast before him. Hastings whisked the tray away, and Gina kissed her uncle's cheek before pulling up a chair to sit at his knee.

"You look much more the thing this morning, sir."

"And so do you. I was foolish to think the worst when

Charles told me you had been grievously injured. But are you truly all right, my dear?"

"Oh, yes, sir. It was a small incident. But the messenger must have got my message wrong. I merely asked for a carriage to bring me home, knowing you would not like it if I walked alone, even so short a distance as from Grosvenor Square."

"Quite right. You must not go unescorted anywhere. Now, Georgina, tell me what happened."

She gave him a carefully pruned version, minimizing the peril. Probably she had been too frightened to judge the incident fairly. "And Lady Granville began to whoop," she continued with her eyes dancing. "I vow that brought more spectators than even the runaway team. How can a well-bred woman lose all her control, sir? It was an embarrassing scene. But Hester did very well."

She chuckled, as she recalled Hester's heartening conversation. Hearing the narrative, Josiah laughed aloud. "You have such a keen eye for foibles," he said at last. "Lady Granville, I happen to know, has been angling for an invitation from the Duchess of Moray for weeks! She would not have missed the occasion if she had gone on a litter!"

"I must add," she said, after sharing his amusement, "that I owe much to Mr. Peregrine for his prompt action in diverting the runaways."

Josiah nodded. "He is a man of—I really hesitate to use such a strong word, since it has been so abused in common usage, but it is the only one that fits—a man of nobility of character."

Gina could think of nothing to say to her uncle's high praise of the man she disliked so much. The man who, with a word to Josiah who trusted him, could destroy her.

At length she said, "Now, Uncle, I must go to pay a call on Lady Granville. Perhaps she will not be receiving after the duchess's party last night, but I am not to know that, am I? She was not at all the thing when I saw her last, and I was not able to thank her for the carriage ride." She looked to him for approval.

"Prickett drives you?"

"Yes, and Agnes comes too."

He barely nodded. Alarmed, she realized his strength had ebbed, and he was suddenly pale and fatigued. She left quickly, pausing only to send Fingle, hovering in the hall, to her uncle's side.

She was vaguely troubled. Something her uncle had said—Lady Granville had been angling for a certain invitation for weeks, that was it! She couldn't have put her uneasiness into words, but she was conscious of something lacking in her new life. The formal promenade along Rotten Row, the inflexible social structure, the framework of calls, of meaningless parties, of seeing many of the same faces everywhere you went, much like the stylized movements of a stately dance: it was a monotonous existence, and as far as she could tell, profited only the jewelers, the mantua makers, and purveyors of fine foods—if their clients condescended to pay them!

But, she reflected, as Prickett turned the carriage into Grosvenor Square, as for monotony, what could be more grinding than scrubbing the same floors daily, seeing the same faces—cook, two other maids, and a footman—at every skimpy meal at Mrs. Potter's? How ungrateful she was! She had talked herself into better humor as she entered Lady Granville's foyer for the second time in two days.

Lady Granville was receiving. Gina followed Peel into the room where she had waited the day before. An elegant room with heavy gold-colored draperies at the window, a preponderance of white and gilt chairs and little tables. A white marble mantel at the far end of the room. A light and frivolous room, matching Lady Granville herself.

"My dear Miss Moffett!" that lady cried, both hands outstretched in welcome. "How good of you to come! You're looking famously—such a pretty shade of green!"

Gina responded as best she could. "I'm glad to see you restored to health, Lady Granville. The accident was upsetting, indeed."

"Yes," said her hostess with an air of casualness that could have deceived no one. "But I managed to be brave. My dear friend—the Duchess of Moray, you know—was counting on me for last night, and I could not bear to disappoint her."

Gina managed to conceal her rising amusement, and deflected Lady Granville from the narration of her social triumph of the evening before. "I failed to thank you for inviting me to drive yesterday," she said. "Have you news of Mr. Peregrine? I hope his injuries are not serious!"

"Nothing much, I understand. A shoulder, not broken."

"I must be grateful to him," began Gina.

Lady Granville interrupted her with a trill of laughter. "Not too grateful," she warned shrewdly. "My niece is to marry him, you know."

"So I have heard," Gina said in a tight little voice.

"She is lucky indeed. Peregrine may have no title, but he is wealthy as a nabob."

"I didn't know that."

Lady Granville eyed her narrowly. "Peregrine's estates border your uncle's in Kent. Surely you knew all about him."

"I am but newly restored to my uncle, you know," Gina responded in a stifled tone, "and he has not discussed Mr. Peregrine with me."

After a moment during which Gina gathered her gloves and her reticule, ready to take her departure, Lady Granville's mood changed in one of the pendulum swings that Gina had learned to expect of the lady. "Too bad," she said.

"Too bad, Lady Granville?" Gina echoed.

"Hester insists on keeping the engagement secret. But I don't see any great signs of regard on either side. In fact, I should not believe an engagement exists, were it not for Hester's assurance." With devastating frankness, she added, "I don't think they will suit."

On the contrary, Gina thought but did not say, *I think they will suit admirably. One spiteful, the other cold and proud.* And capable of cruelty, of threatening Gina with discovery, and then saying no more, leaving her to wait for one dire moment at some undefined future date. She felt exceedingly low in her spirits.

Before she could leave, another visitor was announced. Autherly made his graceful entrance and Lady Granville greeted him brightly. "Here comes all the news! I did not see you last night—at the duchess's, you know. So you must tell me all that has transpired since yesterday morning!"

Thus adjured, the viscount, bowing civilly to Gina, set himself to entertain his hostess. "The greatest bit of news is that Bonaparte has definitely decided to invade England next month!"

Lady Granville expostulated. "But yesterday, he was *not!*"

"Ah, but that was yesterday," retorted Autherly blandly. "And again tomorrow, without doubt. But today's news is that he has a hundred thousand men at Brest, ready to embark."

Lady Granville said, "Preposterous. Where does this secret information come from? Lord Barham?"

"Not likely!" said Autherly. "Barham hasn't spoken to me for three years." He laughed, without amusement.

There was more gossip. Autherly seemed an inexhaustible fount of tales, truthful or not and mostly scandalous, about people Gina did not know. The king's wits sadly addled. The

Duke of Cromarty's inexplicable journey to his lands in Scotland. A duel that would take place on Richmond Hill on the morrow.

Gina's spirits sank lower. She must still be upset by the incident of the previous day, and Josiah's subsequent collapse. She must get back to him. She rose, resolutely set upon escaping from Lady Granville's overly warm drawing room with its spicy atmosphere.

Instantly, Autherly was on his feet. "Pray allow me to escort you, Miss Moffett. It would give me the greatest pleasure."

"Thank you, sir, but I am amply protected," Gina said. "And I would not wish to deprive Lady Granville of your amusing company."

"Which you do not find amusing," he answered with a penetrating glance. "Well, I stand revealed before you in all my frippery. But I am sure you could reform me, if you would!"

"Autherly," said Lady Granville on a warning note, adding lightly, "many a fair lady has tried that, but you are delightfully incorrigible. I must say, you are quite to my taste as you are."

The awkward moment passed. Gina was not sure whether Autherly was at fault with his teasing, or that she herself was too inexperienced to see it as the fribble it must be. At any rate, he made her uncomfortable and she was glad, after she had made appropriate farewells, to take her leave.

She was still somewhat abstracted when she sat with Uncle Josiah after luncheon. He was recovered sufficiently to listen with interest to the account of her visit.

"How much better you look!" she exclaimed impulsively.

"Barham's doctor has done me good," Josiah explained. "Now tell me about your morning."

She obliged, rewarded by seeing his evident enjoyment of her narrative.

"And Autherly said Lord Barham hadn't spoken to him for some time," she said at last. "Is that the same Lord Barham whom I met here yesterday, sir?"

Josiah nodded. "Did Autherly mention his source for news of Napoleon?"

She thought a moment. "No, he turned it off. Is something amiss?"

"No, I think not. A certain amount of information has become common knowledge, although it should have been kept secret by the Admiralty. Somehow we must put a stop to such irresponsible dissemination. But that does not concern you. Nor me, since I live in seclusion now and do not travel to the office. I am sure the one who spreads the information does so from Barham's offices, since only those I trust visit me here—Derwent, René Valois. Edward."

"Monsieur Valois is French, is he not?"

"He lost all his family in the Terror. He was lucky to escape with his life."

Valois had taken tiny Georgina to a place of safety just after her parents died under the trampling feet of the mob that stormed the Bastille. Then, at the summons of Louis the Sixteenth, he had returned to share the travail of his king. "No," said Josiah, "he is fiercely antagonistic to Napoleon. Don't worry about René's devotion to England."

They were sitting in Josiah's spacious bedroom, next to the study where she had first met him. They looked out through a wide window onto the patch of garden, surprisingly rural in the heart of the bustling city. A rectangle of grass, two apple trees. A marble bench, looking uncomfortable in the extreme, and an Italianate statue of some forest demigod. A soothing sight to Josiah, so he had once told her. Now Gina in her turn felt a response to the greenery, a current of a longing long forgotten. . . .

Josiah's voice broke into her abstracted mood. "A word, my dear, of advice. Eschew Autherly. He can only do you harm."

"Of course, Uncle. I promise to have nothing to do with him. It will be no sacrifice, I assure you, since I do not like him in the least." Smiling, she picked up the day's edition of the *Morning Post*, and said, "Shall I read to you?"

Not an hour later, she saw that his drooping eyes had finally closed, and his breathing was heavy and regular. Smiling gently, she set the paper down noiselessly and tiptoed from the room.

In the hall, it was as though she had stepped from the somnolent silence behind her into another world. The household was busy about its ordinary tasks. Faint stirring sounds from upstairs told of maids changing linen, laying fires against the cool April evenings. A door closed somewhere.

And, close at hand, footsteps hurried toward her. Hastings wore a troubled expression. "Miss Georgina, there are callers. I didn't know what to do with them. They asked for the master. I told them he was not receiving today, but they won't leave."

"Who are they, Hastings?"

He did not answer directly. "I put them in the small reception room." Thus, indelibly, Hastings communicated his informed opinion of the visitors. Not of sufficient quality to be shown into the drawing room but not deserving to wait on the steps outside, either.

Her curiosity aroused, she agreed to see them, and went through the door the butler opened for her—and stopped short.

Waiting, in an atmosphere of tension, giving the appearance of a quarrel suspended in midair at the sound of the latch, were a woman of mature years and a young man barely out of his teens, clearly her son.

"Mrs. Potter!"

The woman rose, adjusting her shawl to the accompaniment of jingling bangles on her wrists, and came toward Gina, her hand outstretched. "I don't wonder that you are surprised to see us. My James came home yesterday from his drive—you have no idea how he is getting on, quite the man of fashion I assure you—and told where he had seen you. It certainly knocked us one, you may be sure. Imagine, the little girl I cared for, rescued from St. Clothilde's, clothed and took care of—it's more than enough to send me into hysterics!"

Since Gina's recollection of her sojourn in the Potter household agreed in no detail with Mrs. Potter's version, she could think of nothing to say. James turned from the window where he had taken refuge, and gazed at her with an odd look in his eyes.

Mrs. Potter did not appear to notice Gina's silence. "You must know that it was all a mistake."

At last, Gina found her tongue. "A mistake?" James's stupidity in thinking he could manage a high-spirited pair was certainly more than a mistake!

"Yes, we found the brooch," Mrs. Potter was saying, outrageously. "That stupid Sally had brushed it off onto the floor. But you're wondering why we came all the way across London—"

"You found the brooch?"

"Yes, the day before yesterday. Wasn't that a coincidence?"

Not a coincidence, a lie. "Too bad," said Gina sweetly, "that you did not keep as close an eye on Sally's work as you always did on mine. Imagine, weeks passed before your brooch was found on the floor. Had not Sally swept in the interval?"

Mrs. Potter's face darkened. Clearly she was not used to servants—even servants who had unaccountably been elevated out of all reason to a dizzying social level—questioning her statements, even accusing her of falsehood.

Abruptly, she said, "Our errand is with Mr. Moffett. So if you will just take us to him—"

"My uncle?" Gina felt as though she had spent the entire day echoing Mrs. Potter's words.

"He's the head of the family—at least, so people say now. We've made our inquiries."

"Why do you wish to see him?" Gina interrupted. Head of the family! Surely Mrs. Potter was not proposing to marry James off to her!

Mrs. Potter licked her lips nervously. *Here it comes!* thought Gina. "Why, I've been thinking he will want to show how grateful he is. I gave you a home, didn't I? Took care of you like the mother you never had—"

"I had a mother," said Gina bleakly, the warm arms and the singing voice of her dream vivid in her thoughts. "You sent me to jail. On an accusation you knew was false. Like a mother, you maintain?"

"Now, Gina—"

"Miss Moffett," Gina corrected her, haughtily.

"That affair was only a mother's loving discipline."

A snort from James provided all the comment his mother's exceedingly fantastic remark merited. Mrs. Potter directed a blazing stare his way, and then returned to Gina.

"Now then, let's let bygones be bygones," said Mrs. Potter archly, her piggish little eyes shrewd in their folds of fat.

"My uncle is not well, and he is not receiving visitors," said Gina crisply.

"Well, then, we'll just talk to you," said Mrs. Potter briskly, abandoning any pretense of amiability. "James saw you yesterday in the midst of all your fancy friends—"

"Whom he had just run down and injured badly," interjected Gina, "through his criminal incompetence."

"And it occurs to me," went on Mrs. Potter as though Gina had not spoken, "that you can do him some good. Introduce James to your friends, use your influence—"

Gina laughed inwardly. From that awful moment when she had guessed that a proposal of marriage was about to be broached, the conversation had departed from any semblance of sanity. She barely restrained her amusement, but fortunately she managed.

"Mrs. Potter, I fear I have no influence of any kind. I am myself barely acquainted with the people I was with yesterday."

"I beg leave to doubt that. James said—"

"I'm sorry. What James may have said doesn't interest me. I can do nothing for him, nor would I if I could. I remember too well his testimony at my trial."

James threw his hands out in a gesture of appeal. "I couldn't do anything else, Gina—Miss Moffett, that is."

"You haven't heard the end of this," cried Mrs. Potter. "You haven't finished your term in jail. You can be put back there, you know."

Gina's heart leaped into her throat. She could almost smell the horrid fetid straw, hear the unmentionable sounds of prison. But if Mrs. Potter had expected her threats to cow Gina into submission, she soon discovered her mistake.

Gina stepped to the door. She opened it, her hand trembling on the latch, while she fought for control of her anger, mingled to a degree with sinking fear. She turned at last and said clearly, "Nothing you can say will frighten me into doing what you ask of me. You have admitted the brooch was not even stolen. I am sure you have said all that you came to say. I will ask you to leave."

"Oh, no, Miss Moffett," Mrs. Potter began, scorn spread heavily on the last two words.

But Gina was furious now. She merely opened the door wider, and said, "In one minute, I shall send for the watch. I am sure you remember how quickly they can respond."

They filed out past her into the hall, which was curiously full of people. Hastings at the door, Dabney beside the stairs, Sir Charles Derwent a few steps inside the drawing room, but clearly visible and much interested in the proceedings taking place in the hall. And, Gina noted with a corner of her mind, a dark figure, of the formidably ample proportions of Mrs. Beddoes, loomed at the back of the hall.

The voluntary show of force was not wasted on Mrs. Potter. She gave a comprehensive glance around, and swept huffily through the door, opened promptly by Hastings. James turned and sent a wordless appeal to Gina, who returned his gaze stonily.

The door closed behind them and she sighed in relief. She had outfaced them this time. Would they have nerve enough to try again?

XI

The days following the accident in the park—and the Potters' visit—grew into a whirlwind of activity for Gina so that she was hard put to it to keep track of the days of the week. She found that her uncle's name was sufficient to ensure a rising tide of invitations to the smarter parties of the season.

She accepted most, because Josiah was well again. In fact, this morning he waited with her in the drawing room for her friends to arrive.

"Is it Tom again?" he asked.

"Yes, Uncle. A small party—and we're going to the Tower. Only fancy! Lions and beasts I never even heard of. Perhaps even a unicorn! Hester and Tom and Miss Wood. I believe that Mr. Ranney is coming. You know he positively languishes in the presence of Elizabeth Wood. But Lady Bray will see to them!" Her dancing eyes met Josiah's. "Perhaps others, but I am not sure. It is Mary Bray's party, you know."

"I remember, my dear. You see quite a bit of young Tom. What do you think of him?"

"I do like him! He is earnest, and so frank and kind! I suppose this is an odd word to use of such a boy, but—"

A shadow passed across her face, and her uncle suspected she was looking into her St. Clothilde memories. He had seen that expression before.

"On the contrary, *kind* is a fine word," he said hearteningly. "And accurate. I know the family well. Their land borders mine—ours—on the coast."

She looked up. "Mr. Peregrine's land? I think Lady Granville spoke of it."

Josiah nodded. "Tom's mother was Eleanor Peregrine, Edward's older sister. A very gentle woman, but sadly misguided about rearing young Tom." He hesitated. "How well do you like him?"

The conversation was suddenly serious. She knew what her uncle had in mind, and she answered simply, "I like him very much. *Like*, Uncle. Nothing more. I feel safe with him and I can relax just a little, rather than— Oh, Uncle Josiah, how they all watch for me to make a mistake! Like crows on a fence. And I just know that sometime I shall do the most dreadful thing and disgrace you!"

He burst into a chuckle. "Of course they do. And of course you will make some mistakes. But remember this— you are not pretending to be something you're not. Everyone knows you were lost, and spent years in an orphanage. They'll make allowances." *At least,* he added silently, *most of them will.*

She reverted to his inquiry. "Shall I put Tom off?"

"No, no. I entirely approve of him as an escort for my dear girl. But do not encourage him. I fear—" He allowed his words to die on his lips. He smiled, and the gravity marking his face vanished. "I'm selfish. I just don't want to lose you too soon."

Tom arrived. The April sun was growing warm, and Gina looked forward to a day *al fresco.* Her escort was driving a new sporting curricle, enormous as to wheel, ridiculously small, she judged, as to seat. The paint was shiny black picked out with a clear gold line on the wheels and the body, and a pair of black horses were held at the head, at this moment, by Tom's groom, Chatt.

Gina eyed the vehicle with strong misgivings. "I don't think—"

"Now, Georgina," Tom protested indignantly. "Don't be missish! Just because of that stupid Cit that caused all the trouble, you think no one can handle a pair of ribbons! I've been driving horses since I could sit on the perch!"

"How many bones broken?" she retorted.

"Only three," he confessed, but added brightly, "Mine, never a passenger's."

"What a fine record!" she marveled. "Believe me, I do not wish to spoil it for you. So I shall deprive myself of the pleasure of riding in that absurd conveyance."

Josiah Moffett, listening from the drawing room where they had forgotten him, smiled to himself. They sounded much like brother and sister, he thought, in their wrangling; and he was content. Tom was much too immature to manage a strong-willed wife. Besides, Josiah already had a prime candidate in mind for his niece.

Undeterred, Tom threw himself into a long if unexciting recital of horses he had driven and of narrow escapes from which he had with great skill extricated himself.

"Oh, Tom, stop!" she cried at last. "You are a very nonpareil, I give it you. But I do not wish to ride in that—that collection of wheels and a board or two. Pray do not ask me."

Disappointment flitted over his face and she knew a pang of regret. But whether she still felt skittish from the incident in the park, she knew she could not force herself to get into that entirely unsafe vehicle.

"Well," Tom said, after a doubtful moment, "I suppose I must return home and—"

They were still standing in the hall, looking through the open front door to the street, where Chatt was holding Tom's impatient blacks. Gina waited, twirling her parasol absently. She sympathized with Tom, seeing in his open countenance the crumbling of his hopes to cut a dashing figure in the picnic party.

Unexpectedly, the problem was solved. Behind the curricle in question appeared an elegant landau, a carriage of style and comfort, well-sprung and smart. A coachman driving, a footman up at the back. Chatt, glancing behind him, and recognizing the landau, scrambled to pull up the curricle and allow the landau full access to the step.

Gina examined the carriage in bright-eyed interest. The only fault she could find in it was its passenger—Edward Peregrine.

Hardly knowing how it happened, Gina found herself seated comfortably at Edward's right hand, Tom sulking opposite. Chatt had been sent home with the curricle, and the more elegant equipage was soon threading its way through the busy streets.

"You don't have to *drive* us to the Tower," Tom burst out. "You could have taken my curricle—"

"On the contrary," said Edward smoothly. "It seems nonsense to drive separately to the Tower, when we can all go together."

Tom was openly dismayed. "You mean, you're coming with us?"

"As you see."

Edward's voice was cool and forbidding. Gina was convinced that she was an unwilling spectator at the tattered

98

scraps of a dying quarrel, started at Peregrine's and interrupted by Tom's departure for Kennett Square. Feeling sudden sympathy for Tom—how would it be to *live* with such an unfeeling person as Edward?—she broke into speech.

"I trust your injury, Mr. Peregrine, is mending?" she ventured. "I note you have discarded your sling."

"Very much better, thank you, but as you notice, not quite well enough to handle the ribbons." Edward seemed to welcome her interruption, for he set himself to divert her. "What do you know about our destination?"

"The Tower? A prison," she said promptly. "Haunted by Anne Boleyn's ghost, and Sir Walter Raleigh's. Without his head, I think I have heard, though how anyone would recognize him in that condition, I couldn't say. And of course the menagerie. Pray tell me, have you seen it?"

"Not for a time," he answered. "Not, I think, since Tom came to town to stay with me."

They traveled through the throngs crowding Oxford Street, a wide thoroughfare that held most of London, she thought—on foot or on wheels. Oxford Street became in due course Holborn, and from then they traveled through side streets, always trending generally east and south, toward the river.

Catching sight of St. Paul's dome rising with serenity over the shabby buildings at its feet, she knew where she was, and thanked Edward in her mind for his thoughtfulness in avoiding the ugliness of Newgate Street.

And then she saw the massive gray battlements of the oldest building in London.

Afterward, Gina could not have described the Tower, but she had an overpowering impression of lofty and very thick walls, massive towers in great numbers—she counted thirteen. An unlucky building. A higher fortified line of stone, and then, inside, the Ballium Wall.

The Tower was oppressively melancholy. Suddenly the weight of all the sorrows of centuries fell upon her. Newgate echoed in her mind. Someone's hand under her elbow—Edward's—steadied her for the moment.

Mary Bray was watching for their arrival. She led them through the gates in both walls, and over the grassy moat. Emerging into the quadrangle, Gina stopped short, honestly astonished.

"The sun is shining!" she cried.

Of the several members of Mary Bray's party, only Edward understood her meaning. To her surprise, he said reassuringly, "Only a collection of stones, after all. No brooding spirits left."

She managed a smile. Unconsciously she straightened her shoulders. *I came to enjoy myself, and enjoy, I will!* The other members of the party were in most part known to her. Mary Bray, of course, and her mother. Tom maneuvering endlessly to be next to Gina. Hester Reading, talking continually in an undertone to Edward. Elizabeth Wood, softly pretty and basking in the heat of Gilbert Ranney's worship.

A man introduced as the Honorable Sylvester Fuscue—a willowy figure, with the indefinable attitude of an army officer. Gina regarded him with interest. His married sister, Caroline Taunton.

By the time they had crossed the quadrangle, and strolled inside the wall ending in the Traitors' Gate, where broad steps descended into the river, vanishing in the depths of the Thames, she found Viscount Autherly had somehow appeared and attached himself to their group.

"He must know he is not wanted!" muttered Tom in her ear.

"On the contrary," responded Gina, "it seems that someone is welcoming him." She looked across the few yards separating them. Hester was speaking animatedly to Autherly, and Mary nodded in response to Autherly's apparent question. As Gina's glance traveled, it was caught by Edward, watching her with a thoughtful expression. Feeling her cheeks warming, she immediately looked away.

The Tower lawns and walks were becoming quite crowded. Visitors from the country, up to London on business or to see the sights, dressed in their best clothes, in fashion a few years ago. A half dozen merry youngsters, accompanied by a fondly indulgent older couple, vividly reenacting Queen Anne's beheading with much squealing laughter.

Tom was whispering in her ear, and reluctantly she forced her attention away from the appealing children. "I'm going to call tomorrow," he said portentously.

Mystified, she gazed at him. "Call?" she ventured at last.

"On your uncle," he explained.

"But you saw him this morning!"

A touch of exasperation edged his words. "Georgina, surely you know what I mean? I wish to marry you, and of course I must address myself to your uncle before I say anything to you."

"You just did," she pointed out. "Speak to me on the subject, I mean. Tom, I wish you wouldn't!" Seeing the mulish-

100

ness still in his eyes, on impulse she laid her gloved hand on his sleeve and gazed earnestly into his eyes. "Tom, it's no use!"

"I don't know what you mean," he said. "I can work it out."

"Believe me, you can't. I wish only to save you embarrassment." A set-down by Josiah Moffett, no matter how gently done, would lacerate Tom's young sensibilities, and even if Josiah permitted Tom's addresses to her, she herself must decline to give him any hope.

"Embarrassed!" Tom was saying. "No, no. Uncle Ned must give in if Mr. Moffett is for the match. He'll have to release my funds then. But leave all this to me."

He looked so absurdly ruffled in his determination that she was amused, but rueful as well. Somehow she should have foreseen that his growing devotion would lead to this, but she had not. Not even Josiah's warning had opened her eyes.

She must try again to dissuade him, but not here, not in public. Especially with his uncle watching them. Involuntarily she glanced up and encountered Edward's repressive frown. She returned his gaze coolly, and then, deliberately, looked past him into the growing crowds.

And there—not fifteen yards away—stood Mr. Quinn!

For a fleeting second their eyes met, and recognition flashed between them. The same foxy red hair, eyebrows thick as brush. Little knowing eyes peering through narrowed lids, enjoying her shocked reaction, making sure she understood she was not finished with him, not yet.

She swayed, and suddenly Edward was at her side. "Are you ill?" he demanded. "You lost your color. What is it?"

She took a deep shuddering breath, and when she looked again, Mr. Quinn had vanished. If he had ever been there! She shook her head. "Nothing, Mr. Peregrine. I was faint for a moment, that is all."

"Shall I take you home?" he persisted. "I am persuaded you are ill."

"No, thank you. Miss Bray has gone to a deal of trouble, and I must not spoil her excursion." She summoned up a rather shaky smile, and reluctantly he capitulated.

In fact, seeing Mr. Quinn was upsetting. Almost like seeing Anne Boleyn's ghost, with or without her head. He had loomed large and menacing in her thoughts when she had first come to Kennett Square, naturally enough. But with the passage of weeks without hearing from him, and the influx into her days of new activities and new acquaintances, the fabric of her new life effectively veiled old fears.

But it was clear he had not forgotten her. She had an uneasy conviction that Mr. Quinn had followed her here—that he had, in fact, been aware of her whereabouts all these weeks. There had been no surprise in his sharp little eyes. The thought followed logically—why had he allowed her to see him today?

The rest of the day passed as in a daze. The lions, the grotesque giraffe, even the vast elephant—she looked at them but did not see. Other pictures intruded between her and the pitiful caged animals. Pictures of Newgate, of the frowning judge.

Pictures of James Potter—hot and breathy in the pantry, pale and fidgety in the witness box. Oddly speculative when he recognized her in Hyde Park.

She heard herself laughing, even gay, as they left the Tower and went on to a luncheon in a private room at a restaurant on the bank of the Thames upstream, where the river ran quietly and unmarked by barges and ships, and swans sailed in cool majesty along the reed-bordered shore.

Her thoughts turned to Uncle Josiah—seeing in fevered imagination the love in his eyes turn to disappointment, even heartbreak, engineered by the malevolent Mr. Quinn. She had no doubt that Mr. Quinn boded no good to her nor to Uncle Josiah. She did not see clearly ahead, but of one thing she was sure. The man was not a philanthropist.

On the way home, oddly, a clear picture stamped itself indelibly on her mind—a little horned deer caught with his forefeet in the air in the act of leaping. Grace in every line, and even, so clever had the artist been, a feeling of joy.

A part of her lost dream, her child's dream. It could mean nothing, she told herself crossly, and forced herself to pay heed to her companions. She hoped she had not given herself away. Tom, at her side, gave every indication of satisfaction. With a lowering feeling, she wondered what, in her preoccupation with her own affairs, she had said to him?

He held her hand overlong as he helped her down from Edward's landau. Just before he relinquished her into the care of Hastings, on the threshold, and Agnes, hovering nearby, he said in a low voice, "I'll never forget this day the rest of my life."

In a common-sense voice, she agreed, "Neither will I."

Throbbingly, he promised, "You'll never regret it."

She paid heed absently, wondering if Mr. Quinn were even

102

now spying upon her from a dark areaway, or a shadowed doorway.

Thoughtfully, she said, "I hope not," and went up the steps and into the house without a backward glance.

Once inside Uncle Josiah's house, surrounded by four stout walls and a staff of capable and devoted servants, she lost the ominous feeling that prickled at the back of her neck, the conviction that Mr. Quinn somehow knew her every movement. More than that, she yielded to the persuasion that the encounter that afternoon had been a mere coincidence. The Tower was a magnet drawing sightseers from both the city and the country, and what more likely than that Mr. Quinn had succumbed to the desire for a relaxing afternoon at the menagerie?

She could not quite believe it. She was reluctant to leave the house. She stole long searching glances from her window the next morning, and although she saw no movement in the shadows, no suspicious loiterers, she sent word to Elizabeth Wood, who had engaged her for an afternoon drive, that she was feeling not quite the thing—"a touch of the sun yesterday."

She was in the drawing room in the afternoon when a carriage drew up before the house. She flew to the window in time to see Sir Charles Derwent jump to the ground.

"I must see Mr. Moffett at once," he said crisply to Hastings in the hall.

She hurried to the doorway. "What is the matter?" she asked, her heart jumping in her throat. Mr. Quinn had made her shy at shadows.

"Something at the Admiralty," he said, full of bustling importance. "Lord Barham insisted I come myself with the news."

Nothing to do with her, then, she thought, turning with relief back to the drawing room. She should be curious, she knew, but her own troubles—personified by the lurking Mr. Quinn—seemed large enough to deal with at the moment.

Mr. Quinn was only the beginning, she reflected, moving restlessly from chair to window to chair. He held her in a kind of bondage only because she was unsure of herself. She had only the support of Josiah Moffett to maintain her. She had no true foundation on which to stand.

Was she, in fact, as Uncle Josiah believed, Georgina Moffett? Or was she simply an unknown urchin, with no parents,

—no identity—come full-blown into being, and living and dying without roots?

She searched for hints in herself. Did she remember this house? Did she remember Uncle Josiah? The answers were clear.

No.

But she was grateful beyond words for Josiah's loving her, and she would do anything to keep from disappointing him.

The words echoed; she had promised once before that she would do anything—that time—to escape from Newgate Prison.

The thought suddenly struck her—Mr. Quinn was not the man to be feared! He could not prove she was *not* Georgina Moffett! All he knew was that she had grown up at St. Clothilde's, and that her first employers had sent her to prison. But she had made no secret of that, to Uncle Josiah or anybody else.

No, the enemy—even though he had saved her from serious injury, or even death—was Edward Peregrine. He had claimed to be able to prove beyond question whether or not she was Georgina. And she had no doubt that he believed she was an imposter. How else to account for his coolness, his long, thoughtful looks? And why didn't he bring out his proof instead of setting her on tenterhooks? Instead of setting forth the truth before his friend Josiah was too enmeshed in what she was sure Edward would think of as "her toils"?

As her thoughts darkened, Hastings appeared in the doorway.

"Miss Moffett, Mr. Peregrine."

For one startled instant she thought she must have conjured the man up out of her thoughts. She grasped the arms of her chair, and, arrested in the act of rising, stared.

For Edward Peregrine, coming hard on the heels of the butler, regarded her with eyes glittering like gray frost in December.

He came to stand a couple of yards away, and looked at her, she imagined, as though she were a particularly unpleasant object brought in by the cat. *Here it comes,* she thought. *He's come to prove who I am.*

"In a way," she mused, not knowing she spoke aloud, "it will be a good thing to get it over with."

He stopped short, clearly taken aback. "Well!" he exclaimed. "I had not thought you would be so easy to deal with."

She glanced up at him from under long lashes. "I wonder

104

you thought at all, Mr. Peregrine," she said. "Easy to deal with is not the question. Let us have done with formalities, and give me no apologies."

"I had not intended to apologize," he said icily after a moment. He obviously had not anticipated this attitude on her part, and she could almost imagine the furious rearrangements going on in his mind. It amused her, in a grim fashion.

"No, I did not really think so," she said equally enough, hearing her voice coming from far off. "You are not the kind of man to apologize."

He refused to be diverted. "I must assume that your wish to be settled in life must be paramount in your plans. But I had not expected quite so blatant a scheme."

Mystified, she gazed at him. "Settled? Yes, I suppose you could say so. But you mistake me, sir, if you feel I have initiated what you call a scheme. I was in complete ignorance even of its existence."

"Oh, I agree. But now you know, and you must be guided by whatever scruples you may possess."

She realized with sinking heart that Edward Peregrine was infuriated, nearly out of his mind with anger. It must be so, else he would not be so lost to his accustomed urbane civility. But why, after knowing who she was—or was not—for weeks, had he suddenly become enraged?

She was glad, in a way, that the decision was about to be taken out of her hands. She felt a rising indignation that it should be Edward who was forcing her to act. And his words stung like whips.

"I welcome your strictures upon my behavior," she said, rising to her feet. How disadvantageous it was to sit down while someone loomed over you! Her eyes blazed as she went on. "But I am not clear in my mind where your authority to discipline me—for that is what your words amount to— comes from. Surely I did not give it to you?"

He took a deep breath, manifestly endeavoring to regain control over his emotion. She was puzzled; why should he be suddenly so furious with her?

"I must inform you that I do have a word to say on this situation. I would be neglecting my plain duty not to speak out."

"So. You have spoken out. Although I must say it comes a little late to do any good." She glanced involuntarily toward the window. Perhaps even now Mr. Quinn, or someone he sent, was taking up his vigil across the street, in a corner of the park, watching her. "Too late," she repeated.

Edward in his turn looked startled. "You're so sure of yourself? You have no question about the propriety of your plans? I had no thought that you guided your actions by such low motives."

"Sure of myself?" she echoed, her anger leaving her. She was wrong, she knew it. She should have never given in to Mr. Quinn's proposal. Better to have stayed in her cell and made the best of it. She would probably be dead by now, she reflected in a matter-of-fact way, and never would she have known—the things she knew now. But better never to have known than to go back now, to serve out her term, and remember every waking hour how Josiah had loved her, and she had deceived him.

"Well," Edward was saying, "I must tell you now. This whole foolish enterprise must come to a halt."

She hardly heeded him. He was irritating, and even more, but—her mind was made up. "I will tell him."

"Tell him? And what will you tell him?"

What could she tell Josiah that he did not already know? She could tell him about Mr. Quinn—but even his existence was known to Josiah. She could add that she had seen him at the Tower, and what did that amount to? She had not deceived Josiah at all; her fear of Mr. Quinn, and her deep aching to belong truly to someone, had led her astray, into confusion and false guilt.

She could have laughed aloud. Impartially, she beamed upon her caller. "I'm not going to tell him a thing!"

Edward's face darkened alarmingly. "Don't tell me you are really— No, I can't believe it."

If Edward had proof that she was an imposter, he could bring it out. And then let Josiah decide what to do. She herself had never claimed she was Georgina Moffett.

With that decision taken, knowing that she did not fear Edward, she began to look closely at him. "I believe, Mr. Peregrine," she began slowly, "that you and I may be at cross purposes. Pray tell me what business it is of yours, after all? And why, after these weeks, have you come here in what I must regard as a very crude fashion to tell me what you think I must do? I am really interested in your reasons."

"I have every right to interfere."

"You are not my guardian, I am quite sure of that, and I must decline to believe that you exercise any legal authority over my uncle's affairs."

She was proud of herself—never a quaver in her voice, never a stammer! It was as though someone outside her had

106

taken over and was speaking for her. Left to herself, she thought darkly, she would simply collapse in a swoon on the floor.

"Josiah!" he expostulated in sheer surprise. "I am not talking about Josiah. I am speaking of my nephew Thomas Weston."

"Tom!"

"My nephew has favored me with the news that you and he plan to be married. I collect he was to call upon your uncle this morning, but of course I could not allow that."

Reaction made her furious. So far from luring Tom, as Edward seemed to believe, she had tried, evidently without success, to set him down gently. And now Edward's savage anger, hurled against her without so much as asking for her side of the question! It was too much. She struck at him. "Your standards are so high, then? You have something particularly in mind for your nephew? I collect Tom is of age!"

"Not quite yet. His father set twenty-five as the age at which Tom would be able to handle his funds. And, the way he is going, I doubt that even that age will bring him sufficient wisdom. Tom's mother felt he was overly delicate and kept him by her side far too long. He is too inexperienced to know his own mind."

"Indeed!" she said cordially. "I suppose that no one in his senses would be attracted to me?"

She had the immense satisfaction of seeing him at a loss. His face flushed, and he clamped his lips tightly together. She had the uncanny thought that he might—if he had been a different kind of man—have lifted a fist and sent her sprawling. She smiled inwardly. That would teach him! She could not resist prodding him.

"I will tell you something, Mr. Peregrine," she said, with a spurious air of kindness. "I will not deny Tom's words. But you should know that when I make up my mind to something, I do not turn aside. For anything."

"We'll see about that!" he said furiously. "I must tell you now, that I will never permit Tom to marry you. Never!"

"What will Tom do, then? Go back to the schoolroom? Will you send him to some country place to—'rusticate,' I believe the expression is?"

He took a turn around the room. His rage was waning, and some other emotion seemed to take its place. "Are you then in love with Tom?"

The question startled her. There was a queer anxiety in his eyes that troubled her. But, belatedly, she was reluctant to repudiate Tom, who had been kind to her. It was likely her fault that Tom had misunderstood her feelings for him. And she had a lowering feeling that she must have said something yesterday afternoon to encourage him.

"Does that matter, Mr. Peregrine?" she said, collecting her wits. "Is not the question that I am not well-bred enough? That is what you are saving your famous 'proof' of my identity for? When Tom and I arrive at the altar, will you come running down the aisle after us waving your so-called proof?"

"Proof?" His lips twisted as though he tasted bitterness. "Yes, I can prove whether you are Georgina Moffett, or not. But I am not sure I want to, not just yet."

Queerly, he did not seem threatening, only thoughtful.

Arrested, her thoughts turned privately to a plan that leaped full-blown into being. The plan shone brightly in its perfection. She would make her own search for her identity! Somewhere in the world, besides in the mind of Edward Peregrine, there was a trace of the small Georgina. And she would find it.

"I must go ahead with it," she said softly, more to herself than to him.

"Then your last word is a clear refusal to give up this— this idiotic scheme!"

Once again they were speaking at cross purposes, but she did not care. She wanted time—time to examine her plan. And something about Edward Peregrine exacerbated her beyond caution. He was intolerable!

Summoning all the scorn she was capable of, she said, "You have my last word. Now my advice to you is—go back to Lady Hester, and leave me alone. You two deserve each other!"

To her horror, she burst into tears. She fled from the room blindly, running into Sir Charles as she found the stairs. She did not look back, or she would have seen him watching her with narrowed, thoughtful eyes before Edward joined him in the hall.

She gained the haven of her own room before she gave herself over to the great satisfaction of hysterical and exhausting sobs.

XII

Gina's renewed determination to find out who she really was engrossed her. She had not the faintest idea where to start, unless it was at St. Clothilde's. She had asked Matron many times when she was growing up about the circumstances of her arrival at the orphanage.

"Who brought me?"

"We did not see."

"How did I get here? In a basket, like the babies?"

"No, my child. The bell rang, and Sister Mona answered, and there you stood. You said you had rung the bell yourself; don't you remember?"

Gina did not remember. The years before were gone as though they had never been. Even her dream—of singing, of happiness, of the pert little deer—was not real, and she had considered it only a wish for something she had never known. Finally, she gave up asking Matron. If the woman was hiding something, Gina was then too inexperienced to know. But there was her beginning, as far as she could know now, and there she must go.

It was a simple thing to plan, and yet so difficult to execute. She had not realized how circumscribed her new life was. From the moment when Agnes drew back the green damask draperies and brought her early morning tea, until she lighted herself up the stairs to bed at night, finding Agnes ready to undress her and bring her a glass of warmed wine to help her sleep, every moment was filled with many watching, and caring, eyes.

It was the morning after Edward's descent upon her. She must above all things keep up an appearance of naturalness. She felt instinctively that Josiah might even forbid her to go to the orphanage, saying he was satisfied of her identity and that should be enough. It had been, until Edward had flung his scorn at her, hinting that she was not good enough to marry even that young Tom Weston.

This was the day she had planned to show off her new mare Blossom in the park. Uncle Josiah had sent Prickett and Fingle to Tattershall's auction, with instructions to purchase a certain pretty, well-behaved mare for Gina. Her riding lessons had been intensive, and she had, under her tutor's watchful eye, performed well enough so that he told Josiah she was ready to venture into the public eye.

Sir Charles was to go with her today, Fingle following, of course. Strange how Fingle clung to her, hardly letting her out of his sight. Almost like a guard, she thought, and rejoiced in the safe feeling he gave her. But now, he was the first she must outwit—no, not the first. Agnes would be the first.

Sir Charles was an enigmatic man, she reflected, watching him from the corner of her eye as they trotted slowly into the park. Older, seeming very solid. A dark sort of man as to color, and plain as to feature. She wondered occasionally what ties he had—none that she ever heard of. No wife, no children, and she was not even sure where he lived. He made an extra man in many unexceptionable gatherings, and his manners were faultless. Josiah trusted him, and perhaps he was one she could confide her own project to. He could smooth the way for her.

But she must do the first part herself, she decided. After St. Clothilde's, she would not know where else to go, always assuming that Matron had nothing more to tell her. But that would come later, and time enough then to consult Sir Charles.

The ride along Rotten Row soon engrossed her. Sylvester Fuscue was the first to stop them. "What a topping mount!" he cried. "Is that the one—yes, I am sure it is, that Lord Barham was looking at. And," he added with simple adoration, "how well you look in riding habit, Miss Moffett!"

Her habit too was new—a Lincoln green tailored jacket, a broad and very well-cut divided skirt that showed off her hand-span waist and slim hips to perfection, and a hat of matching fabric with a dipped brim and a curly white feather. She began to glow under the compliment.

Lady Taunton was with her brother, and Mary Bray soon joined them, with Adelaide Gough. Gina was pleased to know how many of the fashionable world, which took its exercise daily in the park, she was acquainted with.

Charlotte Lennox cantered up, halting her steed with a flourish, to Fuscue's disgust. "You'll rack that bay up with that kind of show," he informed her bluntly, "if you don't break a leg."

"Sylvester!" his sister screamed faintly. "Your language!"

"Of the horse, of course," he answered, and the silly rhyme confused him even more, so that he backed off, blushing, and regarded the far horizon with great care.

Before they started on again, to Gina's dismay Lady Hester arrived, with Edward Peregrine. But Tom was not with them.

Fuscue commented upon Tom's absence. "Too bad about young Weston," he said in an undertone to Gina.

She turned an inquiring glance at him, and he elaborated, "He's finally had to see to his estates—that's why he's not in town. His uncle saw to that."

Gina glanced involuntarily at Edward and caught his eye. He stared at her with chilly hauteur, and then turned away as though she were no more than a fly on the wall.

Nettled, she could see that Edward was serious in his resolve to keep Tom away from her. Gina herself could have cleared up Edward's misconception by simply promising not to marry Tom. And she would, since she had no intention whatever of contracting such a marriage. But it was impossible to explain that now, and besides, it would do Edward no harm to worry a bit longer.

She smiled sweetly in his general direction, hoping he noticed, and then said to Sir Charles, "Should we not go on?"

Hester's mare had somehow edged too close to Blossom's rump. The mare stamped uneasily, and Gina looked around. Hester was intent upon her maneuver, her small whip lifted ready to descend.

"Lady Hester, take care," cried Sir Charles.

Hester raised her glance, not to Derwent, but to Gina. While Gina had a good natural seat, and sufficient instruction and experience to stay in the saddle in the ordinary way, she would be unable to cope with a bolting horse. Blossom snorted, and Gina slipped in her saddle. Even without the touch of Hester's whip, Blossom was frightened.

Panic touched Gina's throat. She felt suddenly she had had a great sufficiency of horses—what with one thing and another. She looked wildly to her right for a means of edging out of the close quarters.

It was not her own mare that took fright. A scream rose

111

behind Gina, and Fuscue cried out. It was Mary's mare that suddenly plunged, and it took a good deal of skillful handling to avert disaster.

Gina stared at Hester, letting her see that her maneuver was discovered. With a shiver of shock, Gina recognized the naked hatred in Hester's eyes. How had she merited such malice?

One thing she must do, she resolved, and that was to watch her step. It might be dangerous to plumb the depths of Hester's spite. And once again Gina thought that Hester and Edward deserved each other, and she wished them a merry marriage.

She saw her way clear now, moved free of the press, and set off at a slow canter down the riding path, giving herself over to the soothing rhythm of the mare's rocking gait. If she could leave them all behind, just as she was doing now, she would like it. But of course, she couldn't have both the fine mount beneath her, and be solitary in the world too.

The others caught up with her as she stopped at a small rise to look down upon the ornamental water called the Serpentine. Reflected in it were the high-moving clouds and the nearer trees, against the shimmering blue of the mirrored sky. A placid sight, and she soon grew good-humored again.

Along the shore a little farther, Gina saw Elizabeth Wood and her younger sister, escorted by the ever-present Ranney. Gina waved and the trio trotted over to join the group. Autherly had already appeared, as seemed to be his custom, out of nowhere and attached himself to their growing party. "Where is young Tom?" asked Autherly. "I had a particular question to ask him."

Fuscue was glad to tell him. "He won't be with us for some time," he finished, after explaining Tom's excursion into Kent.

"I hear Tom needs a great sum of money just now," offered Autherly. "I suppose it is a false rumor. People will say anything, you know, just for sensation."

"How cruel!" cried Adelaide Gough. "Poor Tom needing money, I mean. I'm sure he doesn't look hungry!"

"For heaven's sake, Adelaide," said her dear friend Caroline Taunton bluntly. "Can't you tell when Autherly is behaving naughtily? I'm sure there is nothing to the story. Autherly, be so good as to be serious, if you can."

"Oh, I can, Lady Taunton, very serious indeed. Just now I was merely repeating something I had heard. I must confess I wouldn't know why Weston would need any great amount of money. Aha!" he cried, as though a happy thought struck him. "Perhaps he has run up secret bills that his guardian won't pay!"

He looked pointedly at Edward. It seemed clear to Gina that he was determined to embarrass Edward. Even to force him into a duel. That surely could not be allowed to happen. While she hurriedly resolved the best thing to say to divert the argument, she heard Edward say evenly, "My nephew has no need for money, Autherly, and since for an unknown reason you seem to find interest in his affairs, you will feel easier in your mind, I am sure, to know that he has no outstanding debts and does not gamble. I am hopeful that now you will be able to sleep more easily at night." His words were civil enough, but the tone in which they were conveyed was frigid in the extreme.

Autherly considered, to all appearances, that he had gone far enough, and bowed formally, reining his big horse away from the group. But Ranney said, in an innocent attempt to be informative, "I heard Weston's getting married."

An appalled silence fell upon the knot of riders. Edward's gaze fell, seething, upon Gina. As though this were all her fault! she thought, anger sweeping over her and bringing a flush to her cheeks. Furious, she refused to be intimidated, giving Edward glare for irate glare.

A movement caught her eye. Autherly, a secret smile on his lips, moved away. "I must leave you all," he said with every appearance of geniality. "I see the Countess of Sandown coming."

A barouche pulled up beside them, and the countess herself cried out in a scraggly voice, "Autherly! Come here and tell me all the news, you naughty creature!" Stifling a grimace, Autherly did as he was bade, and rode off beside the vehicle.

Gina had had enough. Stifling in the tense atmosphere, she wheeled her mare out of the group, and recklessly set her into a fast canter down the path. She thought, *I am so weary of all of them! Filling the air with spite and malice....* She remembered with renewed shock the look in Hester's eyes as she edged her mount skillfully into Gina's.

Gina felt that only pounding physically down the road would clear out her morbidly churning thoughts. After a hard canter she reined Blossom in, and set her to a steady, more sedate trot. She was pleased with her management of the mare. For someone who had never been on a horse only four months ago, she thought she did well. Her confidence rose,

113

and turned into exhilaration. She could go on riding like this forever!

She was out of sight of the rest of the party. Sir Charles would be irritated, and Fingle, who knew to a turn how well she rode, would be worried. She must turn and go back. But not quite yet. She set herself a limit. *That next meadow and the grove of trees beyond—I'll turn back there.*

She reached the trees and paused. Blossom was warm, and so was she. She reined up and moved into the shade of the trees. It was cool, and she began insensibly to relax. There was no sign of anyone following her. For the first time she began to think she had been foolish to ride so far ahead alone. An uneasy prickling rose at the nape of her neck, as though someone were watching her. She looked quickly into the trees. She saw no one.

At first.

Then she caught sight of him. Mr. Quinn, leaning against a tree trunk not a stone's throw away. She felt a cold lump slip from her throat into her stomach, and lie there like a stone.

"What are you following me for?" she asked tonelessly.

Mr. Quinn laughed, his little brown eyes swallowed up in folds of flesh. "How else can I get to you? Surrounded by your fancy friends all the time!"

"Then it wasn't an accident at the Tower."

"Now, now. You don't really believe that was a chance meeting! I just thought, now the girl's probably been pining like a lost chick to see old Quinn again, to say thank you for all his trouble, you might say, in getting her out of jail. Yes, sir, I thought that. So I made up my mind to put myself in your way. Give you the opportunity."

He beamed upon her, inviting admiration of his cleverness. So might a fox survey his intended dinner in a chicken house! she thought. She heard a horse neigh nearby. Mr. Quinn's, hitched to a ramshackle buggy. She wondered how long he had waited here, on the off chance that he could see her alone. She had, in her own thoughtlessness, fallen into his trap.

She sighed. She was not resigned, but instead, she was wary. Very wary. "What do you want of me?" she demanded, trying to present a poised exterior.

"Not very much," he said, with great good humor. "Now would I want to drive you to the wall?"

She said curtly, "You must know—you seem to know everything—that I have no money."

114

"No, no. We don't want a penny. Just a little favor, that's about it. Now you wouldn't deny that I did you a favor?"

She sat her mount stonily. "Go on. What is this little favor you want?"

"Nothing to cause you any trouble at all. Just a book."

Astounded, she could not believe she heard rightly. "A *book!*"

"Just so. A book about so big—" He gestured with his hands. "I want it."

"Where is this book?" she asked. "Someplace you can't steal it from?"

"Hoity-toity, miss. Enough of this. The book is in Josiah Moffett's house. We saw it taken in."

"You've been spying on me!"

He nodded. "Every move," he said complacently. "You don't like the idea, hey? Then the sooner you get the book for me, the sooner we'll be gone."

"Until the next time."

He didn't answer.

"What if I don't?"

The geniality was wiped from his face as though with a wet sponge. Surprising to note, she thought in passing, how the same set of features could take on a look of sinister threat in an instant. "Now you know the answer to that. And you will wish it was only going back to prison."

His words were spoken evenly, but there was the chill of menace beneath them. What nameless things would he do? She did not want to know. Nonetheless, she could not agree to his demands. So it was only a book. This time. She had no illusions about this demand being the last. And a book? A ridiculous thing even to want—he could buy a book. No doubt, she thought shrewdly, this was only a preliminary, a test, so to speak, of her malleability.

"I won't do it."

He did not seem dismayed in the least, and somehow that was even more frightening. "Think about it."

He stood away from the tree in an attitude of listening. She glanced down the path the way she had come. A little knot of horsemen—too far away for her to be sure of their identity. But she could pretend.

"Here come my friends," she announced. "You'd better be off."

"We're not finished," he warned her hurriedly. "I'll see you again. The book is the one old Barham brought in yesterday. I know you're clever enough to find out where it's kept."

115

"But—"

"I'll find you. You'd better reconsider your answer."

Something he had said earlier caught at the sleeve of her memory now. "Who is *we?*" she asked.

It was clearly the wrong question. His face darkened, and automatically she reined the mare back a step. At that moment, she was mortally afraid of Mr. Quinn.

"Miss Moffett!" came a cry from the approaching riders. Sir Charles wore a look of relief at seeing her, and in moments she was again surrounded by what Mr. Quinn had called her fancy friends.

Friends? she thought as they all rode on together toward a small ornamental Greek structure at the far end of the park. *And not one of them can help me.*

Or—thinking of Edward—*would even want to help me.*

Involuntarily, she glanced back over her shoulder at that fateful grove of elms. Nothing stirred, at least nothing visible from this distance. And she might have dreamed the entire incident.

Except for the spreading chill of fear inside her.

XIII

The encounter with Mr. Quinn had shaken Gina badly. She had been far too comfortable in her new life, she realized with a sinking feeling, far too happy. Such delight must be paid for in the ordinary swing of the pendulum, but she wished that it had not swung back so fast.

Her thoughts were not quite coherent, as she rode home from the park, Sir Charles at her side, and Fingle following dutifully. Sir Charles glanced at her uneasily, until she offered, "I think the sun must have given me the headache." Sir Charles was easily dismissed from her mind. He made no demands, did not seem to possess the slightest curiosity. While she could not read his thoughts, neither, she believed, could he read hers. She wondered for what duties Uncle Josiah employed him.

Dinner with Josiah moved smoothly. She turned over in her mind the task that Mr. Quinn had demanded. What book?

If she could not obtain the book, what then? Mr. Quinn's threats, even though vague, left her imagination to fill in the details. She could not refuse—but she could not agree, either.

Josiah rose from the table. "I think I must leave you now, my dear. Barham wants some answers from me by the end of the week, and I must apply myself."

"Lord Barham? He must have come while I was out," she mused, hardly knowing she spoke aloud. "He comes to visit often," she added. "Is it because—I remember you told me this—he fears a spy in his office?"

"*Probably* in his office. That is why he has brought me the code book."

She felt her color drain away. But in the soft light, pos-

117

sibly, he would not notice. "I don't understand. A code book?"

With a wry note, Josiah said, "I see I have said too much. But believe me, my dear, this is the most vital book of the century. England's security depends on it."

"On one *book*?"

"The new flag code book for the fleet. And if you will excuse me, I think I will say no more."

She smiled sunnily. "I'm glad you won't. I don't want to know your secrets. I hope the book is well hidden."

"Trust me."

He moved slowly to the door. Turning, he added, "I am glad to know that Edward Peregrine made one of your party today. He is as dear to me as my own son."

She went upstairs early, seeking the safe haven of her own room. She was not as sure about Edward, she thought as she climbed the stairs, as her uncle was. Josiah had a great talent for seeing the best in people. But she must not begrudge him that—she, too, was the beneficiary of that entirely admirable trait.

For the first time, she did not enter her room with a lively sense of gratitude. The pale green furnishings, the latest thing when the room was furnished for Sarah Moffett in the new color developed by Josiah Wedgwood, were always soothing to her.

The heavy draperies at the two windows, the carpet made to order on the broad looms of Axminster in Devon, the exceedingly comfortable small chairs with green cushions—all spoke of unerring taste. Sarah Moffett's, or Uncle Josiah's. The colors set off Gina's coloring as though made for her.

She sank into one of the chairs, and rested her head on her hands. She had hoped payment for all this might have been deferred. But the time had come far too soon. Now she must set her mind on what to do about Mr. Quinn.

Three months ago she had been a hopeless prisoner, ripe to be carried off by typhus fever, even in the new buildings at Newgate, rebuilt after the fires set in the Gordon Riots of 1780. Her release had been surprising, and unorthodox.

Mr. Quinn had chosen her partly for her coloring, her resemblance, real or fancied, to a long-dead woman. But more than that, he had chosen her because he believed she had no scruples—once a thief, always a thief.

There was no question in Mr. Quinn's mind but that she

would readily accede to his demands—a brooch or a book, what was the difference?

The difference was this—she was innocent. She did have scruples. Thievery was not part of her. And while she did not wish to say that given sufficiently dire circumstances, she would not have filched something that was not hers, she did know that the idea repelled her.

Perhaps as much a part of her as her long bones that gave her such elegance in walking, as much as her glossy chestnut hair and her fine facial bones, was the innate instinct against Mr. Quinn's request.

Request!

A fine word for his threat, his menacing tone. If she did not produce the book—and just now she had almost no idea where to start looking for it—she would fall into dreadful peril. A situation, so he had given her to understand, from which the horrors of prison would be conceived as a welcome release.

She was convinced she could not accede to the onerous payment demanded. But, equally, she became persuaded that she could not refuse. If she were taken away, kidnapped, or removed by the bailiffs, Josiah would quite likely have another attack, and this time it might well prove fatal.

Only a few days ago, he had nearly succumbed under the conviction that she had been seriously hurt. How much more serious, then, if she were in fact wrested away where his love and concern could not reach her?

How could she, in the last analysis, weigh a book in the balance with Uncle Josiah's life? She could not.

She began to visualize the book—Mr. Quinn's gestured measurements indicated quite a large object—and she had got as far in her imaginings as to put her hands on the book on Josiah's desk, when she thought she felt someone watching her. Turning—still in her mind's eye—she imagined Josiah's eyes full upon her, and in their depths, the ultimate disillusionment.

No!

She could balance Uncle Josiah's life against the book—but, remembering Josiah's words that England's security was involved, she must add her love of her country into the scales.

The result was absurd. Instead of outwitting Josiah, she thought, shaking herself into some kind of common sense, she must study how to outwit the despicable Mr. Quinn.

He had said *we,* and he had been angry when she ques-

119

tioned him. That was a starting point. Mr. Quinn did not work alone.

She pursued this new thread like a kitten intent on demolishing a ball of yarn. *We*—certainly there had to be more than one person involved in the ambitious scheme.

Someone who sent Mr. Quinn to the courtroom to watch for a woman of a certain description; she remembered his words at the time of her apparently miraculous jail deliverance. "They," he then said, "had been right."

So—a certain-appearing young woman, looked for and found. There was the curious insistence, that first night, that she must not fail. The inference that unpleasant things waited for both of them if she failed.

And even this morning, he had said, "We." It was only elementary that he would not be able to watch this house, or follow her, alone. There must be others loitering in the shadows. But they—she dismissed them wisely—were only tools.

Tools, just as she herself was expected to be.

Someone else manipulated the strings that controlled Mr. Quinn. Someone held strings that he thought were attached to her, Gina Buxton, convicted thief.

Chosen by design, by a chance look of the eyes, the slant of the cheekbones. Coming out of nowhere, rejoicing in the chance to find security, to gain respectablility, a place in the world—and determined to do everything she had to do to keep what she had so surprisingly won. Even if England's security was at stake.

This was the picture she guessed *them* to have of her.

She rose and walked around the room. She drew aside the drapery at one window and glanced out into the night. Twilight still lingered, softly veiling London with the deep blue of a spring evening. Lights sprang out here and there, touching the blue with spangles of gold, and she ached with the beauty of it.

If someone lurked below in the street, he would take pains not to be seen, especially by her.

They believed they could use her because she was a thief. And suddenly, all of a piece, she was angry. Not the hot anger of the moment, the traditional ally of red hair—not this time.

A cold anger, pervasive, saturating every fiber. How dared they think she would steal, would deceive her uncle, even betray her country? Out of fear? Nonsense!

120

They would be surprised, she thought with grim amusement, and set herself to scheming.

What would Mr. Quinn do with the book? There was something to begin with. He himself could not do anything with it. He was merely to force her to obtain it, and then turn it over to the dim figure moving in the shadows behind him.

The unknown figure in the obscurity behind Mr. Quinn must have a name. She must ferret out that name, pierce the mask.

It was hopeless. She couldn't even find out her own name! But—maybe she could! And maybe both trails converged somewhere. It was not logical, but she was past logic now, moving by instinct. And instinct is the deepest truth.

The plan she had conceived yesterday, in the midst of her quarrel with Edward, added to the scheme now growing in her mind could, indeed *must*, work together to give her a way out.

A way out, if it worked. But first, she had to gather the ammunition to put her plan into motion. And as she went to bed that night, her plans were all but complete. The first thing in the morning she would deal with Agnes. . . .

It was easier than she expected.

Agnes came in with the morning tray, and Gina set her plans afoot.

"Good morning, miss!" cried Agnes cheerily.

"Is it?"

Agnes halted in her tracks. "You don't feel well?"

"Agnes, I need your help."

"Anything, miss. You know I'll do anything for you."

"I should like to borrow your clothes."

The outrageous demand left Agnes speechless with astonishment. At length she squeaked, "My clothes, miss? *My* clothes?"

Swiftly Gina outlined her plan. "I must get out of the house without anyone knowing. And if I look like you, well—never mind why. I must do it."

Agnes clearly was full of misgivings about the madcap scheme. But the habit of obedience was strong in her, and she even allowed Gina to swear her to secrecy.

"I promise not to tell a soul," Agnes vowed, hand upraised. "It's a foolish idea, and no mistake. What your uncle will say I don't know."

"He won't find out, Agnes. Not if you don't tell anyone.

Now, Agnes, I'll give you—" She fished in her small purse for coins.

Agnes was stubborn. "No telling how it will all come out," she muttered. "I suppose you must have your way, but take something for it, I will not. I hope I know my duty better than that."

The implication was clear. No matter how the *quality* interpreted their duty, Agnes would be drawn into Gina's plot only as far as was entirely necessary, and not a step farther.

"Oh, Agnes, I knew you would help me!"

Once committed, Agnes surprisingly cast her misgivings to the wind, and entered into the spirit of the enterprise as though a lurking dramatic flair had surfaced at last. Hurrying out with the breakfast tray, after Gina had tucked away a hearty breakfast (now that her scheme was in motion she was filled with optimism, and fortified herself against who knew what contingency), Agnes soon returned with an armload of clothing and a scurrying air of conspiracy billowing like a cloak around her.

Arrayed in what she thought must be Agnes's chapel-going clothes, Gina felt a momentary qualm as she surveyed herself in the pier glass. She wore an ankle-length, high-waisted gown of deep blue ribbed material, over a white chemise. White gauzy sleeves came to her wrists. She slipped black cloth slippers on her feet, and tied a gauzy high-crowned cap over her auburn curls.

The stiff fabric of her dress did not lend itself to full drapery, as finer batiste or lawn would do, but it looked well enough on Gina, even hastily pinned in at the waist and a trifle short in the hem. For a long moment, Gina thought she could see herself four months ago. She felt curiously two people at this moment—the old Gina and the new.

And the errand she was setting out on now might destroy them both. She hesitated.

"Here's the shawl I wear, miss," said Agnes, her work reddened hands lingering over the fabric. Clearly it was her treasure, and Gina was touched.

"I'll take good care of it," she promised. "Now, help me slip out of the house."

With Agnes peering suspiciously ahead and to all sides, Gina thought ruefully that if anyone did see them they could offer no possible excuse for such an escapade. Agnes bore strong resemblance to pictures of Guy Fawkes tiptoeing through the cellars of Parliament two hundred years before.

At length, Gina gained the mews behind the house, and

slipped around the corner into the street. She clutched her small coin purse in her hand; she hoped the total would be enough to hire the hackney she knew she would require.

Once away from the environs of Kennett Square, she set off briskly, looking over her shoulder for signs of pursuit. She saw no one she knew, and at length convinced herself that she was not followed.

This was a convenient circumstance for Fingle, following, dodging behind other pedestrians in an effort to keep himself unnoticed.

Agnes had indeed kept her promise not to tell anyone what her mistress had in mind. But she saw nothing in her vow that prevented her from buttonholing Fingle in the kitchen and saying, out of the corner of her mouth, "Better follow her."

Fingle could get nothing more out of her, but the expression on Agnes's face, accompanying the dramatic grimace with which she emphasized her words, sent him out of the house on his mistress's heels.

He followed her down Welbeck Street, into Vere, and across Oxford Street, where he nearly lost her. Only just in time did he emerge from a brouhaha of pedestrians watching a lively dog fight to see Gina climbing into a hackney cab.

Fortunately, he thought, he had sufficient blunt on his person to hire a cab of his own, and he set off behind Gina into the purlieus of old London.

Gina had never ridden in a hackney before. Until three months ago, she had had neither the means nor the reason to do so, and since that time, Josiah Moffett had sufficient equipage in his stables to take her wherever she wished to go.

How much more comfortable her own carriage would have been, she thought, and immediately dismissed the idea from her mind. Her own plans needed her fullest attention, and she could not afford any distractions.

She was on her way to St. Clothilde's. She believed that if she knew certainly who she was—or was not—she could deal better with Mr. Quinn. She did not know how she would go on, but she felt that if she had one single thing nailed down, she would have a firm place upon which to build the scheme that would—that *must*—bring Mr. Quinn down in ruins.

The cab was now traversing streets that seemed familiar. Off the Clerkenwell Road—Woodbridge, Skinner Street— She was getting close to the orphanage, the streets she had crossed on her way to church, the long line of orphans marching along the pavement under Matron's critical eye. All of it came back with a rush.

On impulse she leaned forward and called to the driver, "Please stop here."

He surveyed her from his perch. "Not where you said, miss." He looked sour enough, but after she had stepped down to the pavement, and given him his fare and added a tip, he touched his whip to his cap and hesitated. "Sure you want to stop here? Neighborhood doesn't look too good for the likes of you."

"Oh, but I am very familiar with my way," she answered. "Thank you very much."

He moved smartly on then, and left her to ponder his words. "The likes of you." Didn't she look like a lady's maid? Apparently not so much as she had hoped.

She stepped out upon the street. Here was no raised curb to divide the carriageway from the walkway, as was seen on the better streets. Here were simply cobbles slanted down toward a running ditch in the center of the narrow street.

She looked around her as she walked briskly toward St Clothilde's, enjoying, because she had escaped, the old houses, the harsh soot-stained bricks of the buildings. Even from here she could hear the cries of the gray-uniformed children playing in the yard of the orphanage.

She stopped on the corner to watch, catching her breath with excitement. She could recognize a few of the children. Maggie, surely, with her limp. Young Jemmy; his small brother Ben. No boys older than ten, she knew, since at that age they were put out as apprentices. Those who were smallest, the unluckiest of all, went for chimney sweeps.

She would have spoken to the children, called them by name, but suddenly shy, she hesitated too long. One of the older girls ran out of the building and gathered them all in like sooty chickens in their gray garb.

She nearly lost heart then. She could not make herself cross the street, and pass through the archway that read *Saint Clothilde* and up the steps. Almost she turned, even after she had reached the front door and raised the knocker, to flee back to her comfortable house and let Uncle Josiah tell her again that it didn't matter who she was.

But it did.

The maid Molly held the door open a crack. "You want something?"

"Molly!" said Gina with pleasure. "How are you?"

The maid peered in disbelief, then, recognizing her, opened the door wider, grudgingly.

"Molly?" Gina said, surprised at her cool reception. "You remember me—Gina?"

"Jailbird," said Molly succinctly. "Best come in so as not to stand outside in the street, so all can see what St. Clothilde's puts out. Come in, I say."

Stunned, Gina moved forward into the entryway, smelling of old paint and raw yellow soap. Molly vanished down a narrow hall.

Gina had not thought that Mrs. Potter's displeasure would extend so far as to rebound on St. Clothilde's. Nor that her own character would be so easily forgotten and misunderstood, so that even Molly would believe Mrs. Potter rather than Gina. She stood in the hall and wished with all her heart that she had not come.

She could go back. She could leave without even seeing Matron. She dreaded the sermon that the sturdy and morally rigid woman would feel required to give.

Gina had taken three steps toward the door, when Molly came out of the hallway and said surlily, "Matron will see you."

Well, Gina thought at last, *I may not be able to get anything out of Matron, but at least I can tell her how mistaken Mrs. Potter was.* The prospect giving her some satisfaction, she swept through the door to face Matron.

The woman behind the desk, quickly judging the young woman who had just entered, thought it advisable to rise to her feet to greet her.

"Miss Buxton?" said Matron doubtfully.

Gina looked into the face of a complete stranger. "What—what happened to Matron?" she stammered.

"Matron? You mean Nora Carmichael, of course. She died. Suddenly, of a stroke. Never said a word to anyone after they found her."

So even Matron's memory was lost to her. Gina put her fingers to her suddenly trembling lips. It was no use. She was too late!

XIV

The stranger's face swam before her. Gina clutched at the edge of the desk.

Suddenly she was sitting, and a cup of tea appeared magically before her. "I'm sorry," she said at last. "It was just that I had no idea that Matron was dead."

"Of course not. But we were all in such a taking," explained the woman. "My name, by the by, is Phoebe Nicholas. And yours, I gather, is Gina Buxton?"

"Not my real name of course," said Gina. "At least the Buxton part. Matron told me she had named me for a street." Even now the resentment she had always felt echoed in her words.

She had rehearsed her request—for Matron Carmichael. No use now, but she owed this woman some explanation. "And that is the trouble, of course. I have a need—such a desperate need!—to find out my real name."

Slowly the woman shook her head. "Didn't Matron ever tell you? Of course she didn't, or you wouldn't be here now. But perhaps she thought it best—"

Gina burst in, "She always put me off. She would say things like, 'If they wanted to find you, they could.'"

"And that is true, you think?"

"I always thought that she meant only to keep me from hopeless dreams when I was growing up. You must know the kind—you're a lost princess, and someday the king will find you."

Gina had never before confided such long-ago torments to anyone. But Mrs. Nicholas was uncommonly easy to talk to.

"It is sad, you know," mused Gina, "to believe that no one wants you. That you mean no more to them than a parcel that they set down and forgot. I thought that now I am grown, she might— But of course, all she knew must have been in her memory. And you say she left no word?"

"None at all. One of the maids came in and found her slumped over this desk. This very desk," Mrs. Nicholas repeated, "and there was nothing that could be done for her. She was gone in an hour, and never spoke again. I'm sorry. But what would you do if you did know?"

Gina gathered Agnes's shawl around her and held it with one hand. "That really doesn't matter now, does it? I must thank you for the tea."

"It might matter," said Phoebe Nicholas slowly.

Puzzled, Gina regarded the woman carefully. She liked what she saw, a sensible kindly woman with a round face and plainly dressed hair, showing threads of gray. "I don't know," she said slowly, in answer to Mrs. Nicholas's question, "but I had counted so much on Matron's memory—" Her voice trailed away. Then, firming her trembling lips, she said, "Believe me, I do not wish to harm anyone. Rather, it is harm that I am trying to avert. It is too complicated a story, I think, to trouble you with."

Surprisingly, the woman said, "What about jail? You are free obviously. Did you steal the brooch?"

That dreadful story was going to follow her everywhere she went! Would it never be forgotten? Something of her dismay must have shown in her expression, for the woman explained, "I was not much impressed by Mrs. Potter. She came to us—I think I should tell you this—saying dreadful things about the quality of the girls we send out of St. Clothilde's, but," she added with a twinkle that changed her entire aspect, "she asked for another one to take your place!"

"How like her!" Gina cried. After a moment, she said, "I assure you, I bear no animus against Mrs. Potter. My need has nothing to do with her."

The woman regarded her for a few moments, weighing Gina in her own balance. At length, she made her decision. Leaning forward across the desk, she confided, "Things were in a fine mess when Mrs. Carmichael died. The trustees brought me in at once—and I tell you when I came I almost turned and ran. The maids had been allowed to slack off something fierce, and the first thing I had done was a thorough scrubbing. Yellow soap and vinegar, and lots of elbow grease." She smiled reminiscently. "You noticed Molly at the door? Quite sullen. I don't know whether I can let her stay or not. She was most unhappy with her mop and pail. But this is nothing to you."

Gina's fingers tightened until she could feel nails biting into palms. She felt like a blank sheet of paper, upon which the new matron would shortly inscribe—what?

"Now I must confess," said Mrs. Nicholas, "that I was glad to hear your name when Molly announced you. I hadn't known what to do. Mrs. Potter said you were in jail, and likely to be for some time. And it didn't seem enough to do any good."

"I don't understand," said Gina.

"Of course you don't," Matron said bracingly. "I haven't told you yet. But Mrs. Carmichael never threw anything away. Nothing that ever came into this building went out again. Except the children." She took a deep breath. "I'm getting to it now," she said apologetically, in response to an impatient gesture from Gina. "We had a rare old house cleaning, I can tell you. In the drawers, in the cupboards, everywhere." She indicated with a large gesture the entire nearby area of London.

Something in the woman's manner, even though so exasperatingly long in coming to the point, gave Gina the dawn of a new encouragement. Perhaps there *was* something.

"I found something. It has your name on it—Gina Buxton that is. I don't know what good it's going to be to you, but surely it is yours and not St. Clothilde's."

She got up and crossed to a large cupboard and rummaged around inside. Gina could hardly breathe. Would there be anything—*anything* to show Gina was in fact Georgina Moffett?

Matron laid a small wash-leather pouch on the desk between them. "You will see your name here, on this identification tag. Perhaps you'd like to look at it alone."

Tactfully, she left the room. Gina stared at the small soft leather pouch. It was soiled, apparently the victim of much handling by dirty hands. If indeed the pouch had belonged to Georgina Moffett, what would be in it? Would it have once contained jewels, since rifled? If the story she had heard were true—that Sarah and John Moffett had been killed by the murderous throng rushing to tear down the walls of the hated Bastille—what would have become of the valuables left their rooms in Paris?

René Valois would know—but he had left London, she believed.

Gina tried to envision the events of the infancy she had

128

erased from recollection. If she were Georgina Moffett, she should be able to visualize, from her memory, the marching feet of the mob, perhaps a maid snatching up the small Georgina and what valuables she could find and, with René Valois, disappearing into the turmoil of a Paris in the grip of powerful and long-deferred rage.

Out of the city. Through the gates, before they were closed to all escaping persons, and then—

Gina took a deep breath. It was no use. She could not remember. Surely a child of three should remember something of her early years?

It was small consolation to think that she remembered nothing else of those first three years either—no childhood on the streets of London, for example. No memory of rooms, of houses, of animals, or any person. Only the dream of someone rocking her, singing to her. In French.

Once she knew what she could know, what would she do? She was not sure. For her the world had begun on the day she came to St. Clothilde's, and now, fancifully, she felt her world would end—or at least change drastically—when she opened the small pouch. . . .

There was little enough in it. She spread out the three items on Matron's scarred desktop, and examined them. They were disappointing in the extreme.

A large coin—French, from the writing barely decipherable around the edge. A brooch—how a brooch recurred in her life!—this one of exquisite design. A cameo, so skillfully carved that the little deer on it looked ready to leap out into the air.

Tears stung the back of her eyes. The little deer of her dream! A unicorn, its one straight horn delicately carved in a spiral design in the white stone. Such a beautiful thing!

The pin was hers. But who had worn it? Her mother? Whoever had worn it had sung to her in French—*Mon amie Jeannetot*. And Sarah Moffett was totally English.

The name *Jeannetot* leaped up at her from the third item the pouch had held. A slip of paper, in handwriting that she knew was Mrs. Carmichael's. Notes, no doubt, about the small girl's arrival set down quickly and put away, to be eventually discovered in Mrs. Nicholas's wholesale housecleaning.

Jeannetot, she read, *the only name the girl could speak. Repeated questioning produced no further name. A French name, completely unsuitable for an English child. I have called her Gina Buxton.*

So she was not even *Gina!* Instead of finding out her identity, the one thing she thought was hers—her own first name—was shorn away by a matron devoid of imagination and sympathy. A small child, bereft of parents and all else familiar, was not even allowed her own name. No wonder Gina had put away all trace of her early years.

So she was not Georgina Moffett. Not even Gina. She would one day realize that this was not a great tragedy. But the trouble was, she was French. There seemed to be no doubt about it.

Mr. Quinn had succeeded better than he knew. To put a French girl into the household of the head of the intelligence service—no matter what happened, whether she had known her nationality or not, it would be believed that she was a spy for Napoleon, and that Josiah, through illness or incompetence, had been grossly duped.

She did not know what she did next. She did not remember gathering up the telltale evidence and tying it into the pouch again. She did not remember what she said to Mrs. Nicholas, as she took her leave.

She was conscious, dimly, of walking through streets she did not know. Once a cart nearly scraped her, and again, a horse plunged nearby and someone screamed.

She must leave Josiah. What could she do? *I could be a crossing sweep,* she thought, *living on tips from gentry using the walk. Surely Mr. Quinn could not hurt Uncle Josiah then.* But she needed time. . . .

She was hardly aware when someone came up to her and spoke in a soothing voice. "Come now, Miss Georgina, I've got a nice cab here, and you just get into it and we'll be home in two shakes all right and tight!"

"Fingle?" she said, as though she hardly knew him.

"A rare taking she was in," was Fingle's comment later, when he regaled Agnes, Mrs. Beddoes, and Meg, the new maid, with his experiences of the afternoon. "Came out of that ugly orphanage—and a hard, cruel place it looked too—and it was like she was struck all of a heap. Whatever they said in there sure gave her a leveler!"

Fingle, now, with rare tact helped his mistress down from the cab at the far corner of the street leading into Kennett Square. He had caught a glimpse of Lord Barham's carriage standing before the Moffetts' front door, and he guessed that Miss Georgina might be hard put to explain what she was doing coming home in a hackney cab and wearing her maid's Sunday clothes.

130

"In you go," he said, continuing a stream of heartening words. "Right through this gate, and along here—"

He breathed a huge sigh of relief when he saw Agnes watching anxiously for them from the back door. In moments Agnes and Mrs. Beddoes had his charge by the arms, propelling her up the back stairs.

In a trice her clothes—that is, Agnes's clothes—were removed, and she was bundled into a warm robe. Nonetheless, she began to shiver and her teeth chattered so she could not speak. Mrs. Beddoes nodded ominously to Agnes, and together they slipped out of the room, leaving Gina to whatever thoughts flitted through her troubled mind.

She was half out of her mind with devastating disappointment and with the appalling discovery that she was French—an enemy in the camp of the sensitive heart of England's intelligence service during wartime. And Mr. Quinn lurking somewhere outside either to force her to steal the code book, or to take her away to unnamed tortures, and smear the name of her benefactor, the only man who had been kind to her within her memory.

How she had been used!

She must see Josiah. *At once,* she thought in confusion. *I must tell him all this. There is not a moment to lose!*

She rose from the chair and, stumbling over the hem of her robe, hitched it up with both hands. She emerged from her room into the hall that ran along the head of the stairs. She reached the balustrade.

She stopped to rearrange the folds of her skirt so that she could negotiate the stairs safely, and it was well that she did so. There were voices directly below her.

Uncertain of what she should do, she paused to listen. Uncle Josiah's voice, and Lord Barham's.

Josiah said, "There is only one thing to do. We must set a trap for the traitor. It is a vital time, just now, and Nelson must be given every advantage."

Barham agreed, heavily. "If Bony's fleet is not destroyed, we might as well all start learning French. Nelson is all that stands between England and her enemy. One man."

Josiah's voice came slowly. "And one man can turn England into a French colony. It's a terrible thing, treason. I can't understand why anyone would turn to the enemy."

"Money," suggested the immensely wealthy First Lord. "Other reasons, perhaps. It's not every man who can't be bought, Moffett."

"It's even worse," commented Josiah, "when the traitor is

131

someone close to you. Someone we have trusted. Ah, well, we will find out who, soon enough. Sufficient unto the day is the evil thereof. Is that not true?"

"Always has been," muttered Barham gruffly.

Even in her present state, her wits wandering in a sort of limbo, she could tell that both men were deeply troubled, trying to deal with an appalling fact in a common-sense manner.

A hand tugged at her sleeve. It was Mrs. Beddoes, fearfully glancing down the stairs, and urgently pulling Gina back toward her room.

Gina could not think. All she could do was to stumble along with Mrs. Beddoes to her room. She did not object even when Mrs. Beddoes laid back the coverlet on the immense bed and said in a tone that brooked no denial, "Get into bed, Miss Georgina. I've brought you some milk to drink, and I will stay with you while you drink it. No more of this wandering about the halls."

"I wasn't wandering," Gine protested feebly. "I must see my uncle, at once."

"Tomorrow," said Mrs. Beddoes inexorably. "Now drink this down."

The pillows against her back were comforting and insensibly she began to relax. *It must be someone we trusted*—and surely her uncle had trusted her, even more than she could have dreamed of.

He must know she was the traitor, manipulated by Mr. Quinn.

Something in the milk, she thought suddenly. Mrs. Beddoes had put something in her drink! *My thoughts are muddled*, she thought in panic, *and I'm floating away from them.*

But her last conscious thought was surprising. *How could I be the traitor? I haven't taken the code book yet!*

XV

It was the day after Gina's visit to the orphanage and, while the drug that had made her sleep left her with a conviction that her brains had been turned to wool, she felt surprisingly restored in body.

With the new day, she found no more resolution than she had the night before. Josiah was shut away in his study and was not to be disturbed. Mechanically, she occupied herself with the plans she had already made, and today, to her mild surprise, she was visiting the Royal Academy.

The Academy was no more than half a century old, having been established when Uncle Josiah was a small boy living at Seahaven on the Kentish coast. Sir Joshua Reynolds, a formidable character and painter to the Royal Family, used his considerable influence to bring together certain art treasures so that all of England might feel a pride of ownership in their own accomplishments.

The establishment itself was small and crabbed, with paintings piled on top of each other so that it gave one the sense of being beaten about the head by works in oil that were larger than life-size.

She was too muddled—thanks to Mrs. Beddoes and her warm milk!—to cope with the questions that milled in her mind. She set them aside as well as she could.

Just now she was finding it equally difficult to deal with the excessively lifelike horses of an artist called Stubbs, especially in such close quarters as the small room provided.

She was, of course, not alone. Tom was not of the group, and she remembered his vague duties on his estates. But Edward was there—didn't he have any work to do?—and of course where Edward was, Hester was, also. Lady Taunton seemed to be always of their party these days, and Gina found her, though a trifle light-headed, still possessed of a vast good nature, and a lively, if sometimes excessive, sense of fun.

And serious Mary Bray, who just now was looking pensively at a delightful portrait of children at play.

Lady Granville was seated near the door, not even professing an interest in art. Hester, with great solicitude and in a carrying voice, cried, "How thin you look, Georgina! Are you quite well?"

"Fine, thank you," said Gina, unconsciously stiffening against Hester's spite. "I find all this so interesting, don't you?"

Since she was standing before the famous canvas of Satan calling out his cohorts from the fiery lake, her comment was ill-advised. She forced herself to look with intentness at the painting. Satan was at least twelve feet high, she estimated, awed at the pictorial dimensions of evil.

Satan was here depicted as about to take over the world. Surely she could agree; her recent experience had shown her that. In her muzzy thoughts, she saw that with great acumen Thomas Lawrence had cleverly shown Satan with the face of Mr. Quinn. How had he known?

Well, she knew she was too muddled to see straight. But was she wrong, too, in remembering that she had waked up with a new plan? The details were still obscure but a thread of purpose began to emerge—a purpose changed drastically since the revelation at St. Clothilde's.

Surprisingly, Satan's features no longer looked like Mr. Quinn's. But the intimidating face of the man glimpsed for a moment in a doorway of the room truly did.

This time, she was right. He had told her he would find her. She glanced swiftly around. All her companions seemed to be occupied with the exhibition. In addition, two men had come in from the outside, and she thought instantly that they must be allies of Mr. Quinn, set to prevent her escape. They glanced at her with interest, and if she had been told the truth, that they simply admired the beautiful girl with the glorious hair and the pale gray gown, she would not have believed them. She turned to follow where Mr. Quinn led.

Mr. Quinn was waiting for her at the end of a short corridor. He preceded her into a small room, apparently a workroom of some sort with frames, empty and dismantled, stacked against the wall, and a hammer or two and loose nails strewn around the floor. He closed the door.

"Where is it?" Mr. Quinn's sharp demand came at once.

"The book? I don't have it. I couldn't get it."

Mr. Quinn took a turn around the small room. "You don't appear to have lost your senses. Or are you so tired of living in the lap of luxury that you want to die of it?"

"D-die?"

"The book, girl. Without it, you're good as dead."

She wondered whether he knew what kind of book it was. "Why is this book so valuable? Why not just go out and buy one at the bookseller's?"

He stared at her in amazement. "Now that is a truly silly remark. You can't believe anything so idiotic. That particular book is the one we've got to have. And that is the one that you must obtain for me. You might even say you should stake your life on it, for that is the plain truth."

"I can't do it."

He was totally exasperated. "Don't stand there bleating that you can't do it. You've got to do it!" He took her arm in savage fingers. Advancing his face close to hers, he said, "Understand. You get this book, and get it today!"

"Let me go," she said with icy hauteur, and he reluctantly gave up his hold on her. "There, that's better. There are a couple of things I want to ask. What happens if I get caught?"

"You won't get caught!" he said heartily.

"Suppose I do. It's too dangerous. What would happen to me if they found out I was the thief?"

"Well," he admitted. "It wouldn't be as simple as last time you were caught. Newgate wouldn't be in it." Bracingly, he added, "You don't need to worry. We'd take care of you."

Gina felt more in command of the situation than before. "How?" she persisted.

"Your job is not to get caught," he blustered.

"I don't think you have sufficiently considered the risks," she said. She had no idea where she had learned to act with such steely determination, but somewhere it had been waiting for just this moment. "No, I do not think I wish to rely entirely upon you, Mr. Quinn. I should like money in my own hand," she added reflectively, "to assure my own escape."

"Money!" he exploded. "Haven't you lived in wealth and luxury all this time?"

"But that is not money from your pocket, Mr. Quinn," she pointed out. "You have been at no expense on my behalf except for a simple maid's skirt and blouse and a pair of ill-fitting shoes."

No matter, she thought guiltily, that she had been enormously grateful for them, and for her deliverance. Her overnight scheme unfolded now in great simplicity. "I must be paid, and handsomely, for this."

After a moment, he said, "How much?"

At hazard, she said, "Ten thousand pounds."

He was visibly shaken. "Impossible."

"That's my price," she interrupted.

"Can't be done."

"Very well, then." She favored him with a wintry smile, and prepared to leave.

"When will you deliver the book?"

She looked at him in exaggerated surprise. "I thought you understood. My final word. No money, no book."

Mr. Quinn's face darkened. Against his will, he believed her, and his fury outstripped his control. With mounting fear she watched his hands claw into fists. She took a step backward toward the door. Could she escape from the room before he reached her? The door was closed, and it would take too long—

"I don't have the authority to give you the money," he said sullenly.

"Then," she said with creditable poise, "take me to someone who does."

She held her breath. This was the point she had been aiming for, the gold in the center of the target. If she could somehow penetrate the curtain behind which moved the man who wanted the book, the man who had sent Mr. Quinn to the courts to find someone of a certain description—and find out who he was—then she could in some small way make up to Josiah for his trust in her. *This*, she thought morbidly, *will be just before I leave him forever.*

"I must get back to my friends," she announced, and turned to the door as though his answer were immaterial to the important things of her life, like looking at the awe-inspiring Satan on the wall outside.

From somewhere she heard footsteps. Mr. Quinn heard them too, for he said abruptly, "I'll give you my answer at the masquerade tonight. You'll be going. I'll see that you meet—someone—there."

Before she could say a word, he had slipped through a door in the inner wall of the tiny room, an exit she had not noticed before.

The footsteps in the corridor were nearer now, and she put her hand on the latch. One thing bothered her; she had cer-

136

ainly made progress toward making her point, but Mr. Quinn had revealed that he knew too much about her affairs. Knew, in fact, about the masquerade, a strictly private party. How had he become so well-informed? Uneasy, yet she must think about it later, for just now, she must join the others.

She opened the door to find Edward standing in the hall, apparently wondering which door to open. "Are you all right?" he demanded. There was a quick concern in his voice that led her to reassure him.

"I merely felt faint for a moment," she lied. "All the overpowering paintings out there seemed stifling." Shyly, she added, "I didn't think anyone would notice my absence."

"You fail to give your friends sufficient credit," he said. "But do you feel the thing now?"

He looked over her shoulder into the room behind her. "You found fresh air there?" he said with doubt. "Let me see that you are taken home."

"I am really fine," she said. There was a queer anxiety in his eyes that she could not identify, but it disturbed her.

Had he seen Mr. Quinn or not? She could not be sure. Certainly Edward was rightly dubious about the restorative effectiveness of a lumber room tightly closed against the outside air, and she could not afford to further his suspicions. If she told Edward about Mr. Quinn, no doubt he would take steps to have the building searched. If Quinn were captured, then she would never find out who was behind him. Mr. Quinn would simply be replaced by someone else, and that one she might not recognize. No, it was better this way.

The party, when they emerged into the exhibition rooms, seemed to have dispersed. Caroline Taunton was still there, with her brother Sylvester, and Mary Bray. But Hester was nowhere in sight, nor her aunt, Lady Granville.

Not until later, after Edward had left them and Gina was persuaded to stop at Lady Taunton's for a glass of tea—such dry work, looking at all those dusty paintings, Caroline had cried gaily—did she learn what had happened in the gallery while she was with Mr. Quinn.

"They had a terrible quarrel," cried Caroline gleefully. "Edward and Hester, I mean." Disregarding Mary Bray's disapproving glance, she went on, "All over you!"

Gina looked blankly at her. "Over me?" She turned to Mary. "Tell me Caroline is only funning!"

Mary's sensible face told her that Caroline Taunton told only the truth. But Mary brought the conversation down to earth. "Only that he thought you were not well, and ought not to overset yourself."

"And Hester said—" Too late Caroline remembered the exact words that Hester had used, and she clapped her finger over her rosebud mouth. Surely she did not care to repeat such vulgarities as "guttersnipe," certainly not to the object of the epithet.

"Never mind," said Gina shortly. "Mr. Peregrine's quarrels have nothing to do with me."

"But he told Hester to go to the devil," said the irrepressible Caroline, and, having said all she wanted to say wore a look of smug complacency.

Mary Bray wore a troubled frown. She dreaded scenes of any kind, and the one she had witnessed had been upsetting. Edward Peregrine was a man to be reckoned with, and Mary Bray, who had been at school with Hester Reading, had no illusions as to the depth of malice Hester was capable of. But likewise, she did not feel compelled to warn Gina. Reluctant to gossip, Mary thought it better if the subject were forgotten.

And Gina, all the rest of the day, felt a curious lightness in her spirits that she believed—or told herself she believed—came from advancing one step in her plot to ferret out Mr. Quinn's chief.

While a masquerade was a daring device for a party, yet for a small group, especially one with such respectable members, Josiah had given his approval.

"What kind of costume will you wear?" he quizzed his niece.

"Well, sir," she said, laughing, "we all thought it would be such fun to go as historical characters, but then the scheme was discarded when Lady Bray refused absolutely to countenance any masquerade more than dominoes. I had rather fancied myself in a flowing robe of some sort," she added thoughtfully, with a roguish glint as she smiled at her uncle.

"What character would you fancy?" he said, seeing her amusement and thankful for it, after the last few days when she had been so unaccountably abstracted in her manner.

"I thought perhaps Edith Swan-Neck, the queen, searching for Harold's body after the battle. That would give me excuses to peer into everyone's faces. Do you think I could carry it off, sir?"

"My dear, you could carry off anything you set your mind to," he assured her. "I am so reminded of your mother."

A melancholy look fell across her face again, Josiah saw

138

and wished he had not spoken so. He could not know that she was thinking about the French coin, the un-English name of the small Jeannetot.

And with the thought came the unwelcome presence of the code book in the house. "Uncle," she said, "is the code book safe?"

"Of course it is safe."

"You spoke of a spy in the Admiralty office. Have you found out who it was?"

"Not *was,* my child. *Is.* No, we have not discovered his identity. Yet. But we will."

"Of course you will." *But,* she thought, *perhaps I can help, even find out who he is before you do.*

"But in the meantime," he assured her, "the book is right here in this house. Safe, away from the admiralty office. And, my dear, this is not known outside this house. Except for Barham, no one knows."

No one but Mr. Quinn, and whoever had told him, and Mr. Quinn's superior, and who else? The list might go on for sometime, as far as she knew.

"I must get ready," she said, rising from the small ottoman at her uncle's feet. "I'll stop in before I go." At the door, she paused again. "Uncle, suppose someone tried to take the book by force. What then?"

"Force is met with force," he said, "always. Or almost always. Do not fear, Georgina. If that were to happen, then we would simply change the code. The French are too intelligent to believe that by taking the code book overtly there would be any gain to them."

Slowly she said, "I hadn't thought of that." She opened the door and went through it. She did not see her uncle's thoughtful, appraising glance follow her. Nor did he lose his concentrated expression for some time after she had gone.

She hurried out and into the carriage waiting for her. She had promised Josiah just now to stop in again later, when she returned from the party, and managed to say good-bye to him without confessing her deep fear that she would never see him again. How could she be sure that her encounter this evening with Mr. Quinn and his superior would come off the way she envisioned it?

Lady Bray's carriage contained Lady Bray herself, and Mary. Gina made the third, and she thought they were a frail company to set out across the river into the region called Lambeth, to Vauxhall Gardens. Footpads lurked along the streets, she knew well, and although Lady Bray was not adorned with many jewels, there was certainly some possibility of loot from the passengers in such a fine coach as this one.

But she knew, too, that the servants were armed, and for this occasion at least she was glad to see two extra footmen riding on the steps at the back of the coach.

Vauxhall itself was like a fairyland. Gina had never dreamed of anything so lovely. The gardens were beautiful in daylight, she had heard, but nothing had prepared her for the brilliant illumination, cunningly hidden in the trees so that the light shone down upon the walkways, where fashionable persons met and strolled, taking the air of an evening when the light breezes of May caressed the spirits.

She felt deliciously safe in her pink domino, with the matching pink half-mask, part of her masquerade, hiding her features, and contented herself for a bit with the spectacle of her surroundings. Lady Bray did not walk with them, feeling too lame, she said, to do more than retire to their box in the small round pavilion, built in the Chinese manner, where they were to have their supper later.

Gina was dashed to find that Edward Peregrine was one of their party. She was not quite sure how to greet him, remembering Caroline Taunton's indiscreet narrative of the quarrel between Edward and Hester. But he greeted her with the barest civility, and, since the party was quite large, she did not have to speak again to him.

Sylvester Fuscue, Sir Charles Derwent, Adelaide Gough she already knew. Others she met for the first time—all cloaked, donning the small half-masks, which were surprisingly concealing, before venturing out upon the walks.

But not Hester. Lady Bray mentioned vaguely that "Hester had the headache." Had the quarrel, then, been so devastating? Probably her absence meant only that the quarrel had not yet been made up.

Tom was not in evidence either, and she guessed Edward was making good his threat to keep his ward out of London away from her grasping, no doubt ill-bred, fingers!

And yet Edward had seemed concerned about her that afternoon at the Academy. Perhaps he had caught sight of Mr. Quinn. She could not decipher Edward's thoughts, though, and the best thing was to forget him. She had other matters on her mind this night.

Music played, as though violins had perched in the trees like birds and played their own sweet notes into the air. But
140

other circumstances she would have been ecstatic over the gay gardens.

Lady Taunton went with her down the lighted path. She was in yellow, and the two resembled colorful pastel butterflies as their dominoes floated around them.

Gina was taut as a violin string. Mr. Quinn was to find her here, and lead her to the mysterious Mr. X. But what if he failed? What if the mysterious someone had decided he would not pay the fantastic amount she had demanded?

And then—what would happen to her if he refused?

She thought she had few illusions about the dangerous game she was playing—at least in the beginning. But now, in the mysterious soft dark of a May evening, with the yellow lights of the illuminating lanterns shimmering gently through the trees, all of a piece with the romantic and seductive music, she began to think she had been extremely foolish. It was such a harmless setting. It was nearly impossible to believe that danger lurked here among so many leisured, laughing groups of people. But perhaps especially because her surroundings looked so harmless, the peril she knew she courted seemed to lay violent hands on her imagination.

She was at the mercy of Mr. Quinn. And his chief. She could only wait until one of them found her.

She stared around her, unable to conceal her edgy watchfulness. No one approached her. Perhaps Mr. Quinn was making her wait, playing with her, letting her nerves betray her. She took advantage of a small knot of people approaching them to lift her face-mask and blink away an eyelash, so she said, from her cheek.

It was merely by chance—so she hoped Caroline would think—that she stood directly under a bright overhead light as she did so. If Mr. Quinn were to find her, he must make sure of her identity first.

The approaching group, at least a dozen, converged on them, catching up Caroline and Gina into their midst and then tossing them free again.

The laughing crowd passed by, leaving the two swirling in their wake.

"I thought they would separate us for good, Caroline," said Gina at last, with a nervous laugh. She clutched the yellow sleeve of her silent companion as they went on down the walk.

Surely, she thought, Mr. Quinn had time enough to find her. He said he knew every move she made. Then surely he

141

knew where she was this moment. But perhaps he could not approach while Caroline Taunton still accompanied her.

"Caroline," she said artlessly, "don't you think we ought to turn back? Lady Bray will wonder where we have got to."

She must somehow divert Caroline, and go on alone. Her mind raced furiously to devise a scheme.

They reached a curve in the walk that seemed deserted. Curiously, there were no lights overhead at this particular area, and she felt a prickle of fear. She stopped short.

"Caroline!" she said sharply, but her companion didn't answer.

Instead, the yellow-clad arm reached out and jerked her roughly off the walk and into the shadow of the shrubbery. A man's voice grated in her ear. "Don't fight now. Someone wants to see you. Come along, this way."

So close! In just a few moments, she realized after her first fright, she would know whether her great gamble would pay off. In just a few moments—

She followed her guide through dark paths, roundabout until she was sure she could never find her way back alone. Nor, she thought belatedly, did anyone know where she was—just in case.

But she had made up her mind, and if she were frightened she hoped it would not be apparent to the mysterious someone.

At length, they came to a halt.

They stood on a grassy knoll, lit only dimly from distant lights delineating the pathways of the gardens. Her eyes grew accustomed to the dark, and she made out her guide, standing a few feet away, and—the man she had come to find.

Her guide, in response to a nod of his chief's head, moved aside out of hearing, and the two of them were alone.

The leader—the man who wanted the code book so badly—stood only a yard away. But, to her bitter disappointment, he was dressed from head to foot in a hooded domino. And his face, obscure enough in the darkness to deny recognition, was in addition covered by a half-mask.

"So, you bargain," said the man. His voice was muffled, as though he spoke around stones in his mouth. A disguise, of course. But very effective.

"For my own safety," she said briefly.

"So the affectionate and grateful Miss Moffett is in truth for sale," he said, with more than a suggestion of a sneer.

This time she caught something familiar about his voice.

142

but she could not pin down her impression. If he would just talk some more—

"Isn't that your idea? That I can be bought?"

"What a blow for the fortunate Josiah!" he said in triumph.

There was spite, even venom—not so much in the words themselves as in the feral snarl in the voice that uttered them. Suddenly she had a shattering perception. If the painted Satan in the Royal Academy could speak, it would no doubt be in just such tones.

She faltered, then gathered her scattered wits. "What about the money?"

But he did not rise to her demand. Instead, he motioned to the guide, who joined them again. "I am to ask you when you can get the code book," said the guide. And she realized that she had been too close to the traitor himself, too near to penetrating his disguise. He dared say no more, lest he give himself away.

She answered the guide, but kept her eyes fixed upon the mysterious figure. "When do I get the money?"

"You must realize that we cannot give you any such sum as you ask," said the guide.

"No? Then I fear I cannot obtain the book."

A gesture of impatience from the hooded figure interrupted them. "Too much talk," he said sharply. "Bring her over here."

The guide seized her arm. Too late, she saw her bitter error. She pulled away in panic, but the guide held her roughly and she had no choice. A few yards of struggle, a couple of yards more—

Fighting all the way, landing a sharp heel once in a while on solid flesh, she strove valiantly against the man's hand clamped over her mouth, his viselike arms confining her.

She had been foolish. She had thought she was in charge of the maneuver with Mr. Quinn. And here—

The shadowy bulk of a coach loomed out of the dark, and she heard a horse stamp his hoof.

"Get in the carriage!"

With a great heave, the man threw her into the open door. She jerked at the last moment so that she landed painfully, half on the step and half inside the carriage.

She hit her head on something, and lost her wits for a moment. She heard voiced, blurred, and vaguely she knew they lifted her feet from the step.

And, indistinctly, she heard a muttered curse from the mysterious leader.

Suddenly, she knew that something had gone awry. There were hurried footsteps, muttered voices. And then, miraculously, she was shoved from the open door into the air. She landed with a hard, breath-snatching thud upon the ground.

She gasped for breath. In the distance, the sound of carriage wheels dissolved into silence.

And here, right now, Edward's arms were around her and Edward's stirring voice was saying with savage disgust, "You complete fool!"

XVI

For one mad moment, feeling Edward's comforting arms holding her tight and safe, she felt as secure as in her dream. Safe, but filled with a yearning, aching feeling for something beyond her reach.

Impossible, her returning senses told her; this was Edward Peregrine, and he hated her. She struggled against his encircling arms, and at once he relaxed his hold and helped her to sit up on the ground.

"Are you hurt?" he demanded harshly.

"Hurt? No," she snapped, "I find it exhilarating to be thrown out of a moving coach onto the hard ground. It bothers me not a bit."

To her dismay she felt tears starting, and was glad of the concealing darkness. At least she could hold to a little pride. Tightening her trembling lips, she took refuge in tartness. "You must try it. I recommend it highly."

She made use of his strong warm hand to help her to her feet. Shakily, she tried to rearrange the shreds of her cloak. She could not go back to the supper party with her domino in shreds. She suspected strongly that no story of a fall would suffice to explain how she happened to be alone on the path, without Caroline—and Edward's miraculous arrival would cause more than one raised eyebrow.

She turned a beseeching look to Edward.

"Who was he?" he asked in a conversational tone, as soon as he had assured himself that she was in fact without broken bones and able to take halting steps. "How did he happen to choose you?"

"You mean," she challenged, "why was I separated from the rest of our party? I suppose you would not believe me if I were to tell you that I followed the yellow domino that Caroline Taunton was wearing. Only the yellow domino was not Caroline Taunton after all." Quickly improvising, she added, "As soon as I realized my mistake—"

"Why wouldn't I believe you?"

"Because you think my whole life is a masquerade," she said with a regrettable conviction that she was about to burst into sobs. "Because—"

His stony silence restored her as nothing short of a dash of cold water in her face could have done. She was wrong, very wrong, in thinking he was capable of any sympathy. Uncle Josiah was sadly mistaken in his fond regard for Edward.

Besides, he had come upon her in a highly suspicious manner. Unless he had become worried? Not at all likely!

It was a bracing feeling. Now she did not have to consider him at all—simply thank him, as she had done, and return with him to their party. Unfortunately, her ankle turned as she was about to put her convictions into practice, and she was glad of his hand strongly under her elbow.

"Who was he?" he repeated. "Who was the creature in the yellow domino?"

"I don't know," she replied cautiously. "A case of mistaken identity on his part as well as mine, I don't doubt."

Edward seemed to accept her explanation. He drew her to a halt under one of the brilliant overhead lights they had reached. He looked down into her face, and for the first time she realized that her half-mask was torn partly off. Somehow she felt bare to the world.

His brows drew together in a frown. "You are surely more upset than you realize," he said gently. "I detect a smudge on your face, which you will wish to remove before I take you back to your friends." He proffered her a spotless handkerchief, and she scrubbed at her cheek. She felt stinging pain.

"I am not sure you should go back to your friends," he said thoughtfully. "Will you be guided by me in this matter?"

"Yes," she said slowly. She knew now what she must do. With a rush, she added, "Oh, yes. I must go home. There is nothing else for it now."

Her obscure statement puzzled him, but, to her gratitude, he asked no more questions. Instead, by a series, so it seemed, of magical gestures, he conjured up his own groom who arrived before them in an open carriage, and Edward helped her in.

"Put your mask on again, and turn up your collar," he in

structed her. "This is no time for the proprieties. I must get you home."

"What about Lady Bray?"

"I will straighten it all out at this end, after I get you home. Will you trust me?"

"Yes," she said simply. "I must."

As a civil answer it lacked something, but she forgot the words as soon as she had spoken them. There was no more talk on the way home. Chatt drove, and Edward sat beside her, eyeing her narrowly from time to time. Only once did she speak, and then the question came out without her planning it. "Where is Lady Hester?"

"I don't know," he said briefly, and she had to be content with that.

Edward gave instructions to Chatt, and instead of driving directly to the front door opening on Kennett Square, he turned into the lane behind the Moffett stables. The groom vanished from the perch, and soon Hastings appeared with him out of the darkness. She ripped off her mask.

"Miss Georgina!" the butler said jerkily. "Whatever has happened?"

"A small accident, Hastings," she said, accepting Edward's hand as she descended from the carriage, "and Mr. Peregrine was kind enough to bring me home."

It was certainly a strange way to come home, unchaperoned, in the carriage of a man who knew to a nicety the proper thing to do. So thought Hastings, and Gina guessed shrewdly what was on his mind. But she herself had somehow passed into another country.

Behind her was the hope of living in the cushioned, sunny life that Josiah had afforded her. A life of little care, of little effort. She had enjoyed it, was more grateful than she could ever say for it—and she had hoped somehow to fend off Mr. Quinn's importunities, and preserve the regard of her presumed uncle.

She had come to realize—somewhere on that long, silent journey home with Edward, through the darkened sleeping streets of London—that she had never been serious about leaving Josiah, of renouncing her assumed identity in a noble gesture that even she did not believe.

She had been shocked to her foundations when she realized there was not the slightest chance that she was other than a small French child, abandoned by parents, and brought up in an English orphanage. She had thought that somehow Josiah could make it all right.

Now she knew that Mr. Quinn was not playing games. She had tottered on the brink of disaster when it came to the unmarked carriage that had, at the last, run off without her. She had seriously misjudged the gravity of the situation. There was one chance, and a slim one at that, that the damage done by her amateur dabbling could be retrieved.

And she must set about it without a moment's delay.

She thought, later, that she must have said the proper things to Edward Peregrine. No matter that he hated her. he had saved her, and even now was on his way to mend affairs with Lady Bray. But all that too was in the past, and she would not allow herself to think about certain elements of that rescue; she would forget, soon, the gentleness with which he had cradled her, the real anxiety in his face, bent so close to hers.

Inside the house, she glanced into the glass in the hall. A wavering image returned to her, but she was thankful that her face did not look overly bruised or smudged. Her cheek still smarted, and now she became aware of certain other bruises, one at her knee particularly, that were clamoring, and announcing that they would soon become stiff.

Slowly she removed the pink domino and dropped it on a chair. She turned to the butler. "Hastings, don't worry. I'm truly all right. It was a nasty fall, but fortunately no bones are broken."

She smiled at him, trying to erase the dark worry in his old eyes. "I must talk to—my uncle. Will you be nearby, in case of need?"

He didn't understand entirely, but he caught an element of tragedy in her manner. "Must you, miss? Won't tomorrow do?"

She shook her head. "Tomorrow is too late, Hastings. I really must talk to him now."

She tapped lightly and entered the study. How like that first night! Josiah sitting at the far side of the fireplace, a blanket tucked lightly about his legs. The candles on the table next to him, lighting the book he appeared to be reading.

"My dear, you are home early," he said, surprised.

In her unconsciously elegant walk she crossed the room to the fireplace. She looked at him fondly. Did she wish she had never met him? The answer came with the clarity of a church bell. No! These few months were, to her, enough to last her the rest of her life. They would have to be.

She unclasped the single string of matched pearls from around her neck and laid them on the small table next to

Josiah. She fumbled with the clasp on her gold bracelet, for the oddest reason—her eyes were filled suddenly with tears. The symbols of her renunciation had overset her.

She took a deep, steadying breath, and laid the bracelet beside the pearls. She felt his eyes intent upon her.

At last, she said with deceptive calm, "Uncle Josiah, do you have a few moments? I have a story to tell you."

"Yes, my dear. I have all the time in the world." He gestured toward the chair opposite him, flanking the fireplace. "Pull it closer, and sit down. You have my entire attention. But first, my child, are you well? You have a distraught air."

"I had hoped you wouldn't see so keenly, in the candlelight," she said ruefully. "That is part of my story, but first I must assure you that I am quite whole, and only slightly shaken."

"Some wine, I am sure, will do you good," he suggested. "Pray pour some from the decanter, and then we can be comfortable."

Obediently, she poured a glass of amber sherry, sparkling in the dancing candlelight.

"One for me, if you will," said Josiah, abstemious to a degree in the ordinary way. "Perhaps we will both be glad of it."

Darting a quick glance at him, she almost decided against telling him. But, she must—and, more importantly, he had to know. If Mr. Quinn was what she suspected, then there was more at stake than herself—or even Josiah. It seemed pretentious to say that England was in the balance, but it could be no more than the truth.

She handed him the small glass of wine, and took her seat opposite him. "Perhaps," she said after a long, meditative silence, "the best place to start, after all, is what happened tonight."

"I confess I am curious," said Josiah.

"There was an attempt to kidnap me. At the gardens. I admit I was foolish, but I thought I had taken every precaution. But they are cleverer than I, and so I failed."

Josiah sat so quietly that she glanced quickly at him, fearing that already she had overtaxed his strength. But no, his eyes were bright upon her and his face wore a curious expression.

"Go on, my dear," he said softly. "Failed in what?"

"I wanted to see who was behind Mr. Quinn— Oh, sir, I am telling this so badly. Let me start over."

149

"Of course. Mr. Quinn is the person who brought you to me. I thought I had rid us of him, but I see I did not."

"He has made demands on me that I cannot evade any longer. He has been following me—and finally he was able to meet me in Hyde Park the other day, when Sir Charles Derwent took me riding. I wanted to let the mare out to see what she could do—" Little use in telling him about Hester's attempt to unsettle her mount. It did not matter in the least, now. "And he came upon me there. He told me what he wanted."

"And what was that?"

"The book that you have, the flag code book from the Admiralty. He said it was in the house, that Lord Barham had brought it in. And I thought it must be that same book, sir."

He nodded. "So, they knew where it was, all the time." She had given him something to think about. "And what did you say, my dear? I am positive you sent him on his way, but I should be glad to know just how it was done."

"I don't remember too well. The others came down the path, and he decided it was time to leave. He told me he would arrange to meet me, and I should bring the book."

She set her untouched wineglass on the small table. The candlelight shone on the luminescent pearls, softly on the chased gold bracelet, and touched to life the amber liquid in the glass.

"I said I couldn't," she resumed her narrative. "I told him that I wouldn't. And he said—" She broke off, her emotions lumped in her throat.

"He said," suggested Josiah with keen shrewdness, "that he would send you back to jail. Is that right? I should have told you that your sentence has been stricken from the books. You are safe here. At least from jail," he added, glancing at her set face. "Was there more?"

She nodded. "But—that is immaterial."

"Let me see if I can guess," he said. He was thoughtfully giving her time to recover, she realized gratefully, and she picked up the wine again and this time sipped it. "If the abduction attempt was in fact their effort, then their minds run always along the same lines. So I suspect that they must have threatened you with bodily harm."

Startled, she seized upon one word. "Do you think, sir, that someone else was at the bottom of the kidnapping attempt? I cannot think who."

He did not answer directly. "They did threaten you with physical harm, I see. But why would they force you now,

150

when you do not yet have the book for them? What could they gain by kidnapping you?"

"Well, sir, I told them, you know, that I wouldn't. Then at the Royal Academy rooms this morning, he was there, waiting for me. I told him I could not do as he asked, for fear of being caught."

Suddenly, this calm discussion of the problem that had devastated her for three days now was too much. She leaped to her feet and began to pace around the room. She looked suddenly down and saw that she was wringing her hands, her fingers moving ceaselessly. She cried out, "Say something to me! Tell me that you are shocked, ashamed—something!"

The look Josiah bent upon her was loving and warm. He watched her for a moment, and said, "Believe me, my child, I am far from feeling ashamed of you! On the contrary, it seems to me I have much to be proud of. Shocked at their effrontery, yes. But the problem is not irretrievable, and above all not your fault. The book is here, and you are telling me how strong you were against them." When she did not speak, he prompted her gently. "But you still haven't told me why you think they would resort to kidnapping."

"Because," she said, whirling so that her skirts belled around her, "I was foolish. I thought I could manage them on my own. I told Mr. Quinn that I might get caught stealing the book, and I would need money to get away and live on. He said he couldn't give me the ten thousand pounds I asked for. So—"

She halted, considering how much of what came next would she tell. Wisely, she decided to tell it all. After all, she was fairly launched on it, so she might as well hold nothing back.

"So, I told him I would insist upon talking to whoever gave him orders." She eyed Josiah, but she could read nothing on his face. "He made a rendezvous with me for tonight at the gardens."

"Then he knew you were going to be there?"

"Apparently, and that is something I don't understand, either." Gina was engrossed now by the problem itself. She was no longer worried about Josiah's reaction. He had stood the revelations so far, and now the problem itself was a knot she picked at.

"He knew when the book came into the house, sir. He followed me to the Tower, the day I saw him first. And he said they knew every move I made."

"Then he admitted he was not alone?"

151

She thought carefully. "Three things, sir— One, he said that *they* were right when they sent him to the court to find me. And he said *we* once in a while. He was furious when I asked him who *we* were. And, he made the appointment with someone—he said he was not authorized to give me the money. Do you think he lied about that?"

Josiah did not answer at once. When he did, it was at a tangent. "Undoubtedly he has a staff working for him, to watch this house and at the same time to follow you but, in addition, he probably has access to some very secret information."

"I'm sorry," she said at last. "I have brought such trouble upon you. If I hadn't agreed to Mr. Quinn's proposal at the beginning, this would never have happened."

"I hope you are not shortsighted enough to believe that," Josiah said hearteningly. "Surely you would imagine that if they had not hit upon this plan—whoever they are—then some other would have occurred to them. It is a strange and whimsical thing to think that their plan has backfired upon them. Their wish to spy upon this household has resulted in such happiness for me—for us both, I venture to think. And they really misjudged their tool, didn't they, my dear?"

He caught her hand and held it for a moment to his cheek. "My dear child, I never thought I would be so grateful for the wicked machinations of my enemies!" He laughed gently. "But I will tell you what does anger me."

She stood looking down at him, her hands clenched at her sides. "That I took it upon myself to make such ramshackle arrangements?"

"Not at all. I think you were guided entirely by an excess of zeal, but your reasoning was accurate and without flaw. Except of course you have had little experience in the kind of men with whom we are dealing here. I am proud of you, Georgina."

Her hand flew to her mouth. How could she leave him when he was being so excessively kind to her? And leave, she must.

But he said, "No, the thing that shocks me, angers me, is that they dared to defy the Admiralty in such a wise—by putting pressure on you. I would not for the world have had you troubled in this way. How dare they threaten my niece!"

She took a deep breath. "Well, my dear sir. That is the point. I am not your niece."

XVII

he silence lengthened.

The room suddenly seemed stifling hot, but Gina knew that he heat was generated by her churning thoughts and not the nall fire nestled cozily in the hearth. A log—beech, from the ood at Seahaven—burned through, dropping with a soft lop into the cushion of ashes.

Just as her nerves tingled alarmingly near the breaking oint, Josiah said, with astounding calm, "What kind of fool-hness is this?"

At first Gina could not find her voice, could not force ords from her cottony mouth. But she managed to say, "I'm ot your niece. Georgina Moffett is not my name."

"Now, Georgina—"

"I can prove it, prove that I'm an imposter."

Josiah raised an eyebrow. "But why should you? I thought e had settled that the first day you were here."

"But you see, I came here as an idiotic masquerade. Any-ing to get out of Newgate."

"And very wise, too," said Josiah judiciously. "You were t guilty, and the trial was a ghastly mistake. But now you e here—"

"But—"

"Enough of that, my child. I am convinced that you belong re with me. Isn't that enough?"

She couldn't speak over the lump in her throat. Finally, she anaged, "Believe me, I am more grateful than I can ever d you, sir. But you don't know—"

Gently he interrupted. "Some sort of issue that I am una-re of, I collect. Now, my dear, is it— Forgive me if I am forward, but your welfare is so dear to my heart, and

153

that must be my excuse. Is it that some question has arisen a[s]
to your true birth—by someone wishing to marry you, is tha[t]
it?"

She shook her head.

"I have thought these weeks that young Tom had falle[n]
under your spell. If he has such a foolish thought in his hea[d]
I will soon set him straight."

"No!" she said with emphasis. "Tom has nothing to d[o]
with this. Besides—"

She was vividly in the grip of recollection. Edward Pere[-]
grine holding her close, holding her safe, because he had bee[n]
watching her—it meant nothing. As a matter of grim fact,
must mean nothing except that he was watchful to see th[at]
she did not steal his young ward away from him while he wa[s]
engrossed in his own marriage plans. And, she reminded he[r-]
self bitterly, Hester deserved such an unobliging husband a[s]
Edward Peregrine would be. Selfish, and full of his own righ[t-]
teousness! Hold to that thought, she advised herself.

"No," she said to her uncle. "Marriage has nothing to [do]
with this. I must—I dare not think of marriage. No, sir, t[he]
problem is much more immediate."

Her uncle watched her with growing concern. He thoug[ht]
he knew her well, because he had made it his study to unde[r-]
stand the niece so fortuitously cast up on his doorstep. B[ut]
this was a new facet of her, and it was a disturbing one.

She was almost hysterically restless, moving from boo[k]
shelves, picking up small figurines from the niches and setti[ng]
them down again, and then flitting to the window, where s[he]
opened a slit in the dark red draperies and peered fruitles[sly]
into the night.

Josiah was a man who recognized a need for ste[rn]
measures when it arose, and he took them. "Georgina,"
said with firm authority, "come and sit down. I think y[ou]
must tell me at once what has happened to distress you so."

His implied rebuke was salutary, and Gina, knowing s[he]
must tell him everything, knew that the moment had co[me.]
No longer could she indulge in the luxury of letting her em[o-]
tions drive her.

She came back from the window, and sat on the edge [of]
her chair like a wind-tossed gull settling upon the waters.

"I went to the orphanage yesterday. St. Clothilde's."

"Why?"

"You have asked me that before, sir, and all I can say [is]
that I have a deep need to find roots for myself. Believe [me,]
it is not for any lack that has forced itself on me here."

"Had you not asked for information from the orphanage before?"

"Of course."

"Then one might think you were satisfied that there was no information concealed from you."

"No, sir. On the contrary. I stopped asking when I was perhaps eight. Now that I am grown, it occurred to me that Matron might reconsider."

He nodded. "I admit it is hard for me to put myself in the place of one who truly does not know who she is. The Moffetts have always known—at least in recent generations." A wry smile crossed his face. "Before that, in Tudor times, I think one shouldn't inquire too deeply into the characters of our ancestors."

She went on, almost to herself. "I need to know who I am. Not who you *believe* I am." A small sound that could have been a snort escaped Josiah. She paused a moment, but he said nothing. "Nor who Autherly thinks I am."

His head rose sharply. "Autherly? What has he to do with this?"

"I don't really know. I think I just use him as an example. But I do say that I don't like the way he looks at me. I have seen just such looks on Mrs. Potter's guests, when I served at table."

Warmth flushed her cheeks, as she remembered certain pointed stares of the Cits that had dined with the Potters. She was not even amused when she realized she had thought of them by the unflattering term that was used disparagingly by the *ton*. Cits they were, and she knew it.

"Autherly dares to cast his sights this high," mused Josiah, and she could tell by the grim lines suddenly on his face that her uncle was becoming overwrought. Instantly alarmed, she protested. "Believe me, sir, he has been all civility. He has offered me no affront."

"I'll have Autherly dealt with," said Josiah in a dismissing tone. "Now what did Matron tell you at St. Clothilde's?"

She told him of her grave disappointment when she learned that Matron had died suddenly, without giving any of the precious information stored in her mind alone to anyone else. "I thought then that my errand had been foolish in the extreme."

Since she did not continue for some time, Josiah nudged her. "Was that all of it?"

"I wish it were. No, the new matron, a very pleasant

155

woman, told me that they had had what she called a 'rare old house-cleaning' when she took over."

"And found something!"

She nodded. "A small leather pouch, that's all."

"Where is it?"

"It's no use, sir. The pouch doesn't tell me who I am. It only tells me who I am not—your niece."

"I should like to see the pouch."

Struck by a new note in his voice, she looked up quickly. Josiah, she knew, was not a man to be trifled with, especially when he had reached a point he considered important. Now, she believed, was such a point. Obediently she rose and went in search of the pouch.

Up the broad stairs and down the hall to the room she had been given. She stood just inside the door for a moment. The room stood ready to receive her, the cool apple-green color soothing and soft. The fire laid ready in the grate, her night robe laid out on a chair, the bed coverlet turned back invitingly.

It should have spoken to her. She was momentarily surprised that she felt no emotion, not even the familiar rush of happiness at her good fortune. Just now, she was numb—in emotions, in mind. Even her thoughts lay inert, deadened by frustration.

It is better this way, she thought. *Perhaps I can get through this; in an hour it will all be over.*

She found the pouch where she had tucked it away in the back of a drawer in the great chest. She weighed it in her hand, probing with fingers through the leather; all was there, the firm round outlines of the coin, the uneven surface of the pin.

She returned to Josiah's study and found he had moved. Now he sat behind his desk. It was indicative of his changed mood. She laid the pouch on the desk before him.

"Now," said Josiah in a businesslike tone. "Before we go into this famous pouch, I wish to show you something. Here are some papers that I wish you to read."

"What are they, sir?"

"Look at them, Georgina. This first one is my will. My *new* will."

She could only stare at him. What did that have to do with anything? He told her.

"The other day when the news of your accident was brought to me, unfortunately I was overcome, and Barham called his own doctor to see me. I learned that I had alarmed

156

the household greatly, and my enforced inactivity gave me time to think. Suppose I had truly succumbed to that—indisposition? What then? What would happen to you? I could not rely on the good nature of my executor to protect you, although I believe Edward would be completely scrupulous. But—there were too many variable factors, so I simply changed my will so that you are my principal beneficiary."

"Why do you tell me this, sir?" She read the first lines of the top page. "I do not understand. It will not apply to me—here I see that you speak of a daughter. I was not aware that you had a daughter."

"Oh, yes," said Josiah, suddenly grinning like a small boy with a secret. "See this paper!"

She scanned it briefly, and then went back and read it with great care and mounting bewilderment. "Why, sir," she said, giving it back to him, "this—I don't understand it!"

"Simple, my dear. I have adopted you legally as my daughter, Georgina Moffett. A legal term, it is true—*daughter*, rather than niece. But it serves the purpose I wished—to simplify matters so that you will in fact inherit all my goods. So you see, the pouch is irrelevant. You are my legal daughter, and there's no use protesting. Your consent was not required."

Clever Uncle Josiah! she thought. Stopped every hole, made all as binding as could be. There was nothing she could say. except what he was clearly not expecting to hear.

"How good you are, sir! But don't you see, that makes it worse than ever!"

Gina faltered. She didn't have to tell him anything more. Her future, once totally dark and undefined, was now bright and shiny, and she would never have to worry again. She had gathered, from what Edward and others had said, that Josiah Moffett was a wealthy man—and it would all be hers.

But the thought of Edward, sneering and haughty, told her she could not accept this, not in this way. A Moffett she wasn't, but honest and truthful she was.

She pulled up a chair to the desk and sat opposite her uncle. The candles flickered restlessly, and Josiah's face came and went in the shadows. "I must tell you the rest, sir," she said, and thought she saw a look of high approval in his eyes, but because of the shadows she could not be sure.

"This is how it will look, sir. You will see when you look in the pouch. I am French. A French girl, planted in your household by that scoundrel Quinn, in time of war. You have mentioned to me the lack of security in the Admiralty. Now

157

that is serious enough to bring Lord Barham with the cod
book to hide it safely in your household—the same househol
where a French girl, who may or may not be a spy, has bee
introduced."

Josiah nodded. "You are exceedingly intelligent, my dea
This is how it would look, of course. If you were French. B
you are not."

She brushed his objections aside. He was a dear perso
but, she began to think, strongly opinionated. Could she ev
convince him of her point of view? She tried again.

"I tried to make amends by at least finding out for you th
identity of your spy. For I think your spy and Mr. Quinn
superior must be the same person. Don't you think so?"

Josiah nodded. "I feel there's no doubt."

"You must realize that I failed to find out what I set m
self to find out. Foolishly, as it happens."

"Most dangerous," he agreed solemnly.

"And therefore I must leave."

"I agree completely," said Josiah, surprisingly. Had it rea
ly been so easy, after all?

"I think you must go down to Seahaven," he continued.
believe I can keep you safer down there."

She was aghast. "No, absolutely not. That leaves you he
with the book, and it's all my fault." Suddenly she peered
him intently. "Are you feeling well, sir? This must have be
such a shock to you."

"I'm fine," he assured her. "Barham's doctor gave me ne
medicine. Very efficacious. Besides, I confess the need
straighten things out for you has enlivened my spir
greatly."

The will and adoption papers set aside, for putting into t
safe later, Josiah turned his attention now to the pouch. I
pulled open the drawstrings, and upended the bag on t
desk.

The three objects fell out, the pin upside down, the cc
rolling a few inches and then flattening, and the paper flutt
ing momentarily in the air.

"See, sir?" she said after he studied them in what s
thought was puzzled silence. "The coin is French."

"That means nothing," he pointed out. "If Georgina—I a
assuming for the moment a total impersonality for t
child—were taken from Paris by René Valois, it is likely tl
this French coin was his, or one of John's. This may ha
been the child's only funds."

"I hadn't thought of that. But—there's the slip of pap

My name on it, Jeanne—too Frenchy, so Matron said. And I remember—"

"What?"

She told him then about the dream. The sweet voice singing, *Mon amie Jeannetot.* "In French," she said stubbornly. It was almost as though she were unwilling to have Josiah knock down her suppositions, one after another. Almost as though she were afraid to be happy.

"That of course is a point. Except that Sarah and John both spoke French fluently. As I do. This note of Matron's means nothing. A three-year-old, especially one hearing more than one language for days or weeks, may not speak either one distinctly. And Matron, while she may have been a good soul, was probably not highly educated."

"Then the pouch means nothing. Either way."

"Not in itself," Josiah agreed, absently poking at the other object. He picked up the cameo. He turned it over and looked at the design on it. The color drained from his face, and the hand holding the pin shook wildly.

She sprang to her feet with a cry. "What is it? Let me call Hastings!"

"No," he whispered. "Just give me a moment." She brought brandy and held it to his lips. Nothing else in the pouch had moved him—only the cameo of the tiny graceful unicorn.

She waited until the brandy had brought color back into his cheeks, and then, still watching him narrowly, returned to her chair. She didn't dare speak, but she was nearly frantic to know what in the little pin had touched him so deeply.

Finally, he said, musingly, "My instincts were right! Your looks, my child— you are a beauty, you know—the unconscious way you move, tilt your head, all the little mannerisms that you have when you are thinking of other things. Especially, my dear, your sweetness of disposition and your great intelligence—an unusual combination—all convinced me without a doubt that you were in fact my lost little girl. My great-niece for whom I searched so long. But no real proof—that is why I took these steps." He tapped the legal papers. "But now—"

Her thoughts subsided from chaos into total bafflement. It was possible that all this was real, she supposed—possible, but not very likely. Was she really Georgina Moffett? She shook her head slightly. She could not accept that.

She was content to sit in silence, letting the burden of her recent days, of Mr. Quinn and his fellows, sink into tem-

159

porary oblivion. But Josiah had not yet told her what had affected him so deeply. Now he stirred, and indicating the pin with his finger, said, "Does this cameo mean anything to you?"

She told him then the rest of her dream, of the little white deer, gracefully carved with one spiraled horn springing from the center of his forehead. "But, sir, this dream can mean nothing as proof. You forget that I have had the cameo in my hands since yesterday, and I could easily have contrived such a dream to impress you."

"It would take more than that to impress me," said Josiah with a faint chuckle. With shaky triumph he took from the center desk drawer a small oval-framed miniature. "This was painted at my request by Richard Cosway. Look at it closely."

She took the miniature in both hands and looked at it with absorbed interest. A portrait of a woman only a few years older than Gina herself. Deep auburn hair, waved softly in timeless style over her forehead. Eyes more gray than green. A mouth wider that Gina's, a chin perhaps a trifle more pointed.

But the resemblance was striking. With the minor differences she had noted, she could have been looking into a mirror.

But the object in the miniature that had nearly the same effect on Gina as the pin on the desk had on Josiah—was the cameo pin of the white unicorn!

The dream was true, then. The sweet cherishing, the warmth of loving, the surrounding of hopes and gay delight in their child, all of these were true. And she had the distilled attar of her memories that came to her in dreams. She had had a mother, and a father.

And now she had an uncle—a real uncle, who was making up to her for all the empty, rootless years.

The roots were real, drinking in the waters and holding her safe.

She had been gone a long time, so it seemed, when she was recalled by Josiah's voice. "I had this cameo carved special for your mother, on the occasion of the birth of a daughter to her and my nephew John. And you had this very pin with you when you arrived at St. Clothilde's. So you see, my dear, there's no escape!"

Then the trouble came back to her. "And see how I have repaid you, Uncle Josiah! With Mr. Quinn, with—"

"With all I ever wanted, my child. Now, we will have more nonsensical talk, if you please, about deserting me. I have the power, you see," he added, chuckling mischievously.

and indicating the papers at his right hand, "to bring you back."

"No need," she said, giddy with happiness. "Not even will I go as far as Seahaven."

"I really think you will be safer there."

"But it's my fault that Mr. Quinn has become such a menace. . . . Sir, I remember something that happened yesterday."

The day she returned home from the orphanage with the leather pouch—that surprisingly proved the opposite of what she believed. She had gone out to the landing, to tell Uncle Josiah that she was obliged to leave him.

"And you and Lord Barham said you were going to set a trap for the spy in his office."

"You heard that?" Josiah was startled. "We really should have been more circumspect. Not because of you, of course. But on general principles."

"And you said the spy was someone you knew and trusted."

"It has to be. No one else has access—or had access, rather—to the flag code book, and yet there are those who know it exists, and those are on the enemy's side."

"Two copies exist."

"One in Lord Nelson's hands, and this one," confirmed Josiah. "I must take steps to see that this copy is better guarded. Do you think— You said earlier that it might be removed from here by force. Do you think it possible?"

"But then the code would simply be changed, sir. I believe you told me that. But I don't understand. How can the new book be made up quickly enough and a copy sent to Lord Nelson?"

"It can't be, of course. No, we must keep the code book safe, and catch the villain too. I must evolve a scheme. In fact, I have been thinking how to do this very thing. Now, my dear, it's been a long day for you. You have fortitude enough for an army, but surely you will wish to rest now, and I—"

"You plan to stay up and spin your web," she said, rallying him. "Well, I should like to ask a favor."

"Of course," he said, then catching the glint in her eyes, added prudently, "within reason."

"You're going to set a trap. Please, Uncle, I have such an overwhelming desire to help catch the traitor." She bent forward eagerly, earnestly.

"Please, Uncle," she begged. "Let me be the bait in your trap!"

161

XVIII

In the end, Gina had her way.

It took much persuading, and a certain persistence that Josiah said pointedly was certainly a Moffett characteristic but at length the snare was set.

The traveling coach was ready at last. Baggage was strapped to the roof and the back of the coach, leaving hardly room on the back seat for Kane and Gibson, the two grooms armed heavily against footpads. On the perch in front was Prickett the coachman, and beside him, conscious of his heavy responsibilities, sat Fingle, a mammoth shotgun ready to hand under the seat.

Josiah was seeing her off on her trip to Seahaven. Charles Derwent too stood on the threshold, watching her departure.

"Here is your bandbox, my dear," said Josiah. "Take good care of it." He handed her the satin-covered article in question. It was surprisingly heavy, as anyone passing by on the street could see. Gina took it in both hands. She stowed ceremoniously under the seat, saying, "Never mind, Agnes I'll look after this case. It has all my valuables in it."

"It seems strange to send her down to Seahaven before the season is over," said Sir Charles to Josiah, sourly eyeing the preparations.

"That's just the reason," said Josiah blandly. "She is looking a bit pale, and I feel she needs a rest. A quiet sojourn peaceful surroundings."

Gina cast a knowing glance at her uncle. How clever he was! A quiet sojourn was just what they did not expect.

The coach at last trundled out of Kennett Square, and she waved at Josiah until they turned the corner and left behind the little patchwork of green, surrounded by elegant town houses.

Agnes, in the opposite corner of the seat, still wore the grumpy expression that had marked her since the previous day, when it was announced to her that she was to pack Miss Moffett's clothes for a long stay at Seahaven. And—worst of all—that she herself must go and wall herself up in the country, she complained bitterly to Mrs. Beddoes, right in the way when Bony comes across the water. Who knows what awful things would happen to a pretty girl?

Mrs. Beddoes said briskly, "The men will look after Miss Georgina."

Since Agnes was clearly speaking of herself, the housekeeper's remark was not well received. And to crown it all, thought Agnes morosely, Miss Georgina wouldn't let her pack the bandbox. Trunks, yes. Valises, to be sure. But the bandbox, no. What was in it? Agnes knew to a certainty every item of Gina's possessions. There were none unaccounted for. It was certainly a puzzling thing, the maid thought, looking dourly out of the window across the Sussex countryside.

For her part, Gina was not much worried over Agnes's sulks. She had a thing or two to think of, herself. She began to wonder whether she could carry it off, after all.

The bandbox was the crux of the scheme. In it was the flag code book. At least, this was the story that Josiah would spread, whispering to all possible suspects, in confidence, that he was sending his niece with the book to a place of safety.

And of course, that place was his own home of Seahaven, a house kept in readiness for his own return at any time.

The decoy was to draw the bird of prey. And she was not worried about the danger—not much, anyway. The coach attendants were, as a matter of course, armed against the risk of highwaymen.

But also there would be other persons along the way whose duty was to protect her. "You won't be aware of them, I promise you," said Josiah when she objected. "And neither will our game. You will be watched all the way. I could not let you do this otherwise, you know."

She owned she was grateful for knowing that she was not alone, carrying the decoy flag book, riding into the grasping and cruel hands of Mr. Quinn.

Or his superior, the mysterious Mr. X.

They stopped at noon at a small coaching inn in a town she did not know. An excellent lunch, served with snail-like service. The afternoon was getting on when she mounted into the carriage again, and Fingle said, "We'll have to put them right along, miss, to get to Rothbury tonight."

Nodding agreement, she settled back to enjoy the ride. She gave full rein to a new feeling that bubbled just under the surface, threatening to break out in ill-timed exhilaration. She had promised herself that she would not dwell on the unbelievable event, that she was really Georgina Moffett, and really adopted by her uncle—not until the traitor was caught.

What an amazing coincidence that she should have been brought to Josiah, and yet, it was not by chance. She knew that someone had been on the lookout for a girl resembling Sarah Moffett, and that resemblance was not coincidence. It was clearly, so Mrs. Beddoes had said much earlier, the workings of Providence.

And she would snap her fingers at Edward Peregrine! How she longed to see the crestfallen expression on his face when he learned the truth. What did his "proof" matter now?

The regular lurching of the coach was monotonous, and the rising heat made her drowsy. She had dropped off to sleep, when one jolt of an excessive nature brought the coach to a rumbling, broken-rhythmed stop.

Thrusting her head from the window, she saw that Fingle was already down from the seat, and one of the grooms had hurried forward to take the horses' heads.

"What is it, Fingle?" said Gina in a low voice.

He was looking alertly around him, suspecting an ambush behind every tree. "Best stay in the coach, miss," he warned "till I find out what's what."

There were conferences out of her hearing at the front of the coach, and at last, Fingle returned to inform her, lugubriously, "It's only a broken trace, miss, but it can't be mended here."

"What shall we do?"

"Send for a carriage to the next town, I suppose." Fingle abruptly withdrew his attention from her, and looked down the road the way they had come.

"A small vehicle, Miss Georgina. Only the driver. Best let me handle it."

She peered down the road too, and then exclaimed, "Oh, Fingle, what luck! See, it's Sir Charles!"

Sir Charles's astonishment upon seeing the disabled coach was plain. "I thought you would be much farther along," he said.

"How fortunate that you came along just when you did," exclaimed Gina. She was impressed with Josiah's arrange

164

ments for her safety. He must have sent Sir Charles to follow them, on the off chance of some emergency just like this.

"Nothing to be done," he said, after consultation with the coachman, "at least until help comes from the next town. But you can't stay here on the road. Let me carry you to town, and see you safe."

"How good you are," said Gina. "Is there room for us all in your calèche?"

"All?" said Sir Charles sharply. Casting an eye to the roof of the coach, he added, "Not the baggage."

"Oh, no, I am not so foolish. Prickett will stay here with the coach, and Kane and Gibson too. But Agnes and Fingle must come with me." Seeing Sir Charles prepared to protest, she added, "Or I myself cannot go. Uncle Josiah has given me such strict orders that I fear to go against them."

Sir Charles allowed Gina to sit next to him, putting Agnes at the outside of the seat. Fingle crowded Sir Charles's groom on the back step. "Do you require your bandbox?" he asked.

"It's a part of me," she said, laughing. "Agnes won't mind being crowded."

If Agnes minded, it did her no good. The bandbox was wedged between Gina and her maid, with Gina's hand firmly on the handle.

"A valuable piece of luggage indeed," Sir Charles commented dryly.

An hour later they reached Bornley, and pulled in at the *White Rose*. Warm yellow light from the inn windows streamed out into the azure twilight, in a most comforting fashion. There would be food, she hoped, and clean beds. It looked that kind of place.

The landlord was clean and efficient, his wife eminently respectable. The room given to her and Agnes was spotless, and the bed felt soft.

And supper, later, was well-cooked, even if plain.

The windows in the private parlor were open to the warm evening breeze. Candles flickered fitfully, and suddenly, at the end of dinner, Gina had an overwhelming sense of well-being. The mishap of the afternoon would be mended by morning, and she had safeguarded the bandbox. So far, no attempt had been made on it.

But by far the most exciting thing was to sit here in an inn, far from London—even farther from St. Clothilde's—and know that she had a true name, a true family. Her mother had in fact adored her—and, assuaging a lurking doubt that had lived with her for years, her parents had not simply cast

165

her off, unwanted, but had been prevented by death from caring for her.

And surprisingly, her thoughts, as she faced Sir Charles across the small table, dwelt upon Edward Peregrine. She would be pleased to point out to him that she was in fact not an imposter.

The door to the private room opened and Fingle stood just outside, making queer motions with his head. "What is it, Fingle?"

He said stiffly, "Sorry, Miss Moffett. The coach will not be ready in the morning."

"What?" she demanded. Turning to Sir Charles, she said, "Can that be true? Fingle said it was only a broken trace, a piece of leather that can easily be replaced."

Sir Charles said slowly, "So I understood. I don't understand this, Fingle."

He made as though to rise, but Gina stayed him with a gesture. "I shall see to this, Sir Charles," she said. "I will speak to the landlord."

She swept out. Fingle closed the door sharply behind her and hissed, "Miss—wait a bit, if you please."

She was puzzled by his strange manner. "What is it?"

"I didn't know how else to speak to you alone, Miss Moffett," he said in a conspiratorial undertone. "The trace didn't break."

"Of course it broke!" she said, unconsciously lowering her voice to match his. "The coach—"

"No, miss. The coach will be ready in the morning. But the trace didn't break. It was cut."

"Cut?"

"Half through," he affirmed solemnly.

"When? We were traveling all the time. No one could have got near it. Except," she remembered, "at lunch. Is that possible?"

"I suppose so," he said doubtfully. "Don't seem as though it was alone for long. But it could have been done before we left London."

"Do you think we were meant to be hurt?"

Slowly thinking, Fingle at length said, "No, miss. For you see, all that could happen was just what did happen. The coach fell lopsided on the road, but it didn't turn over, no anything."

She nodded. His logic was clear. "We'll start early in the morning," she said, "to make up for this delay. I hope that no one has been inquiring for us at Rothbury."

166

Josiah had expected them to stop there for the night. She hoped that the forced change of plans had not upset his arrangements for her safety. The bandbox and her obvious apprehension over it were expected to lure Mr. Quinn's fellows into the snare, and—once fairly trapped—Josiah's men would close in. Worried, she wondered whether the damaged trace had already served its purpose, putting her beyond the reach of her unknown guards.

"Where did they lodge you here?"

Fingle told her, and then saying good night, she turned back into the room where Sir Charles was standing at the window. Well away from the door, she noticed. Well, Fingle had spoken in too low a tone to be overheard, she thought. And then wondered why the thought came to her. Sir Charles was her protector, sent by Uncle Josiah.

"You spoke to the landlord?" said Sir Charles.

She turned over in her mind various answers, and settled for partial truth. "A misunderstanding with Fingle, that is all. It is straightened out now," she said carelessly. Stifling a yawn, she said, "I am so sorry, but I find I'm exhausted. I wonder if you will excuse me?"

"Of course. Then you travel in the morning?"

Something made her say, "Late, I fear. But certainly before noon."

Agnes was already asleep in the trundle bed. Getting into bed as quietly as she could, Gina found she could not sleep. *If I were as sleepy as I was downstairs,* she thought with irritation, *I'd be snoring like Agnes.*

The night was noisy. Two or three guests arrived after the inn had gone to bed. For one mad moment she thought she heard French words rising from the yard, and quickly hushed. The invasion?

She raced to look from the window, and saw the landlord himself carrying a light, wearing trousers with his nightshirt only partly tucked into the waist. He wore the air of one disturbed from his rest, and nothing more. She laughed at herself, seeing Frenchmen behind every bush!

And then, long after everyone had gone to bed, and the inn was silent again, the only sound reaching her being a mouse in the wainscoting and an owl hooting softly far off, she heard a sound, stealthy and furtive, close at hand.

Footsteps in the corridor.

Footsteps that stopped outside her door!

The latch made the tiniest snick of a sound. She would not

have heard it had she not been awake. Surprisingly, she heard Agnes turn over. "What is it?" cried Agnes, frightened.

The footsteps hurried away, not quite so stealthy as before. No use to look into the hall. "You must have had a dream, Agnes," Gina said persuasively, and soon the maid's heavy and regular breathing showed that she slept again.

But Gina could not. Instead she sat up in bed, pulled her robe around her shoulders, and set herself to think. Not until the faint light of dawn appeared did she nod to herself in satisfaction, and fall asleep at once.

The shock came in the morning. She went down to breakfast, leaving Agnes to pack. She hoped that Sir Charles was lulled by her remark about leaving late. Her job was simply to draw attention to her flight from London, showing exaggerated care for the decoy bandbox. The cut trace was evidence that her journey had been noted, and the footsteps in the night told the same story.

The continued presence of Sir Charles might warn off the prey. The traitor—would he be someone she knew? She was sure of it.

She entered the breakfast room. And there sat Tom Weston.

She gasped. He rose to his feet and stared at her with an odd expression. "Then here's where you are," he said abruptly.

"As you see. What on earth are you doing here?"

"Escaping."

His response matched so closely with her suspicions that she could only echo him faintly. "Escaping? From what?"

"From my uncle's house party. By the way, I can recommend the ham," he added, spearing another pink slice and sitting down to enjoy it with relish.

"Bother the ham!" she exploded. "House party?"

"He says to enjoy the yachting in the Channel with all his friends. Foolish if you ask me. Who's going to sail back and forth in sight of the French fleet, even if his yacht has just been fitted with new sails? Not me!"

In a daze she bespoke breakfast from the hovering landlord. Edward, having a house party? She regained her common sense enough to realize that her own adventure filled her mind to the brim. She had forgotten for the moment that the rest of the world was still going blithely about its business.

Tom was still grinding along with his list of grievances. "I could abide them all, even Frenchy Valois and that idiot Ranney—they're all invited, you know. But I cannot stomach

Hester. She is an antidote for certain. In a way," he said with an air of considered judgment, "I'm glad he's going to marry her. She's poison when she doesn't get her own way."

"Did you come in the night?" she asked him, as her breakfast was set steaming before her. "I heard several late arrivals."

And someone after that came down the corridor and tried my door, she thought but did not say.

"I don't like the idea of a lady traveling alone," he said, after admitting that he had come after midnight.

"You know," she said, buttering a muffin, "I agree. It would be much easier if you rode with me in my carriage. Then you could be sure to keep an eye on me."

He stared at her, reddening. With a crestfallen air, he said, "Then you've guessed."

"That you were looking for me? Of course." Sent by Mr. Quinn? Or Josiah? "What about the house party?" she asked lightly. "Was that a fiction, too?"

"No, it's real enough. But I wasn't truly escaping. I was sent to protect you, and not let you know. But you guessed."

"But why would you be here if my Uncle Josiah sent you? He expected me to stay the night at Rothbury."

"But you didn't arrive. So I backtracked. No trace of you. So I meant to continue my search this morning."

A very plausible explanation, and one she wanted to believe. Her breakfast was delicious and she was ravenous. But not too hungry to think. Tom clearly lied about his destination. He could have informed Mr. Quinn of her visit to the Tower. He could have returned, even, to London without her knowing it—especially if he had a reason for avoiding her. His following her now was suspicious in the extreme. She could not trust his assurances that his errand was to protect her. And he had not mentioned her uncle's name—she had.

He was a fumbling boy. She could not picture him as the arch traitor, giving instructions to a cagey and vastly experienced man like Mr. Quinn. No—someone else moved behind Tom, pulling his strings as well as those of Mr. Quinn. She must get rid of this boy, and lure, in some way, the man behind him into the open.

"Come now," she said craftily, "ride with me? I'll be ready after a while."

"Well." Tom sighed in evident relief. "I could surely protect you better that way than riding some miles behind."

She smiled brilliantly on him as she left the room. He would be content to wait, she knew, and in the meantime—

well, she had not realized how scheming and devious a mind she really had!

Rousing Fingle, she sketched her plan briefly. A smile broke over his face as he understood the ruse that would leave Uncle Josiah's coach in full view of anyone who planned to follow it, and hopefully keep Tom glued to the window lest she escape him! And very shortly she left her room, carrying the bandbox. She started toward the back stairs, and heard someone moving in the corridor.

She shrank back into the shadows. To her unbounded amazement, she watched René Valois pass by on his way downstairs to breakfast. Almost she called to him, but she did not. He was on his way to Edward's house party. So Tom said. She decided she could not trust any of them.

Instead, glad that she had foresightedly settled her account with the landlord the night before, she slipped out through the back gate into a side street and down a lane, to a certain corner on the main road from London. There, the hired coach, with fresh horses put to, waited for her.

Fingle helped her up into the interior of the coach, where Agnes was already installed. Gina slid the bandbox under the seat, and Fingle closed the door behind her.

The coachman and one groom had been left behind at the *White Rose*, along with the Moffett coach, prominently displayed in the innyard.

But Gina and the bandbox were tooling merrily down the road to Seahaven.

XIX

Gina, in her hired coach, arrived at Seahaven late that day. They had driven hard for nearly nine hours, making up for the time lost the day before. An uneventful trip, as it happened.

Seahaven was an impressive sight. They entered between stone gates, and drove along a winding road, ever rising, to the promontory at the end of the land where the massive gray stone house stood, surrounded by wind-bent trees of great age but low stature.

If she had expected to feel pangs of recollection, the stirring of some memory from the three forgotten years when she must have visited here often, she was disappointed. A handsome house—but that was all.

She sighed and stretched. "I'll be glad," she confessed to Agnes, "to stand on something that doesn't jolt my wits loose!"

"We always take three days to the trip," reproved Agnes. "I'll be surprised if anyone expects us. Damp beds more'n likely, and we'll all get our death!"

"From a damp bed?" doubted Gina, remembering some rigorous circumstances prevailing at St. Clothilde's. Damp feet from broken-soled boots, for example, and none to change into.

"*And* the night air," corroborated Agnes, morosely.

They were expected, to judge from the prodigality of candles blazing from the windows, pale and futile against the deep rose and saffron of the sunset.

"See, Agnes?" commented Gina, amused. "How warm and welcoming it looks!"

But Agnes was not cheered. "Beacon light for Frenchies, if you ask me!"

Gina sobered at once. Out there somewhere lay the powerful fleet of Napoleon Bonaparte, the conqueror of Europe, poised at Boulogne and other Channel ports waiting only for tide and favorable wind. And the certainty of victory that a knowledge of Nelson's new flag signals would provide. Hastily, she pulled the symbolic bandbox from beneath the seat and held it tightly on her lap, until the carriage stopped before the wide front door and Bowles stepped from the house to make her welcome.

The next morning Gina got her first look at Seahaven. Her father had lived here as a boy, her mother had visited often after their marriage. Gina, too, must have run across these polished floors, scurried out into the open air, looked, perhaps, fearfully as Gina did now, over the cliff-edge into the cove forty feet below her. But she did not remember.

She felt uneasy. She told herself that the excitement of the past few months had at last deserted her, leaving her limp and spent—like, she thought with wry humor, sea wrack at high-water mark. And just now these months all seemed like a vision. Finding Josiah, learning she really was his great niece, learning, too, to take her place in the world she knew was rightfully hers—all unreal, as though, waking, she yet dreamed.

Even the yacht below, riding on the green water of the cove like a white gull, was part of this dream-world of air and sun. She remembered that Edward Peregrine's land bordered Moffett land, and although she had no idea where the boundaries were, she suspected that this cove lay somewhere between the two estates. Witness the small yacht below, at anchor. It must be Edward's.

"I saw a yacht in the cove," she commented at lunch. "Mr. Peregrine's, I suppose?"

Mrs. Bowles, serving fluffy omelet, dismissed the yacht with a gesture. "Always out on the water, even as a boy," she explained. "He'll be glad of it after he's married. Anything to get away from Lady Hester, although I shouldn't say so. She's going to redo the whole house, so Crawford says—Mr. Edward's butler, you know. She came yesterday from London."

"Lady Hester? Here?" cried Gina. Then that part of Tom's rambling narrative was fact. The quarrel between Edward and Hester was clearly made up.

172

"To look the house over. So *she* says. I mind Mr. Edward when he was a boy. Happy all the time. Too bad," Mrs. Bowles added darkly.

Then it was true. Lady Hester's rumored engagement turned into fact. And Edward would soon be out of reach.

Appalled, she realized the truth. She cared not a whit for Hester, but she cared a great deal, a great deal too much, for Edward.

When had this feeling stolen upon her?

It did not signify. He was out of reach, and besides that, he despised her. He had said as much, more than once.

Resolutely she turned her mind to other things—to the prime reason she had come to Seahaven, the flag code book. She took the bandbox down from the wardrobe shelf, and opened it. There lay, amid crumpled paper to hold it from shifting, the famous book. A small volume, to hold the fate of England inside its covers! Wrapped in plain paper, tied with red tape, and secured with great masses of sealing wax. Impressive!

The parcel she had helped to wrap, and now held in her hands, contained a book, it was true. Identical in shape to the code book, this one was merely a bound collection of blank pages.

The previous code had led to a disaster at the battle of Chesapeake Bay in North America. The English admirals, Graves and Hood, had sent up messages to their fleet on the flagship's mast, but there were so many flags, and each one could mean more than one order—the English ships turned the wrong way and De Grasse and his French navy annihilated them, saving the day for their American allies.

What the French wouldn't give for this new, vastly improved, code! They would then be able to read Nelson's orders as fast as the British themselves. With Nelson's fleet destroyed, Bonaparte's dreaded invasion would become a reality.

There was no need to contrive a safe hiding place for the blank pages of the book she held in her hand. Yet it might serve as a delaying tactic under circumstances she could not now imagine.

She was surprised that no further attempt had been made to secure the book. Possibly "they" had learned it was only a decoy. Or perhaps they were even now planning another try.

With the addition of her own guards—Fingle, the groom that had come wtih her, and Prickett and the other grooms who had just arrived with the repaired coach—to Bowles and his men, she felt safe.

But she took the package from the bandbox and hid it, all the same.

The day wore on serenely, without incident. Cloud towers rose, pink and gray, in the west.

Now it came to her that Uncle Josiah had in fact got her out of the way while the real business of catching the spy went on in London. She suspected that Uncle Josiah meant only to keep her safe and occupied—busy as a child with "pretend" horses and toy soldiers. Only she would have been given dolls by her mother!

Suddenly, all the grief, the years of yearning ache over her lost parents, and the finding of her real uncle broke through barriers lowered by the disappointment of her mission. She broke into a storm of weeping that was prolonged enough to encompass all that distressed her, and strong enough to sweep it all away.

"Stuck out here at the end of the earth," she fretted, wiping her still streaming eyes. "Might as well be in prison!"

Then, horrified, she regretted her outburst and went for a brisk walk to atone for it. When she came back, a note lay in the salver in the hall. Addressed to her, she did not recognize the handwriting. "Bowles, who brought this?" she queried as she broke the seal.

"A messenger I did not know, Miss Georgina," said the butler, who had told her he had once dandled baby Georgina on his knee. She nodded thanks, and read the message.

Culprit discovered. Will be captured as he sails. It was signed simply, *J.M.*

"Something amiss?" worried the butler.

"N-no, Bowles. You did not recognize the messenger?"

"No, Miss Georgina."

She read the message again, worried. Edward's yacht, newly fitted out, ready to sail, rode at anchor in the cove. And as Edward prepared to cross to France, bearing the prized book, bailiffs were this moment closing in on him.

Vividly she imagined the rest of it—Edward stumbling in the dock, the judge horrified at the heinous treason. The sword of judgment, sharp point toward the prisoner. Not "the prisoner"—*Edward*!

She knew the interior of prisons. She simply could not bear the thought of Edward Peregrine hurled into a loathsome cell, as she had been.

She really had no choice.

When would he sail? She knew nothing about the tide. The oppressive air grew hotter, and, far off, thunder mut-

174

tered. Thunder—would this be the way the attacking guns of the enemy would sound? She shivered.

She could not take time to run upstairs for a shawl. She waited, chafing under the delay, till Bowles was out of sight, and slipped out a side door. As she hurried toward the clifftop, she feared she might already be too late. Her mind worked at speed. All her anger, all her resentment of Edward's arrogance, had been clear signs that she had ignored—or chosen to ignore.

She had had so little experience in love! She did not know it when it stood face to face before her. How does one learn to know love? By bits and pieces—starting with the warm cradling in loving arms, and going on.

But she had nothing else, and yet she knew—as surely as she knew that storm was fast approaching up-Channel—that she would herself go to prison again rather than know that Edward suffered.

And that—no matter how stealthily it had approached her, no matter what mask the face of love wore—told her all she needed to know.

She had thought she hated him. Where had she read that love was a coin, the reverse side of which was hate? Well, no matter. She had the coin right side up now.

The mutter of thunder seemed closer, and ragged lightning flickered over the Channel. Rising storm clouds darkened the sky as though it were already late evening.

The lovely boat was still there, its sails folded as though asleep. She thought she saw movement on deck. She found the rugged path leading down from the clifftop. It led around a craggy boulder, where her handhold was merely a wisp of scrubby bush. Sliding the last yards on rattly scree, she stood at last on the shingle.

She did not call. Instead, feeling the wet sand and pebbles of the shore soaking through her thin slippers, she hurried around the head of the cove. On the far shore she found what she was looking for. A small dory, beached on the sand. Oars on the bottom of the boat.

She eyed the dory with misgivings. Best call first, she decided, before trusting herself to *that*.

"Edward!" she called through cupped hands. "Edward Peregrine!"

Only a startled smew answered, taking flight. But she had the unmistakable sensation that someone watched her from the shadows on deck. If he were Edward, why didn't he answer?

Gingerly, she shoved the dory to water's edge. With concentrated care, she stepped into it, feeling the water in the boat slopping at her wet feet. If the dory sank, she thought, she would be lost. It might well sink, she discovered as she poled the dory away from the shore. The waves were choppy, and slapped loudly against the wooden planks of her craft. She could scarcely keep the dory headed into the gusting wind.

The wind and the tide fought over her dory. She could not control the boat. Her muscles screamed, and suddenly a quick gust turned the boat.

She was speeding past the yacht!

She made one vital thrust, and caught the boarding ladder. Just in time. The dory floated off into the distance, bobbing toward the open Channel.

She clung for some minutes to the ladder, feeling the strong pull of the tide on her skirts. She felt with one foot for the rung of the ladder. After several thrusts against the tide, she gained a foothold. Eventually, hand over hand on the swaying ladder, she gained the deck.

She leaned heavily against the railing, gasping for breath. She could not even call Edward's name. She could only frame the syllables, as a figure appeared at last in the open hatchway.

"You got here," the man said. His features were hidden in the dark. But he was not Edward.

And suddenly, with a sinking feeling of disaster filling her, she recognized him. "Autherly!"

"And you came aboard to sail with me," he drawled lazily "I confess I did not think you would come."

"Why should I?" she panted. What had Autherly done with Edward? She must get away.

A glance over her shoulder into the pitchy dark below made her shudder.

"Didn't you get Hester's note? I must admit she had difficulty in persuading me it would bring you here. She must be possessed of second sight."

He crossed the deck quickly. Glancing skyward, he said sharply, "Come on, let's get out of here. That sky will break open any minute!"

She pulled away from him, in vain. He held her wrist in an iron-fingered grip and half dragged, half carried her across the intervening space to the hatchway.

He pushed her into the cabin below. She fell, surprisingly on soft cushions.

"This is *your* yacht?" she cried.

"Edward's."

"Where *is* Edward?"

"Occupied with Lady Hester, I devoutly hope."

"But the note spoke of a culprit! What could Hester have meant?"

Thinking swiftly, she played for time. This was quite possibly the worst trouble she would ever find herself in. And Edward would not come this time to rescue her.

"Some rumor in town about a spy," Autherly said impatiently. "Hester is far more intelligent than anyone gives her credit for. Your flight from town, for instance. Hester remembered the old Scripture saying. What is it? The wicked flee—"

"When no man pursueth," she supplied mechanically.

Autherly grinned. "So Hester devised the trap, reckoning that if you knew more than you should about this spy business, you would come running. Especially since you are supposed to be old Moffett's niece. And you did just as she predicted."

"Then the note was a hoax."

"Of course. You must see that you are a threat to Hester. She wants to marry Edward—or rather Edward's fortune—and everyone knows he prefers you to Hester. It's working out well. I already have what I want, thanks to your gullibility. And Edward will find out how wrong he was in thinking you virtuous. His disgust, Hester believes, will send him directly into her arms."

Gina scrambled to her feet, her heart pounding. "What if I hadn't come?"

Autherly shrugged. "Another way, then. For I am determined to have you." He laughed then, a cruel, mocking sound in the tiny cabin. Overhead the thunder rolled, seeming to echo the mood of Autherly's triumph. "And the more you struggle, my dear, the better I shall enjoy this night!"

He reached for her.

There would be no escape.

She was caught between a table and the banquette wher he had thrust her. The yacht was pitching wildly now. Sh could not even stand in the narrow confines.

Crouching like a panther beset by dogs, she reached blin ly with one hand in the dark. Her groping fingers found half-full glass on the table. The yeasty smell of whiskey ro when she moved the glass.

Instinct took control. Her hand, without volition, lifted th glass and tossed the liquid in Autherly's eyes. He recoile with a curse.

She had not stopped him—only slowed him for a momen And worse than that, her resistance seemed to add spice his anticipation, for he chuckled. "Aha, I knew that red ha meant something. Peregrine will never know what a prize has missed!"

No time now to reflect on her stupidity—that would con later. Now she ducked and slid under the tabletop. Gropi her way, she made a mistake. This table had a folding leg, add support in foul weather. Her hands missed finding it the dark. She was moving, she thought, toward the cab door, when her head struck the table leg. The flat boa thudded down on her head, and she was pinned between t slanting board and the wall.

The world reeled. She thought it was the blow on her hea but Autherly staggered, too. Puzzled, but wary, she remain still—letting her head clear. Waiting to detect his next move.

"Where are you, you little wench? Pretending to be dainty. Not one for a romp? All serving-maids are willi

178

"You won't get—" His taunting voice stopped abruptly. "This cursed boat—"

Then she knew that the violent and unsettling pitching of the floor beneath her knees, where she crouched, was not in her bruised head. The yacht was riding rough seas—the approaching storm had struck.

Autherly was quiet, too quiet. She knew he must be listening, listening for her breathing. She made her lungs take in slowly, exhale gently.

But she was wrong. Autherly was listening, but not for her. He muttered, "The anchor's gone!" and she heard his striding footsteps away and up the companionway. The moment she realized the import of his words, she scurried from her hiding place. *I have no desire to be drowned in that hole,* she thought, and on leaving the cabin was inordinately relieved to gain the open air.

But only for a moment.

The storm was upon them. Lightning illuminated in vivid green light the roiling clouds, spinning round and round. The sea beneath the keel was surging as though the ocean floor were moving. Gina grabbed with both hands a post of some sort and clung for dear life.

The wind parted her hair. Screamed in her ears. Water ran down her cheeks—tears or spray, she did not know.

Shouts reached her ears, and she turned to look. The headland was nearing fast. The boat was adrift on the ebbing tide!

The pitifully small yacht, lovely at anchor, was now no more than a painted white chip in the roaring seas!

Her landsman's eyes saw no way to escape. Slipping swiftly on the tide out to the Channel, she had time only to reflect on Josiah's grief when the seas cast up her broken body.

Then the squall hit.

A whirligig of wind, freakish and powerful, rounded the headland from the southwest and pounced like a playful kitten on the waters of the cove. It picked up the lovely yacht and dropped it on its beam ends, spilling everything movable into the water.

Gina felt herself sliding down the sloping deck. She hit the icy water with a gasp. She flailed out mechanically and her hands fell upon some unnamed piece of floating debris. A minor miracle, which would only prolong her misery.

The lightning was less. Already the storm's fury was moving up the Channel to the northeast. She had no very clear idea of what was happening. She saw Autherly once, as he floated past. A long dark trickle of blood snaked down his forehead. He was as near to her as he had been in the cabin, but his eyes stared and he did not see her as the current took him toward the open sea.

Her mind, overflowing with horror, went away for an unmeasured time. Hands reached down to grasp her, strong arms drew her from the water. Voices, angry, authoritative, spoke over her head. A voice—surely she knew that voice?—spoke tenderly in her ear, and roughly she was bundled up in a coat.

She was riding in a boat, that was it! A dory, which mercifully ceased to move on the moment.

"We're here," said Edward Peregrine. "Pull us up, Fred." When the boat was beached, and the men sent to look for Autherly on the shore, Edward helped her out of the dory and set her on her feet on the shingle.

"What were you doing on that boat?" he demanded. Even in the darkness she could tell that he was furious. Autherly was right, she thought bitterly. Edward could not contain his disgust with her. But surprisingly his voice moderated, very slightly, as he added, "Did you know it was my yacht?"

"I supposed—or, I don't know!" she cried. "Surely I didn't think it was Autherly who should be warned!"

She didn't even try to explain about the note. She shrugged and turned away. The borrowed coat slipped from her shoulders and she hardly noticed. But she began to shiver. She stumbled blindly toward the foot of the cliff. She didn't even want to see Edward anymore. *Leave me alone in my misery* she pleaded silently.

Edward was beside her. He placed the rough coat again around her shoulders, and let his arm stay shelteringly around her. Forlornly, she reflected, this would be all she remembered. She seemed destined to hold small fragments of love to her heart, tiny fragments—the little French lullaby, and now this moment—and that was all.

She must have made a sound, for Edward dropped his arm from her shoulders as though scalded.

The path up the cliff was far steeper than it had been on her way down. It was an endless climb, and Edward's firm grip on her wrist was all that kept her going. She thought they must be near the top. Someone was sobbing. She stopped to listen, but she heard it no more.

"Crying won't help," said Edward coldly. He added grudgingly, "Want to rest a minute?"

They had climbed only as far as the huge boulder set the middle of the path. She slumped against the stone, feeling

180

its chill seeping through her drenched clothing. Edward knelt beside her, his face on a level with hers.

"Keep your voice down," he ordered. "Tell me who is in the house."

"Why?"

If, as she had believed, Tom lay in wait for her on the road from London, who was the man behind him? It must be someone whose authority Tom respected. Poor Tom! First his overly doting mother and then his guardian kept him on a tight rein—no wonder she had thought him her own age when she first met him!

The conclusion was inescapable—and this of course was why she had thought Edward must be warned. Behind Tom, only Edward was strong enough, powerful and intelligent enough, to compel Tom to do his bidding.

Her instinct, honed to a fine edge by the usages of her orphaned past, had been right. Logic served only as a buttress to conviction. Rightly, she dismissed Autherly and Lady Hester as a mere diversion. The real issue was treason.

"Why don't you kill me here?" she added bitterly. "Why bother to take me to the house?"

A flame of anger kindled in his eyes. With careful control, he pointed out, "I could have left you there in the water, you know."

Perversely, she argued. "You had witnesses. I suppose even your own men might not approve of murder."

He laughed, without amusement. "That might be a solution at that. I confess it had not occurred to me. I shall give it my serious consideration. In the meantime, perhaps you will be good enough to answer my question. Who is in the house?"

Reluctantly, she told him. "Bowles, and Fingle. The maids, and cook." She did not mention Prickett and the two grooms. They might be useful, she thought obscurely, as a diversion.

"I know all the staff," he brushed them aside. "No guests?"

"No."

"But the book is still—safe?"

He had made a mistake. His interest in the book was too lively, too intense. She stiffened, and seeing in him the traitor she had convinced herself he was, she hardened her resistance to him.

Surely she had lost Edward. No man would want a wife who had spent any time alone with Autherly. What a fool she had been! It was useless, she thought, to try to explain to Edward the amazing change in her own feelings toward him.

181

She herself did not quite understand such a swift alteration. Besides, her pride would not allow such a confession.

Had it not been for the storm, by this time she would doubtless have been the smirched woman that Autherly intended, that Hester had counted on to fill Edward with revulsion, so that Hester might shine, flawless in purity.

Gina shuddered in spite of herself. She had nearly lost her life, as well as her honor. But at least she could salvage something from this *débacle*—Josiah's book.

"What book?" she said with exaggerated innocence. "If you will let me pass, sir, I shall not trouble you further." With simple dignity she tried to stand. The effect was spoiled when her sodden hem clung to her slipper and she nearly fell. He caught her, and began the upward climb again without another word, pulling her roughly behind him.

He knew Seahaven better than she did. Guiding her through the wet night, they approached the side door through which she had slipped, how many aeons ago! Leaving Edward to pour himself restoring liquids, she hurried up the stairs to her room. She stripped off her wet clothes, reflecting upon the miracle that Providence had performed this night. Perhaps she had been saved for a purpose. The only purpose she could see was to mourn what might have been.

Brisk toweling began to revive her, and her skin's tingling spread inward. Just before she left the room, feeling much better, physically at least, she looked around. Something was not quite right. The candlestick awry? A drawer not quite closed? The bed a trifle mussed? Perhaps all of these, perhaps none—she could not remember the details of the room, having lived in it only since yesterday. But she strongly suspected that in her absence just now someone had searched her room.

Edward? There had been time between the moment she left the house and the time that Edward plucked her out of the water.

She shook her head to clear it. The note hinted that Edward was the culprit. But the note was Hester's fiction. Yet Gina was convinced that Edward was in truth the mysterious Mr. X.

Strangely, that did not matter greatly anymore. What did matter was Autherly. He said Edward was more than interested in her. How glad she would have been to know that *before* Autherly lured her to destroy her reputation by climbing aboard that yacht!

She had caught no one in her snare set with the decoy bait. She herself had been the victim of Hester's device.

She was done with traitors, with code books, with setting traps. Let Josiah deal with Edward. She could not raise her hand against him.

Stonily, she wished strongly to see the end of Edward. She hesitated a long time, thoughtful. At length, the solution came to her. She would *give* him the decoy package, if that would be the end of it. By the time he found out he had been hoaxed, he would, she hoped, be far away.

She took the package downstairs. Stealthily she tucked it into the drawer of a small table standing in the hall. Close enough to get to it quickly, yet out of sight.

Edward seemed to have lost his savage anger. "I've been thinking," he began. "You seemed to think I should be warned. Why?"

"It doesn't signify. Not now."

"I think all this needs explaining," he said judiciously.

"What good is that?" she cried. "I'm weary of the whole horrendous evening. In fact, the whole—*business*!"

She had the lowering feeling that she would burst into tears in another moment. "Please don't cry," said Edward, reading her mind. "I have a word or two to say to you, but first we must get some misunderstandings cleared away."

She sank into a chair, and regarded her folded hands seriously. Edward's tone was so reasonable that she was lulled into listening. "Now," he said, "what led you to board my yacht?"

"The note." Seeing his uncomprehending expression, she amplified. "It said the traitor had been identified."

"Let me see it."

She fished out the slip of paper from a desk drawer, where she had hidden it lest Bowles find it. "Will be captured—" she read again. Her voice died away, as she remembered.

"What's amiss?"

"Autherly told me," she said painfully, "that this was a hoax to get me aboard. And if this didn't work, they—he—would try something else. Oh, I was soundly tricked!"

Edward took the note from her nerveless fingers, and too late she remembered, too, that Autherly had implicated Hester in the writing. *Hester!* She glanced at Edward. Amazingly, he seemed unmoved. He read the note through, with a strange expression on his face.

"Hester's handwriting," he said at last. "So this was how they did it."

Slowly, comprehension crept into his face, followed by a

grim tightness she did not like. He lifted his gaze from the note to glare furiously at her.

"So, you thought I was the traitor?" he demanded savagely. "Why?"

She shook inwardly. She took refuge in a spirited attack. *"Think,* not *thought.* For all I know, you are here to get the book. Didn't you ask me just now, out there on the cliff, where it was?"

He was as pale as if she had struck him. "I may have called you a fool, before," he said, clenched fists showing his struggle to control his temper. "But my reasons then are nothing compared with now. Pray tell me, how has your logical mind led you to this conclusion?"

He was in deadly earnest. His intense glare, holding her eyes with his, forced her to be honest with him.

She told him. "You were always there," she finished. "At the Royal Academy, in the gardens that night. Here. Sending Tom to steal the book."

He laughed, a short bark without amusement. "Tom was Josiah's idea. He was to keep an eye on you if you needed help."

"Tom?"

"I know he's of little help to anyone, but he should have a fair chance to accomplish something on his own. So Josiah persuaded me."

He took a turn around the room. "Is that all?"

"Enough."

"I don't think so. But perhaps you had not realized there could be another explanation for all your suspicions?"

"Perhaps," she said in a voice full of doubt. "But you claimed to have proof that I was not Georgina Moffett. And yet you did not bring it forth. Why not, unless your purpose was to keep me in Uncle Josiah's household? To steal the book for you at the proper time?"

His savage temper no longer rode him. Somewhere it had dissipated, leaving only a rueful relic behind. "I underestimated you," he said surprisingly. "I had not thought you so acute in your thinking."

"Much good it has done," she said quietly. "I am here alone and at your mercy, and all you need to do is to take the flag code book and leave. You must know I will be unable to stop you."

Amused, he queried, "Why should I take that very fancy decoy that you wrapped with enough sealing wax to sink it?"

"You know it's blank?"

"I suppose there is no reason for me to expect you to be-lieve what I say—"

None, she could have told him, *but my own wish. How much I wish to believe you!*

"But the villain is not I," he said, striving to be reasonable.

"All right," she said unsteadily. "If not you, then who?"

"Your journey, and my own house party, were to provide the answers. So far, of course, they have yielded nothing except a tragic accident for Autherly—if they ever find his body, I shall be surprised; a strong current there—and a monumental misunderstanding between us. And of the two, let me assure you it is the latter I regret."

"Your house party? I don't understand."

"No, of course not. Josiah did not wish you to know all his plans, lest they somehow divert your attention. But he was not sure of the loyalties of certain of his acquaintances, and I devised the scheme of bringing those whom Josiah, even against his will, suspected into the same region as the decoy took itself."

"Even Hester? Was she one—?"

"No, no. The countess. You remember she was one who did certain small favors for Josiah."

"Such as schooling me."

He nodded. "And after that, a few other small chores. She is deeply in debt."

And Edward Peregrine's fortune was to pay off her credi-tors, Gina remembered. So Autherly had said.

"And René Valois must be here," she said aloud. "I saw him at the *White Rose.* Just before I hurried away."

"Throwing all your protectors into consternation," said Ed-ward, reprovingly.

"I thought it was clever of me."

He shot a dark glance at her, but his faint smile told her he agreed. She suddenly felt much warmer inside.

"Did it never occur to you," he said in a different voice from any she had heard before, "that I was close by, not for any clandestine purpose, but simply because I wanted to watch out for you, to protect you—to be near you?"

She would have spoken, but her mouth was dry and she could only shake her head. After a long moment, knowing his eyes were fixed on her, she managed to quaver, "But, sir, how did it happen that you were down at the beach just now?"

"Having heard from Hester that you had gone aboard my yacht to meet Autherly—she could not wait to tell me, you know, of what she called your wanton proclivities," he said

185

with a wry smile,—"I simply went down to the yacht—to kil
him."

She half rose from her chair. "Kill Autherly?" She gape
at him. "But Hester—"

"Hester and her mother are at this moment on their wa
back to London." He added after a significant pause, "
hoped, of course, that I would find you unharmed. I did nc
know to what lengths he would go—drug you, perhaps. But
had no idea the storm would make the situation so perilou
for you."

She thought for a long time. His story had moved her. H
had gone to great lengths to save her, and to avenge he
honor. But—Autherly's thorn still stuck in her mind.

She rose in agitation. "But, sir, you do not know what ha
pened to me before the storm came up."

He said with deliberate calm, "It does not matter."

"Does not matter!"

He had the grace to redden. "I phrased my thought badl
I see. What I mean is this—I cannot of course enter int
your experience, nor do I know just how to help you de
with the terror you must have felt. What I meant was—" F
broke off momentarily. "I find it very difficult to expla
without taking too much for granted."

He crossed to where she stood at the window. Fiddlir
with the hem of the curtain, she hardly knew what she w
doing.

"Georgina, will you do me the great honor of marryi
me?"

The room reeled. The lump on her head throbbed and sl
thought the bruise had addled her wits. Such as they wer
They had surely misled her into thinking—

"Sir, I don't believe I understand."

"Georgina, I've been in love with you for longer than y
know. Since you were three years old, I think." His sm
grew lopsided.

"Me?" The word was strangled in an unaccountably tig
throat.

"You. Do you remember when you fell from the swi
Bowles had made for you, and hit your head on a stone?"

She shook her head. "How brave you were!" he exclaime
caught in the grip of strong recollection. "Your ear bled f
ages. I was only fourteen, and frightened to death."

Involuntarily she reached up to touch the concealing cu
over her left ear. His face suddenly wore an arrested loo
"You don't remember?"

186

"No." Then with a rush, she added, "I wish I did!"

He was standing very close to her. She put out her hands in an oddly appealing gesture of denial. "You don't want to marry me! You don't know what happened on the boat. I will have no reputation left. You don't know whether Autherly—"

"My dear girl," he interrupted in a voice that thoroughly overset her strong resolution, "you are alive. And, I hope, mine."

He opened his arms, and she walked into them. This was more than love. This was the cherishing that she had longed for, ached for—and, as it happened, nearly died for.

Edward was still explaining. "That was why I could not believe you were the real Georgina. Because I wanted so much for it to be true, and yet I could not credit it."

He was not making sense to her. But she did not care. Someday she would tell him that Autherly had not touched her, that the storm had come to her rescue.

An idyllic moment—shattered by a voice from the doorway behind them. "A pretty sight!" said Sir Charles Derwent. Gina broke abruptly away from Edward, and glared at the visitor in anger.

Edward, with glittering fury, said, "Have you never heard of having yourself announced? How did you get in?"

"Through the side door. As I did earlier this evening. Sorry about interrupting such a happy occasion!" said Sir Charles sincerely. "If you will give the flag book to me, Miss Moffatt, I will be on my way."

Edward started toward him, but Sir Charles said calmly, "Don't make trouble. Josiah sent me down to get the flag book, that's all. He says the danger is over, and the book should be returned to the Admiralty."

Gina whirled toward the door. "But I don't understand—" She felt Edward's warning glance upon her, and changed what she was going to say. "Why shouldn't *I* take it back?" she objected.

"In his infinite wisdom," Sir Charles said with unconcealed bitterness, "Josiah has ordained that I bring it."

Edward interposed, "I don't think so, Derwent. I don't believe you. . . . Where is Valois?" He seemed strangely intent on the answer.

"*Hors de combat,*" sneered Sir Charles, "as he would say. On the *White Rose,* nursing his head."

Edward laughed. "Josiah underestimated you, I see. But I can't believe he would trust you—"

"Quiet! All the years I've worked with Josiah, done exactly

187

what he told me to, trotted around on his errands, played es
cort for his reputed niece—" He stopped for a moment, t
regain control of his raging emotions. Then he said, "Don'
question me, Peregrine. I want the flag book and I will hav
it. Get it!" he added sharply to Gina.

She had been thinking. If Edward would just play along—
"Why not, Edward? Let him have it."

Edward's eyes flickered. His rage at Derwent gave way t
a comprehension of her stratagem. The flag book was fals
so why not give it to him? Then she realized somethin
more—and Edward's thoughts paralleled hers.

"So it was you all the time, Derwent," said Edward. "Wh
didn't you just take the book from Josiah's desk?"

"And lose the pleasure of seeing you all running aroun
not knowing who it was that outsmarted you all? And the d
light in proving to Josiah that he is not quite the genius h
supposes himself to be?" He laughed, loudly, harshly.

Suddenly Gina experienced a revelation. The room gre
bright with the force of the understanding that blinded her.

Derwent was the same height as Edward—more than on
she had mistaken the two. And it was Derwent that night
the gardens.

"What would you have done with me," she ventur
boldly, "if you hadn't been frightened away that night?"

"Frightened? I have never been frightened in my life." S
Charles's eyes rolled wildly. "I only paused to reconsider n
next move. You see, you turned out not to be the kind
woman I told Quinn to get. I thought you would be easy
manage—a jailbird!"

"But would you have killed me?"

"What did your life matter? I got you out of prison,
you'd be dead anyway. No, it was Josiah who was going
pay. Your life in exchange for the flag book. Simple, was
it?"

How could she ever have thought that it was Edward th
night? Only Derwent could have radiated so much hatr
that she had felt its force even in the darkness. Now, frustr
tion had intensified his insane envy until it sent waves sprea
ing out to destroy everything they touched.

"So now you know," Derwent continued. "I only wish
could see Josiah's face when he finds your bodies. I am r
sure how I can leave it so that he thinks you are the traitors.'

Puzzlement swept over his smooth face, distorting it u
he looked much like a baffled child. And Gina recogniz
that Sir Charles had crossed the borderline into madness.

Edward pretended to notice nothing strange in Derwent's manner. "Why are you doing this, Derwent?" he said in a reasonable voice. "You've admitted to treason. But I confess I do not understand why you insist upon this tedious fiction that you came down on Josiah's business. Your journey itself shows a sad lack of intelligence. I wish you will explain to me why you trouble yourself to follow Georgina here to Seahaven, and then burden yourself with two murders, just to escape with a book full of blank pages."

Sir Charles allowed his jaw to drop. For the first time in her life Gina saw color literally drain from a man's face. "Blank?" Furiously he roared, "I don't believe it! Get the book! It's the real one, I know it is!"

Edward stepped forward again, but suddenly Derwent had a gun in his hand. "Don't worry," said Edward with a reassuring glance at Gina. "Give him the decoy. You should have known about the decoy book, Derwent, if you are really here on Josiah's business."

"It's not true!"

"Oh, yes, it is, Sir Charles," said Gina. "But I will get it for you. Then you will see."

She led the way into the hall, and pulled out the drawer of the small table. The light from a wealth of candles shone down upon them. On Edward, looking unutterably weary from his exertions—a hard ride from London, a harrowing scene, no doubt, with Hester, and then the disastrous affair in the cove—but yet giving every evidence of sustained interest.

Candlelight shimmered along the barrel of the gun in Sir Charles's shaking hand. And on a vague whiteness somewhere in the shadows at the back of the hall. She must not look in that direction.

Sir Charles was breathing heavily. "Open the package."

Suddenly Gina had had enough. Was this man simply to come in and order them about like dogs before he shot them? He might be dead the next moment, but she would at least not crawl to him.

Defiantly, she refused. "There is the book," she said scornfully, "in the drawer. Take it if you want it. I shall not give it you."

Cautiously, he edged toward the table. He was wary, suspecting a trap. Edward looked ready to leap at him, and Derwent allowed himself a sly grin. "Don't try it, Peregrine," added Sir Charles. "One wrong move from you, and this girl gets it first."

"That isn't going to help you," said Edward.

"The fair-haired boy," taunted Sir Charles. "You're the on
they picked to head Intelligence after Josiah's gone. You. No
me. I haven't a chance now. But—" he leveled the gun at Ed
ward—"neither will you!"

His attention distracted for the moment, Gina acted auto
matically. She was facing Sir Charles. One hand, behind her
groped for the package in the drawer. Without thinking, he
fingers closed on the package—heavy with sealing wax, an
bulky—and she hurled the decoy code book at Sir Charles.

The next moments were filled with great confusion. Sud
denly the hall was filled with men. The gun went off, stun
ning her with the sound. There was such a hurly-burly goin
on in her poor head—a buzzing that went with the ache th
had been rising since something had struck her as sh
clutched at debris in the cove.

Edward was holding her, turning her face into his should
to hide the thing that lay on the floor. But she had on
glimpse of it before, shuddering, she closed her eyes an
wept.

Sir Charles, on hands and knees, crawling for the gu
Crawling for the decoy book. As each was kicked away fro
his groping hand, he babbled—senseless syllables, edged wi
vitriol.

René Valois and Fingle swiftly brought him to his feet a
secured his wrists behind him. René looked quite rakish, s
perceived, after she had revived somewhat. His head swath
in bandages—the pale splotch she had seen in the darkness
the hall—he showed little signs of the injury dealt him by
Charles.

Edward set her on her feet. With a searching look,
smiled reassuringly, and turned his attention to Valois. "Gi
you're all right. Josiah is gathering in his net in London no
But thanks to you we have the leader of the ring right here."

"The Monsieur Quinn and all the fishes, big and little,
will leave to Josiah!" agreed Valois with glee. "And the li
Georgina is safe now! *Formidable!*"

Edward nodded. "Leave that to me."

With what Gina could describe only as a very *French* lo
René Valois left them alone.

"You are mine," said Edward. He took her face betwe
his palms, and kissed her. Soon, she knew, he would ger
push her hair back and probably be surprised to find
three-cornered scar on her ear, where she had fallen from
swing so long ago. But now his proof no longer mattered.

"A miracle that you were found," he said softly.

"Formidable!" she echoed, and lifted her lips to his.

About the Author

Vanessa Gray grew up in Oak Park, Illinois, and graduated from the University of Chicago. She currently lives in the farm country of northeastern Indiana, where she pursues her interest in the history of Georgian England and the Middle Ages.

Have You Read These Big Bestsellers from SIGNET?